PRAISE FOR THE ALEX MARTEL THRILLERS

"Alex is a formidable addition to the pantheon of kick-ass heroines of military thrillers."

—*Publishers Weekly*

"*Perfect Shot* was a fantastic ride. Steve Urszenyi rolls on the throttle in *Out in the Cold* to make it even better! Alexandra Martel is one terrific protagonist!"

—Marc Cameron, *New York Times* bestselling author of *Tom Clancy: Shadow of the Dragon*

"With *Out in the Cold*, Steve Urszenyi delivers another electrifying, world-class thriller. The writing is precise, poignant, and utterly compelling. A jaw-dropper from start to finish."

—Simon Gervais, former RCMP counterterrorism officer and bestselling author of *The Elias Network*

"In the world of espionage and high-stakes thrillers, few authors can match the adrenaline-fueled intensity and pulse-pounding action of *Out in the Cold*. He's only two books in, but if Urszenyi can keep this pace, his name will soon be mentioned among the pantheon of today's master storytellers. Prepare to be captivated from the very first page!"

—Ryan Steck, The Real Book Spy and author of *Out for Blood*

"Alexandra Martel is the heroine readers are clamoring for, and *Out in the Cold* delivers the goods. Steve Urszenyi skillfully crafts a narrative as chilling as the Arctic winds, brimming with action that grips readers from start to finish."

—Jack Stewart, retired Navy fighter pilot and bestselling author of *Unknown Rider: A Battle Born Thriller*

"Opening this book is like trying to jump onto a fast-moving train. Urszenyi is the real deal."

—Linwood Barclay, *New York Times* bestselling author of *Take Your Breath Away*, on *Perfect Shot*

"Gripping and on target, *Perfect Shot* hits with maximum impact. Steve Urszenyi's debut thriller never lets up from the first page to the last."

—Jack Carr, *New York Times* bestselling author of *The Terminal List*

"A stunning debut heralding an extraordinary new character and series. Alex Martel is a kick-ass special agent in an action-packed, on-the-edge-of-your-seat espionage thriller with a jaw-dropping finish."

—Robert Dugoni, *New York Times* bestselling author of the Charles Jenkins espionage series, on *Perfect Shot*

"Urszenyi's powerful debut starts fast and finishes faster. Full of high-octane thrills and intricate details that bristle with authenticity."

—Mark Greaney, #1 *New York Times* bestselling author of *Burner: A Gray Man Novel*, on *Perfect Shot*

"Urszenyi brings his background as a police tactical medic to this boldly authentic debut, introducing an impressive female warrior in the first of an anticipated series."

—*Booklist* on *Perfect Shot*

Also by Steve Urszenyi

Perfect Shot

Out in the Cold

BLOOD OATH

AN ALEX MARTEL THRILLER

STEVE URSZENYI

MINOTAUR BOOKS
NEW YORK

This is a work of fiction. All of the characters, organizations, and events portrayed in this novel are either products of the author's imagination or are used fictitiously.

First published in the United States by Minotaur Books, an imprint of St. Martin's Publishing Group

EU Representative: Macmillan Publishers Ireland Ltd, 1st Floor, The Liffey Trust Centre, 117–126 Sheriff Street Upper, Dublin 1, D01 YC43

BLOOD OATH. Copyright © 2025 by Steve Urszenyi. All rights reserved. Printed in the United States of America. For information, address St. Martin's Publishing Group, 120 Broadway, New York, NY 10271.

www.minotaurbooks.com

Designed by Meryl Sussman Levavi

Library of Congress Cataloging-in-Publication Data

Names: Urszenyi, Steve, author
Title: Blood oath / Steve Urszenyi.
Description: First edition. | New York : Minotaur Books, 2025. |
 Series: An Alex Martel thriller ; 3
Identifiers: LCCN 2025030409 | ISBN 9781250393029 (hardcover) |
 ISBN 9781250393036 (ebook)
Subjects: LCGFT: Thrillers (Fiction) | Novels | Fiction
Classification: LCC PR9199.4.U78 B58 2025
LC record available at https://lccn.loc.gov/2025030409

The publisher of this book does not authorize the use or reproduction of any part of this book in any manner for the purpose of training artificial intelligence technologies or systems. The publisher of this book expressly reserves this book from the Text and Data Mining exception in accordance with Article 4(3) of the European Union Digital Single Market Directive 2019/790.

Our books may be purchased in bulk for specialty retail/wholesale, literacy, corporate/premium, educational, and subscription box use. Please contact MacmillanSpecialMarkets@macmillan.com.

First Edition: 2025

10 9 8 7 6 5 4 3 2 1

*For James Urio and all the Guardians of the Wild.
This story was born in the dust of safari tracks and beneath
the sprawling African sky you helped me understand.
Asante sana.*

May the God of vengeance now yield me His place
to punish the wicked.
—Edmond Dantès in Alexandre Dumas's
The Count of Monte Cristo

Whoever sheds the blood of man,
by man shall his blood be shed.
—Genesis 9:6, *New International Version*

BLOOD OATH

CHAPTER 1

SERENGETI NATIONAL PARK, TANZANIA

Somewhere ahead in the fog lurked her quarry, and as she stalked through the grass she remained vigilant, watching and listening for any hint that she had been detected. But only the muffled sounds of the savannah filled the air—the whispering rustle of the grass, the distant bray of a zebra, the low grunt of a wildebeest chasing off a rival. All other noise was muted as if swallowed by the fog that crept in and enveloped her.

Special Agent Alexandra Martel, contract CIA paramilitary officer, pushed forward. Each beat of her heart sent a rush of blood coursing through her veins, echoing in her ears like a Maasai drumbeat in the stillness of the heavy air.

Alex had always trusted her instincts. They had served her well as a young combat medic in her Ranger regiment, and with every posting and assignment ever since. Now, having lost sight of her quarry, she hoped those instincts wouldn't let her down. But as the minutes ticked by without another sighting, she wondered if perhaps she had lost her edge, and the moment had escaped her. Maybe she'd been outsmarted. Maybe they were on to her. Or worse, maybe they had circled back and flanked her.

Then, as if someone had lifted a veil, she saw her target and adjusted her aim through her optics.

A little to the right, she told herself. And ever so carefully, she slithered sideways on her belly, making the required adjustments to bring her subject back into range and focus.

"Eighty-five meters," called her spotter.

But Alex wasn't satisfied. The thorny branch of a blackthorn acacia partially obscured her primary target through her lens, so again, she waited.

"Alex," whispered her spotter. "Take the shot."

Moments slipped by as Alex watched and waited for the image in her mind to align with the sight picture presented through her optics. Luck was the intersection of preparation and opportunity, and she was content to await a stroke of it to achieve success.

"Take the shot! You're going to lose him."

"*Her*," she whispered.

"What?"

"It's *her*, not *him*. Now be quiet for two seconds."

She was losing time. The sun was setting, and the rays reflecting off the thin layer of fog set her subject off in a hue of golden light that wouldn't last more than an instant. But the wind shifted behind them, carrying their scent on the warming air currents up the slight grade to the kopje, an island outcropping of ancient granite in a sea of grass.

The female leopard she had been watching through her camera's telephoto lens pressed her nose into the air, lifting it to sniff the wind. Then Alex saw her chest give a slight heave. Though she couldn't hear it, she knew the mother cat had issued a warning call to her three leopard cubs poking their heads over the edge of the rock high above. They scampered down the rock face toward their mother. Together, they disappeared into the many small trees, shrubs, and hollows that provided plenty of cover and concealment options from predators.

"I told you," said her companion.

"For an old man, you can be such a twelve-year-old girl," she said, noting his frown. General David Martel didn't seem amused by the analogy—or the snipe at his age. "Truth hurts, huh, Pops?" she said.

"Yeah, well, the truth is you missed the shot."

"For your information, I got some great shots."

"Maybe, Little Miss NatGeo, but you also miss one hundred percent of the shots you don't take."

"So now you're channeling hockey wisdom?"

"If the skate fits . . ."

He was right, of course. Although she had gotten a few photos that would probably turn out well, she had been so focused on the *great shot* that she might have let the best of them slip away. But there was no sense telling him that and inflating his already robust ego.

She sat up and slung her camera over her shoulder, the long, heavy lens weighing down the front of her Nikon. She reviewed the images on the camera's display. "Look at this one," she said, tilting the screen toward him. "See how the light catches her eyes?"

It still amazed her that, after all these years, she still wanted her dad's approval. She guessed she would always be her daddy's little girl.

Retired US Army general David Martel leaned closer, his weathered face softening into a warm smile. "Beautiful shot, Allie."

Alex grinned. For once, she wasn't calculating wind speed or counting heartbeats between trigger pulls. No lives hung in the balance. There were no targets to eliminate. Just this moment of perfect stillness in the Serengeti, sharing her father's company and the simple joy of photography—a passion she'd neglected during years of deployments and operations.

She had come out a few days ago to meet her dad for a safari vacation. She couldn't remember the last time she'd taken a vacation, let alone one with her dad. Despite being unable to spend much time together over the past few years, they quickly fell back into their usual banter and good-natured chirping. They were having fun, and she found herself smiling more than she had in a long time. She was relaxed, enjoying her time with her dad.

"Come on," she said. "Let's get back to the truck."

They didn't hike far before finding the Toyota Land Cruiser, where their guide awaited their return. James was a native of northern Tanzania, descended from the Chagga people who inhabited once-sovereign kingdoms within the Kilimanjaro Region on the mountain's southern slope. When he wasn't guiding safaris, he still called the town of Moshi, two hours east of Arusha along the Arusha Himo Road, his home.

"I was wondering if I was going to have to send a search party," said James, exuding a cheerful facade through a robust accented voice.

"Alex thinks she's a famous nature photographer," the general replied as they climbed into the SUV.

"My daughter has much the same delusions," he said, shaking his head, his puffy jowls shaking as he laughed. "We are in Tanzania, David. Africa is a magical place that elevates notions of our own greatness." He sniffed like a lion checking a scent on the breeze. "It's in the air," he said.

Alex sniffed the air herself. "The only thing I smell here, James, isn't coming from any magical place I've ever been," she said. "*Mavi ya tembo.*"

He laughed even louder. "Now I am sorry that I am teaching your daughter Swahili, General. When she starts speaking about elephant dung, I know she is becoming too fluent in our language!"

"She's a fast learner, alright," said David Martel. "Just a slow photographer."

"You're a pair of real comedians," said Alex. "Home, James."

"And *you* seem to have lost your sense of humor, Ansel," Alex's dad teased, summoning the legacy of the groundbreaking American photographer Ansel Adams.

"Yes, but I'll have the last laugh when I'm awarded a prestigious juried prize for wildlife photography for my photos of the leopardess and her cubs."

James and the general burst out laughing as they headed along the two-track red dirt road toward their lodge.

The Land Cruiser featured a closed-cab design with a pop-top roof, sliding windows, and creature comforts like air-conditioning and a refrigerator. Alex and her dad preferred to ride with the roof up and the sliding windows fully opened rather than with the A/C cranking. Most of the time, they stood with their heads and shoulders protruding through the opened roof, taking in the majesty of the land and on the lookout for animals. But, as it was getting late, the pair lounged in their seats, one on either side of a center aisle.

Alex picked a traditional Maasai *shuka* off the seat in front of her, then wrapped the red, green, and black cloth around her shoulders like a shawl. She leaned her head against the 4x4's window. She had almost drifted off into a much-desired slumber when two staccato *pops* in rapid succession reached her ears. Immediately, she sat bolt upright in her seat.

"What is it?" asked James, who had caught her movement out of the corner of his eye.

"Did you hear that?" she asked.

"I heard nothing."

"Hear what?" asked the general.

James eased the vehicle to a stop on the narrow two-track road, its tires crunching softly on the gravel below. Surrounding them, the savannah unfolded in a vast tapestry of golden grasses gently swaying in the whispering breeze and rising to waist height. The air was filled with the earthy scent of sunbaked soil, mingling with the sweet perfume of the wildflowers scattered around them.

Nearby, acacia trees gracefully dotted the horizon, their feathery leaves and umbrella-shaped canopies creating a soft silhouette against the fading azure sky. The sun hung low, casting long shadows and bathing the scene in a warm golden light that danced across the rolling plains, inviting a sense of tranquility and wonder at the timeless beauty of the savannah. But the tranquil tableau was shattered by two more high-pitched reports that pierced the serenity of their surroundings.

"That I heard," said General Martel.

Suddenly, the vehicle's radio squawked with activity. Frantic radio chatter erupted from the speaker.

"What are they saying?" asked Alex.

James didn't reply right away. Instead, his eyes grew wide as he listened.

"What is it?" asked the general. "What's going on?"

The two-way radio was used so guides could communicate animal sightings to each other and coordinate tourist activities, including emergency procedures, should danger or threats arise.

"That is a ranger patrol," said James. "Two of them have been shot."

"*What?*"

"Poachers," James continued.

More chatter on the radio was almost unintelligible to Alex, but she recognized panic when she heard it.

"From the sounds of the gunfire, they're not far away," she said. "Take us there."

"No, Miss Alex. I cannot. That message was meant for the ears of other rangers and the police. It would be too dangerous for us to try to help. And besides, it is strictly forbidden to take safari guests toward known danger."

"Do you have a rifle?" she asked.

"No, Alex. You know the guides are not armed."

"Well, we have to get there to help."

"No!" said James. "I cannot put you and your father in jeopardy."

"Alex, I agree with James," said her father. "We can't go barging into the middle of a shoot-out unarmed. Never mind us; we'd be putting James in harm's way. Someone else will answer their call."

CRACK! CRACK! . . . CRACK!

Alex's hackles went up at the sound of gunfire, and she was determined to intervene.

Send me! a voice in her head shouted. She had never been one to disregard the call. She wouldn't ignore it now.

"James, get us there."

He turned to look at General Martel.

"Don't look at him for an answer! Let's go! Now!"

"Yes, Miss Alex."

CHAPTER 2

SERENGETI NATIONAL PARK, TANZANIA

Despite the word *Serengeti* meaning "the place where the land runs on forever" or "endless plains" in the Maasai language, the vast 5,700-square-mile national park was more than just a flat, featureless landscape. With a total area larger than the state of Connecticut, it was a land of varying topography. As Alex, her dad, and their guide chased down the sound of gunfire, they found themselves surrounded by hills that rose two or maybe three hundred meters above the plains.

Two ranger vehicles came into sight at the entry to a bend in the road. James slowed the Land Cruiser down just as more gunshots sounded from somewhere up ahead.

"We really should turn back," James protested. "General, perhaps you are comfortable in this situation, but let me take your daughter to safety. It is too dangerous for her."

Alex wasn't the least bit offended by his assumptions. How could he know who she was beyond being the general's daughter? But her father's expression was priceless—somewhere between amusement and pity for their guide.

"She'll be okay. I used to take her on hunting trips when she was younger. Besides, she has some first aid training that might be useful." He winked at his daughter.

"Yes, but . . ."

She tried not to laugh. She felt sorry for James and would have chewed out her dad for toying with him, but there would be time for that later. There would always be time for that.

The pair dismounted from the Land Cruiser. The general stuck his head through the open passenger-side window of the right-hand-drive vehicle. "Go back down the road," he told James.

"But how will I know to get you?"

The general snatched a portable radio off the passenger seat. "I'll take the walkie-talkie and call you over the truck radio."

James looked exasperated and worried. Not for himself but out of concern for his guests. "General, please, this is foolhardy."

"Five hundred meters. Not an inch closer. Now go."

"Yes, General. Alex, listen to your father. I will coordinate with the incoming authorities."

Whatever was happening would all be over by then. "I will, James," she lied. "*Kwaheri.*"

"Not *goodbye*, Miss Alex. *Jihadhari, rafiki.*" *Be safe, my friend.*

"Let's go," said the general, clutching at the Ka-Bar knife he carried in a well-worn leather sheath on his belt. It was stamped with the insignia of the 1st Armored Division, under which fell the unit he had commanded during Operation Iraqi Freedom.

"We might need more than that, Dad."

"Let's hope not," he replied.

Alex assumed point and ran up to the first Toyota Hilux pickup truck they came to. It was angled off the two-track roadway. Alex peered inside and opened the door, searching for a weapon or anything that might be useful. Finding nothing, she moved to a second vehicle ten meters down the road. The general searched it with the same discouraging results.

Every so often, a single shot would punch through the sounds of the African savannah. Insects buzzed and birds chirped and sang around them. She gestured for her father to follow as she moved toward the gunfire, advancing quickly but staying as low as she could while still maintaining forward movement. Aside from the waist-high grass along the side of the road, there was no other cover or concealment, and she really didn't want to think of what else could be in the tall grass. Out here, one never knew.

Twenty meters ahead on the two-track road, Alex found the body of a ranger. He was face down, a large exit wound prominent below the margin of his rib cage in his back. She felt for a pulse at his neck, but there was none. She looked at her dad and shook her head, then checked in the grass around them for any sign of a weapon—a rifle or a pistol—but again came up empty. The body of a second ranger—a woman—lay just ahead of the first. It wasn't often that Alex had encountered other women bearing arms in combat situations. Her reaction surprised even herself. It felt more tragic, more of an affront. It shouldn't have, but it did. She assessed her for signs of life. The female ranger was dead, same as her compatriot, and there were no guns left to collect.

They held their squat, trying to home in on where the battle was being fought.

"What's your thinking, Alex?"

"Someone's still shooting, maybe a quarter klick that way." She pointed ahead of them along the road. "There are two distinct guns and calibers being fired."

As if to illustrate, two more gunshots sounded in the near distance.

"Come on," she said. "Let's keep going."

The road curved right, but the gunfire came from their left. Someone (or *someones*) was likely shooting from an elevated position. If she led her father along the road any farther, she would most likely be exposing them to direct gunfire. Odds were good that whoever was engaging the rangers held the high ground and possessed better sight lines. They would likely be able to see them—if not now, then soon. She led them off the road and into the tall grass, following a game trail toward a rise of rocks.

"There better not be any snakes in here," whispered the general.

"You're okay with lions and hyenas, though?" she whispered.

He stopped in his tracks. "*What?*"

"Come on, Pumbaa," she teased. "I think we're good."

She led them along the base of a rocky mound, keeping low. She heard the scraping of boots on gravel and halted in her tracks. At least, she hoped it was boots. There was no telling who or what was ahead of them—blue force or red, friend or foe—so she crept slowly, hoping to get eyes on whoever was around the rocks in front of her. As she advanced, the back of a forest-green shirt with wildlife ranger patches on the shoulders appeared in front of her. Now, how to let him know they were here without scaring him into opening fire on them.

"*Psst*," she tried. Nothing. "Hey," she whisper-yelled.

The young ranger spun around, AKM rifle in hand. In his haste, he lost his balance and fell backward. Alex and her father raised their arms in the air.

"Americans!" she said. "*Rafiki!*" Friend.

His eyes were wide, his pupils as big as his brown irises.

She pointed to herself and her dad. "We are soldiers. American. *Rafiki*," she repeated. "How many?" She pointed to the hill ahead of them that the young man had been focused on.

"Three or four," he said, his English accented, his rifle still trained on her, center mass.

"Lower your gun," she said, gesturing while smiling casually. Or, at least, she hoped she was smiling and looking nonthreatening.

She held her hands in the air as she edged forward, keeping low so as not to present a target to the shooters on the hillside ahead. As she emerged from the grass, she noticed another man lying on the ground, a large pool of blood beneath his legs. From what she could see, he was breathing but unconscious.

Shit.

"I'm going to help him," she told the ranger, pointing to the unmoving body on the ground. He nodded, and she moved closer and knelt beside the body. A bandage fashioned from a bandana was wrapped around his leg and tied ineffectively below his knee. The makeshift tourniquet hadn't stopped the bleeding underneath it.

His popliteal or tibial artery had likely been disrupted, either from a bullet or from a bone fragment that had been turned into shrapnel. Without a proper tourniquet, he would bleed out. It might already be too late to save him.

"Dad!" she hollered. "GSW!"—gunshot wound—"Get your ass over here and put pressure on this. And you," she said to the ranger whose gun was still trained on her, "point your weapon the other way—at the bad guys would be good."

He seemed to gain courage from their presence and turned with intent back toward the enemy.

"Don't fire," she told him, "unless you see something to shoot at. Okay?"

She had wanted to say, *Until you see the whites of their eyes.*

He nodded.

The general came over and got down beside her, wrapping his large hands around the downed ranger's leg. Blood oozed like water from a sponge, and he withdrew his hands, startled.

"That's normal," she told him. "It's all the blood that's soaked into the dressing and his pants. Get your hands back on it and squeeze hard, like you were wringing somebody's neck."

The general nodded and obeyed her instructions. "Thankfully, I don't have much experience with that exact scenario, but I get the analogy."

A tear-away individual first aid kit was strapped to the man's thigh. Alex emptied the contents of the kit onto the ground and picked up a triangular bandage, still wrapped in its square cellophane package. In lesser hands, this piece of cloth would usually be used to make a sling to cradle an injured arm or shoulder. But to Alex, it was the Swiss Army knife of bandages, its usefulness limited only by the imagination and experience of a good medic.

She unpackaged the bandage and fashioned it into a cravat, which she wrapped around the man's leg above his knee. She tied a square knot snugly, then grabbed the pair of trauma shears from the first aid kit and tied them in against the knot. Blood still streamed through the general's fingers from the dressings that covered the gunshot wound, but the stricture formed by the triangular bandage tightened as she rotated the shears. As it did, the man moaned, but the flow of blood slowed to a stop. She tucked the handle of the shears into the band formed around his leg by the bandage to keep it from unwinding itself, then tied it off securely.

"You can let go now," she said to the general. He did as instructed and wiped the blood off his hands into the grass. "That should hold for now," she continued. "But he needs a hospital, fast."

"Nice work, Doc," her dad said.

She made eye contact with her dad, not confident the man was out of the woods yet. "We'll see," she said, turning the man onto his side in the grass.

Next to him lay his rifle.

CHAPTER 3

SERENGETI NATIONAL PARK, TANZANIA

Alex embraced the threat posed in moments like these, choosing to confront rather than evade the possible—and sometimes highly probable—risk of death. It was her nature. She scooped up the AKM rifle that lay within arm's length of the fallen ranger.

"Call James on the radio," she said to her father. "Tell him to update the cavalry."

"What do you want me to say?"

"Standard sitrep, Dad. You're the general—figure it out."

"Right."

Alex located the magazine release in front of the trigger guard, thumbed it forward, and removed the mag. Pulling back the charging handle on the side of the weapon, she cleared the chamber. A bullet dropped out, and she let it fall to the ground to be reclaimed later. Or not. She looked down the barrel to ensure the muzzle was straight and free of obstructions, then worked the charging handle to test its operation. She examined the receiver for visible cracks or deformation, running her hands along the steel to feel for damage that might cause catastrophic failure. The last thing she wanted was for a defective receiver or barrel to explode in her hands the first time she pulled the trigger. Finally, she reinserted the magazine and worked the charging handle. Less than fifteen seconds after she began the procedure, she and the gun were good to go, with a round chambered and ready to fire.

"Any sign of them?" she asked.

"No, miss. Not since you and the old man arrived."

She was sure it was merely an observation and not a judgment—something wherein the tone of intended respect had gotten lost in translation, she told herself—but she was glad her dad hadn't overheard his remark just the same.

"Alex," she said, pointing at herself.

The small-statured ranger considered this strange white lady for a moment. "Anga," he said.

"Anga," she repeated, then nodded.

She wondered why the poachers hadn't bugged out. They had inflicted serious damage on the ranger patrol, killing two and critically wounding another. They should have been content to quit while they were ahead—*ahead* being *still breathing* in this case. Their focus should have been to make their escape and resume their illegal hunt another day, assuming that's what this was. But she remembered what her father often said about assumptions, that to *assume* risked making an *ass* out of *u* and *me*. He got that wisdom from a sitcom, but it seemed apropos.

She scanned the bush-covered hillside for any sign of movement, any suggestion that they still faced a lethal threat nearby.

"Are they gone?" asked Anga.

"I don't think so," she said.

Nothing indicated the aggressors had left, and she wasn't ready to declare that the danger had passed. In the absence of proof, she wouldn't risk her own life, let alone her father's or those of the rangers. So she waited, crouched behind a translucent veil of grass. Waiting was something she did well with a rifle in her hands.

Even though poaching for bushmeat and ivory was routinely controlled by gangs that answered to larger criminal entities—often with the lead players in faraway lands—the poachers themselves frequently came from local villages close to the boundaries of national parks like Serengeti. Whoever had ambushed this patrol was likely an unsophisticated crew wanting nothing more than to shrink away to the safety of their own homes.

The *crack-thump* of a rifle shot broke the silence and dispelled that theory. The bullet hadn't missed her by much. The time between the two sounds was less than half a second—more like only a third or less—the *crack* being the mini sonic boom of the air being split by the bullet traveling between three and four times the speed of sound and the *thump* being the report of the gunshot itself, its sound traveling only *at* the speed of sound. From these two sounds, Alex estimated the range of the shooter to be less than one hundred meters, but there were too many variables to make a precise guess.

So much for shrinking away.

There were multiple bogeys on the hillside facing them. They'd killed two rangers and critically wounded a third. Why hadn't they bugged out? Surely they knew they held the upper hand. Opening fire again when they could just as easily have made their escape didn't make much sense. Was there another objective?

What the hell is going on?

She peered down the AKM's iron sights, scanning the area to their front, left, and right.

There! A sliver of light glinted off glass—a rifle scope—maybe seventy-five meters ahead of her. She flicked the safety down two clicks, putting the rifle into single-fire mode, and aimed where she had seen the flash of light. The trigger felt mushy beneath the pad of her finger as she squeezed it, but it broke crisply, yielding to around five pounds of pressure. The gunshot was deafening. A split second later, a wisp of dirt kicked up from the ground on the hillside where her bullet had impacted below the shooter. Through her iron sights, she tracked as the figure broke cover—a tall man with broad shoulders, a ballcap perched backward on his head. As he turned to look up the hill for better cover, she recognized the unmistakable logo of the Philadelphia Eagles gleaming under the Tanzanian sun, its sharp lines and green accents almost surreal in this desolate place.

What the hell is an Eagles fan doing here? she thought, her mind briefly snagging on the absurdity of it.

The man turned, raising his rifle to fire. Alex didn't hesitate. She exhaled slowly, her finger squeezing the trigger in a smooth, practiced motion. The shot rang out, and he crumpled to the ground.

"Hit!" called Anga from beside her. "You shot one of them! *Risasi nzuri!* Great shot, miss!"

His joy was short-lived, however, as a fusillade of rifle fire rained down on their position, and Alex mashed her face into the dirt as bullets buzzed overhead like an angry swarm of killer bees. When the torrent died down, she risked a glance downrange and saw that the body that had fallen was being carried away by a trio of men. From this distance, she couldn't make out many details besides that they were dark-skinned and wore camouflage-patterned clothing.

She aimed again but hesitated. Her assailants were in the process of collecting a casualty she had inflicted on them. Now it was she who held the advantage, as they were out in the open and vulnerable to her rifle fire. She could have reengaged the various targets of opportunity, but that wouldn't have been sporting, let alone copacetic. On the other hand, the ranger beside her didn't feel the same disinclination.

BOOM! BOOM! Both his bullets missed their mark.

"Hold your fire!" she shouted.

"Why, miss?"

Well, for one thing, you're wasting ammo.

She didn't say that, though, and she didn't feel like lecturing Anga on the various rules of the Geneva Conventions, so she replied, "They're leaving."

"But they killed my friends."

Fair point.

Shooting them as they retreated with a fallen comrade, though, was more akin to vengeance than justice. Lord knows there was a time for revenge, but this wasn't it.

Alex assessed that the bogeys would likely bug out around the back side of the hill to waiting vehicles. She considered taking Anga with her to pursue them, but ultimately, she resisted that urge. This wasn't her fight, purely speaking, and she and her father were alone with one dying ranger and one whose combat skills were untested at best against an enemy force of at least three or four. Well, three, anyway. Going against her instincts, she decided it was better to let them escape than to chase them and risk more lives.

The injured ranger lying on the ground stirred.

"Dad, check on him."

It was still daylight, but the sun had settled behind the surrounding hills. Alex kept low as she moved forward to a better vantage point. She hoped to catch sight of the men who had shot at them, hoped even more that they had chosen to get in their vehicles and abandon their plan—whatever it was—rather than circling behind her and their small party.

She turned back to rejoin the general.

"He might make it," he said, standing beside the fallen ranger whose eyes were open now while his partner spoke to him in a low voice. Alex's Swahili was limited to a few polite phrases and food orders—not enough to understand the conversation being shared—but she was a survivor of enough battles to recognize the efforts of one warrior comforting another.

Then, from behind her, the sound of approaching trucks reverberated off the hills.

"Get down!" she called.

They did as she directed, and seconds later, three Toyota pickup trucks rolled around the bend, visible above the grass and shrubs. Anga lay almost on top of his fallen comrade, shielding him, while the general lay next to them, obscured by the vegetation.

She trained her sights on the windshield of the lead vehicle, ready to put a bullet into anything that posed a threat. The truck was identical to the ranger vehicles they had passed on their way in, but she couldn't be sure who its occupants were yet.

Anga popped up unexpectedly, waving his arms and shouting.

Shit! You better be right, little man, she thought.

The trio of trucks came to a stop not more than ten meters away, and six men armed with AKM rifles, like the one she was holding, piled out. She was wary about showing herself too quickly—or at all—but the jig was up when Anga pointed in her direction. She stood up slowly, laying her recently acquired rifle down in the grass, hoping this would appease their unease. More than one person had been shot by accident when jittery nerves got the better of the one who held the upper hand. The newcomers didn't seem to fully comprehend her gesture, however, and she suddenly found herself looking down the business end of half a dozen rifles.

"*Rafiki!*" she announced, expectations and hope buoyant.

Despite what their guide, James, had been telling others, she hadn't yet mastered conversational Swahili. Stammering the word *friend* might be the icebreaker she needed.

Anga jumped between the newly arrived crew of rangers and Alex, explaining animatedly about . . . something. The conversation fluctuated in raised voices, with fingers pointing. Finally, he backed up and put an arm around her shoulder, guiding her toward the man who appeared to have seniority in this outfit. Then her dad, ever the brave general, stepped out from the tall grass next to the injured ranger with his arms raised, and the process was repeated.

One more time, the leader in front spoke.

"He says you should follow him," Anga translated.

They walked to the back of the third truck while the other men in the party retrieved the downed ranger. Once he was settled into the back of one of the trucks, Alex went to him to check on his injuries.

She spoke to the group's leader. "His condition is critical," she explained. She racked her brain to see if she could cobble a sentence together from words and phrases she had heard others speak.

She tried, "*Anahitaji kufika hospitalini mara moja.*"

She hoped she had just told him that the man needed to get to the hospital immediately, but she might have just told him his mother was a cow. She wasn't sure.

The man's eyes grew wide as he began speaking to her rapidly. Then he made a gesture she thought indicated a helicopter was coming as he got on his portable radio.

It took some time, but eventually, the commanding officer of the wildlife ranger detachment conceded that Alex had not been the aggressor in the incident that had resulted in the deaths of two of his rangers and left another in critical condition. That young man had been medevacked by helicopter to a trauma center just across the border in Nairobi, Kenya, less than an hour away, his life saved by Alex's quick and improvised actions.

In fact, once the commander was convinced of that significant mitigating detail, he determined that Alex's actions had been justified and that her continued detention or questioning was not necessary. She and her father were released from his custody and free to go.

As they prepared to depart, Alex felt her father's hand on her shoulder.

"You okay?" he asked quietly.

She nodded, though the adrenaline was beginning to ebb, leaving her hands with the slightest tremor. "Just another day in paradise, right?"

He squeezed her shoulder. "Let's get back to James before he has a heart attack."

They found James in his Land Cruiser, parked behind the three ranger vehicles. As they approached, he rushed to them. "That was bad—very, very bad," he said.

"It's okay, James, we're okay," Alex said.

"No, no, no. I am responsible for your safety, Miss Alex. You cannot go running into danger like that."

"It's okay, James, it's what she does," said the general as they climbed into the vehicle. Driving back to the lodge, Alex couldn't shake the image of the man she'd killed. Something told her this wasn't over. There was no way these men were poachers, so what had they been hunting for?

CHAPTER 4

MARA SERENGETI LODGE, TANZANIA

The night sky over Mara Serengeti Lodge pulsed with stars, brilliant pinpoints against the pitch-black darkness. Alex sat across from her father at a linen-covered table, the afternoon events replaying in her mind like combat footage on a loop.

"Come meet me on a safari . . . we'll have a few laughs," her father quipped, his voice rising to a theatrical falsetto.

"Stop your whining," she replied, a smile breaking through despite herself. "It wasn't exactly Nakatomi Plaza out there, Pops."

The general sipped his bourbon old-fashioned, studying her over the rim of his glass. His large, calloused hands dwarfed the tumbler—hands that had commanded armies and comforted the dying with equal conviction.

"Well, it's still the last time I'm going on vacation with you, Allie," he teased.

She laughed. "You're losing your edge. How'd you get your Army call sign Condor anyway? Maybe they should have called you Sparrow or Chicken instead."

"Ha, such a comedian! Okay, *Shooter*."

She laughed again at hearing him mock her call sign.

Around them, other guests dined in blissful ignorance, their conversations a gentle murmur beneath the African night. None of them had spent their afternoon applying tourniquets or dodging bullets, nor did any feel the weight of unasked questions lingering in the air.

As the grounds of the lodge grew darker, lanterns were lit, casting warm halos against the encroaching night. Beyond their light lay the vast, unknowable darkness of the savannah—beautiful, dangerous, and filled with predators that hunted in the shadows.

During the day, the Mara Serengeti Lodge was a marvel of architecture in harmony with the landscape. Built in the traditional circular design that mimicked the Maasai bomas, the main pavilion rose from the plains with its soaring thatched roof and walls, constructed from local stone, that appeared to have grown organically from the earth itself. Tall windows stretched from floor to ceiling, framing postcard-perfect views of the endless plains.

She had been struck by its beauty when they first arrived—how the wooden beams overhead had been hand-carved by local artisans, how the parquet floors guided visitors past plush couches and settees to the curved bar and the restaurant beyond.

The grounds were a testament to careful cultivation in this harsh environment: lush gardens of native plants surrounded the individual guest cabins, each designed to resemble the traditional Maasai houses yet featuring luxurious interiors. Behind the main pavilion, a stunning infinity pool appeared to spill directly into the savannah, creating the illusion that one could swim right up to the wildlife that occasionally wandered by.

It wasn't uncommon to find dik-diks—tiny antelope no larger than house cats—grazing on the manicured lawns, or to require an escort after dark because a Cape Buffalo had come to drink from the pool. James had warned them on their first day that the wildlife considered the lodge to be part of their territory, not the other way around. "The animals were here first," he'd said with his characteristic smile. "We are merely visitors in their home."

The outdoor dining patio where they now sat was her favorite spot—positioned perfectly to catch both the sunrise and sunset, with comfortable seating arranged to encourage conversations among strangers who would soon become friends, united by their shared wonder at this magical place.

"Isn't it incredible?" she said finally, her gaze fixed on the horizon where the last vestige of sunset glowed like embers.

Her father was smiling but not at the view.

"What?" she asked, catching his stare.

"You have that same look on your face you'd get at the cabin when you were a kid."

"I remember those trips."

"You'd be staring up at the mountains as the sun set behind them while your mom and I stared at you, watching you soak it all in, your face lit up like it was just now."

Those were precious times—her father home from deployment, her mother away from her medical practice, the three of them together in the Wyoming wilderness. Family time had been rare and, therefore, treasured.

As darkness thickened around them, her feeling of being confined within the glow of the tiki lamps lining the patio intensified, and the euphoria of the previous moment was overshadowed by the predations of her own thoughts. She wondered what lurked beyond the light. Would the faint illumination keep predators at bay or draw them in for a closer look, their prospective meals softly lit for easier selection, like squishy cream-filled puff pastries in a bakery display?

As if reading her thoughts, her dad said, "You've paid a heavy price, Allie." He was trying to comfort her.

She pushed the thought and his comment aside with a wave of her hand and a swig of ice-cold beer.

"No, really," he continued. "I don't say it often enough, but I'm proud of you." Alex turned away, rolling her eyes. "And I know your mother would be, too," he continued.

"Come on, Dad. I was doing what I do—what you instilled in me to do."

"I need to make a point of saying it more often. I watched you out there. You have the heart of a lion, Alex. And you've accomplished more in your brief career—*careers*—than I did in twice the time."

"Stop, Dad. That's such bullshit."

But he continued. "It's not. It took me a lot of years to find my feet, but from the very beginning, you picked a specialty where your actions would directly impact your fellow soldiers. Being a combat medic isn't an easy road. It's tough, and it's noble." She could see he needed to get it out, so she leaned back with her beer in hand and let him, meeting his gaze across the table.

"By fate or bad luck or horrible timing, you ended up having a Silver Star pinned to your uniform by no less than the vice president of the United States. Like it or not, Allie, you earned that honor and are among an elite warrior class. You're not just any grunt; you're a soldier's soldier."

"Okay, enough already. Fate brought me into the midst of those wounded warriors. After that, I just did my job."

"Fate loves the fearless, Allie. You did something few could—or would. You picked up a sniper rifle to save your platoon mates and the elite soldiers you were sent to help. Your actions that day saved countless lives. And you shed blood for that Silver Star."

"For which I also received a Purple Heart, so can we just knock it off, Dad? You're embarrassing me."

He glanced around. "There's no one listening. Fine," he conceded. "But that's my job. Never let anyone tell you you're anything less than one of our nation's finest warriors."

Across from her, he took another bite of roast . . . *something*.

"Whatever," she said.

They dissolved into silence.

The general's phone buzzed on the table. He glanced at it and frowned. "Sorry, Allie, I have to get this." He stood and moved toward the edge of the patio, phone pressed to his ear.

Alex watched him go, noting the subtle straightening of his posture, the way his free hand clenched and unclenched at his side. Whatever the call was about, it wasn't good news.

Around them, a mix of animated chatter and breathless quietude permeated the camp. People engaged in conversations about the beauty of their surroundings, their food and drinks, and other more personal matters. Young couples exchanged flirtatious glances, while older couples shared a level of comfort and familiarity born from years of shared experiences that the young could only envy.

Alex wondered what it would be like to be so comfortable with someone that you could finish each other's thoughts without outright annoying each other. Even with her late husband, Kyle, there had been times when they would sooner kill each other than make love. Passion ran deep. There were things about Kyle that drove her crazy—his boyish fascination with video games, his delight at seeing her naked, regardless of how inappropriate the moment or the circumstances were—but what she wouldn't give to be able to hurl her sports bra at him in mock anger one last time as he pulled her close with well-muscled arms when all she wanted was to get dressed.

You smell amazing.

Kyle, I have to go to work.

Come on, it'll just take a few minutes.

Oh, be still, my beating heart! The words of a poet.

Right?

Go away, Kyle!

Looking back, those moments gave life meaning and energy. Being loved, however adolescent the expression of that love, was priceless. It was love all the same, deeply felt and expressed with the innocence of a man who didn't care who knew how much he loved her. Kyle was a proud man, yet he was as vulnerable as a child when he finally opened his heart to her.

And then he was gone. In one senseless act, he was taken from her just as their life together was beginning.

CHAPTER 5

BUTEMBA, ON THE SHORES OF LAKE VICTORIA

An early summer storm blew in from the northwest. It arrived not as a whisper but as a roar—a tempest born from the collision of Ugandan highland winds and the humid breath of Lake Victoria. The village clung to the lakeshore like a stubborn weed, its skeletal fishing boats tethered to weathered piers, its homes cobbled together from corrugated iron, sun-bleached driftwood, and the plastic detritus of a globalized world. It was yet another chapter in an unending saga of survival.

Children scrambled to secure tarpaulin roofs as the first raindrops fell, fat and heavy, their laughter drowned out by thunder. To the people of Butemba, it mattered little where the storm began. Like the misfortune that had plagued the continent for centuries, once trouble blew in, it became a local problem.

This was the story of Africa.

The tempest unleashed torrential rain that flooded the village's fragile homes and damaged its minimal infrastructure. From the townspeople's perspective, yet another storm was assailing the village. Whatever was lost would not be regained anytime soon. Such was the nature of the land they lived in: it was unforgiving and cruel, but the people here were resilient and had lived through worse, and would again.

At the village's edge, where the shanties gave way to dense bush, stood Lemarti's compound. The prefabricated Nissen hut—a relic of British colonialism—dominated the clearing, its curved steel ribs groaning under the onslaught of rain. Surrounding it, a makeshift barracks had formed: tents patched with UNHCR tarps, a cookhouse belching smoke, and a rusted Toyota Hilux on blocks, its bed converted into a sniper's nest. This was no ordinary rebel camp; it was a hybrid of tradition and desperation, where Maasai spears leaned against crates of Chinese-made AKMs and AK-47s.

The compound was well away from the lake, nestled in a pocket of land surrounded on three sides by lush green hills. While they often buffered the winds, at times the hills directed the rain into circular patterns, trapping the people inside a lashing storm with rain that fell sideways. Into this maelstrom, the men returned. As they pulled into the large compound, they parked their trucks in front of the Nissen hut. The semicylindrical shape allowed the rain to flow off the building quickly, making a sound reminiscent of muffled steel drumbeats and white noise at night.

Lemarti watched the storm from the hut's doorway, his lean frame silhouetted against the flickering light of a kerosene lamp. His skin, the deep umber of fertile soil, bore the ritual scarification of his people—three vertical lines on one of his cheeks, earned not in a rite of passage but in a battle with a lion years ago. The memory still haunted him: the hot stench of the beast's breath, how its claws had ripped through his *shuka* as he drove his *rungu* between its eyes. Back then, he had been Laioni, "the lion," a young Moran guarding his father's cattle. Now, he was Lemarti—"the courageous one"—a title that tasted like ashes.

Displacement had forged him anew. When Saudi investors and Tanzanian officials conspired to seize Maasai grazing lands for a luxury safari lodge, Lemarti's *boma* had resisted. They'd been promised compensation, schools, clinics. Instead, they'd received bullets. He could still hear the screams of his mother, her body shielding his younger sisters as the bulldozers advanced. Only he and his brother, Saitoti, both already young warriors, had escaped, fleeing into the bush with nothing but their knives and the scarred hide of the lion Lemarti had killed.

Above and beneath his skin, he bore the scars, anger, and shame of a survivor, one who had been forced to flee as most members of his *boma* were exterminated, the sounds of their pain and terror reaching his ears as he crossed the dusty swath of land where he pastured his cattle, then fled to safety. He had learned to turn his pain outward and mastered skills that a cattle herdsman ordinarily didn't possess. The leadership skills he had learned growing up as the son of a Maasai chieftain came to the fore, and he found he could lead in ways others could not; all it took was to lead with bravery. And when that didn't work, to lead with brutality.

Next to him in the doorway stood a boy no older than fourteen, cradling an AK-47, its stock sawed down to fit his frame. Lemarti watched him—Kijana, orphaned when Burundian rebels slaughtered his family. The militia was full of such boys: raw nerve endings wrapped in skin and bone, their laughter too sharp, their eyes too old. They called Lemarti Baba, meaning "father," though he'd sired no children. His own family tree had been chainsawed for tourist cabins.

Kijana was Maasai by birthright, but he was not yet a Moran—a Maasai warrior. He barely reached the height of Lemarti's rib cage. His bravery was not a divine gift, as was Lemarti's, nor had it been earned or born of an innate strength or finely honed martial skill; instead, it stemmed from the hubris of youth and the roar of cordite.

The compound stirred as Lemarti's men returned, their trucks sliding through the mud. Lemarti drew on a Ugandan-made cigarette cradled between his fingers, a habit recently acquired. Armed men on either side of him stood poised to assist the arriving crew with their cargo. He French-inhaled the smoke, then noticed the most important cargo was not there. *The general.* He flicked his cigarette onto the drenched earth, its sizzle drowned out by the deluge from above.

His second-in-command, Desmond, exited into the rain. Silently, he moved behind one of the trucks. In the back lay a body wrapped in a tarp that pooled rainwater and blood. It was Saitoti, his face frozen in a snarl, the scar on his cheek a remnant from his youth.

"What happened?" asked Lemarti.

"*Mwanamke*," hissed Desmond, Lemarti's lieutenant, as they unloaded the body.

The general's daughter. He had been warned about the American soldier-woman—the child of a warrior.

Lemarti knelt beside his brother, fingers tracing the scar he had earned defending their herd from hyenas as a boy. Saitoti had always been the thinker, the one who'd memorized constellations to navigate the savannah. Now, his eyes stared at a sky that wept for him.

"She dies slowly," Lemarti said, his voice low as the thunder. "Not with a bullet. Let her taste the fear we've swallowed."

With a flick of his head, he directed the men to carry his brother inside. They laid the tarp on the floor, the blood and rain running off it in a stream that bumped and curled against cracks in the concrete as it flowed, collecting in small pools here and there before reaching the drain. Lemarti watched the river of his brother's blood leave his lifeless body, intermingling with the rainwater and dirt on the floor.

As rain drummed the Nissen hut's roof, Lemarti addressed his men. They sat in a semicircle, Saitoti's body at their center.

"The *mzungu* thinks we are animals to be culled," he said, switching between Swahili and Maa, the liquid syllables of his mother tongue. "She forgets—the lion may flee the hunter, but he always returns."

He unsheathed his panga, the machete's edge catching the lamplight. With ritual precision, he sliced his palm and let blood drip onto Saitoti's chest.

"*Enkitok Enkai!*" he cried. *By the blood of God!* The ancient Maa oath tore from his throat as he smeared crimson across Saitoti's lips. "Until the plains run red or my bones bleach in the sun, I pledge vengeance!"

Men rose and blades flashed in the gloom as the warriors followed suit—pangas, bayonets, even a rusted machete taken from a Rwandan death squad. Their blood rained on Saitoti's corpse, mingling with Lake Victoria's tears pooling on the concrete floor. Kijana cut deepest, his slash across the forearm drawing approving nods from warriors who'd once mocked his trembling grip.

The men echoed the oath, blades flashing. Outside, the storm raged on—a mirror to the tempest in Lemarti's chest.

"We will hunt the ones who took our land, our blood, our people!"

Lemarti smiled, khat-stained teeth gleaming in the dark. Let the storm come.

CHAPTER 6

MARA SERENGETI LODGE, TANZANIA

Alex's father returned to their table, mercifully interrupting her thoughts about Kyle. His expression was carefully neutral. "I have some bad news," he said.

"What is it?"

"I have to leave first thing in the morning."

"What? Why?"

"Something's come up at work. I have to fly back tomorrow and smooth over some problems."

"What kind of problems? Isn't anyone else on your team able to manage a crisis?"

He shook his head. "I'm afraid not. When government officials get used to working with someone, they're not very keen to adapt to others."

A familiar sense of disappointment welled up inside her. She tried to tamp down the childlike feelings that came flooding back from her youth. But damn, she had been looking forward to reconnecting with her dad and enjoying his company over the next few days. Now, this sudden change of plans was setting off warning bells. Her father had been deliberately vague about his post-military work in the nearby Okavango Republic. She had only recently learned of his intelligence connections—more by accident than admission.

"You haven't told me much about this project of yours in Okavango, Dad."

"And I can't." His voice softened. "Look, Allie, you understand sensitive, compartmented information better than anybody, so I won't give you some song-and-dance cover story about what I do."

She recognized the truth in his words, even as part of her bristled at being kept in the dark. Her own work for the CIA—and before that, with Intelligence Support Activity—had taught her the value of compartmentalization.

Okavango's government was among the few in the southern African region that still welcomed an American presence on its soil, unlike many others on the continent that had been seduced by the promise of cold, hard (American) cash offered by different state actors. The OR was a country half the size of Tanzania, making it small by African standards. Nevertheless, it punched well above its weight in strategic importance and through its influence within the African Union and the United Nations, thanks to its wealth of natural resources and rare earth minerals, along with its more stable regime, admirable security status, and relatively well-educated and affluent citizenry. It was an ally the US couldn't afford to lose. Okavango posed an uncommon barrier to Russian and Chinese inroads on the continent, and there were other projects rumored to be in the works that the White House routinely denied, but were understood to be critically important to American interests.

"Well, I guess I can cut this trip short and head back to work after you leave," she said.

"I don't know why you would."

The conversation from the nearby pavilion grew more animated. A familiar voice emerged from the throng, but before Alex could place it, her father continued.

"You could stay here."

"What, and just finish the safari alone?" she asked.

The sound of approaching footsteps rose behind her. Before she could turn, a voice rang out from the darkness.

"Hey, Shooter!"

Alex whirled around to face the voice, her long hair whipping like the tail of a horse. There was usually only one person who called her that, and he had been doing it since long before it became her code name at the Agency. The man stood just over six feet tall, with wavy, chestnut-brown hair that was a bit too long in the back, showing silver strands at the temples—he could use a haircut. His rugged face sported a broad grin, and his shoulders strained against the seams of his safari shirt. Smoky hazel eyes bored into hers.

"Caleb?" she asked, disbelief coloring her voice.

It didn't compute. How could he be here? Last she saw him, he was back in Washington. Specifically, she had left him behind at the team office on Leesburg Pike in Fall's Church, Virginia.

"Hey, Caleb!" her dad said. "Pull up a chair and join us."

"Don't mind if I do." He plunked a sweating bottle of Kilimanjaro Premium Lager onto the table and slid into a chair. "Good to see you, General."

"How was your flight?"

"Oh, you know—"

"You knew about this, Dad?"

"I sure did," he boasted, a smirk dancing across his face. "I invited him . . . Surprise!"

She eyed her father with a mixture of grudging respect and a healthy dose of irritation.

Caleb, meanwhile, scooped up his beer and gave it a healthy swig.

"Man, nothing beats a cold beer after a long day of traveling." Then, turning to look Alex straight in the eyes, he winked and asked, "So? How's the photo safari?"

The general chimed in. "About that. We had a bit of a complication."

"Oh?"

David Martel summarized the altercation and shooting for their new arrival. Caleb assessed Alex warily. "You okay?"

"I'm still stuck on the part where my father invited you to join us on an African safari without talking to me about it first."

"I wanted it to be a surprise—"

"Oh, I'm surprised, Dad."

"You guys have been working your asses off for Uncle Sam, and after that job in Helsinki kind of blew up in your faces back in Virginia, I figured it would be good for the three of us to spend some quality time together."

"Dad," Alex said while eyeing Caleb sideways. "I say again, maybe I should have been part of that discussion."

"I'm not feeling very welcome," said Caleb.

"Call your therapist. Or go stroke your Kubotan, or whatever."

"Now, Allie—"

"Don't *Allie* me, Dad."

She pushed her chair away from the table and walked to the pavilion, leaving the two men to nurse their beers together.

"Well, that went well," the general said.

"Yeah," responded Caleb. "Surprises aren't really her thing."

CHAPTER 7

THE BAR, MARA SERENGETI LODGE, TANZANIA

Alex entered the main pavilion of the lodge and headed for the bar. The interior was more spacious than it seemed from the outside, its circular shape creating an openness like the savannah itself. She strolled along the parquet floor, past plush furnishings, down a few steps, and toward a curved bar, her long cotton skirt flowing in the gentle breeze.

Other guests and lodge workers greeted her cordially as she passed. She nodded politely, maintaining the professional distance that had become second nature. She sidled up to the bar, the bartender eyeing her as he wiped tumblers, hiding them out of sight behind the counter.

"What'll it be, miss?" he asked, an Australian accent on display.

She considered the row of bottles on the shelf behind him. There were whiskeys, scotches, and vodkas, but tonight, she was in the mood for none of those. Her nerves were already raw enough without adding fuel to the fire.

"Gin and tonic."

"Going full colonial, eh?" He waved a hand toward a high shelf. "Pick your poison?"

Hemlock, she wanted to say, but instead, her eyes surveyed the bottles—the blacks, blues, and greens. Their colors reminded her of bruises. Fitting, considering how her pride felt at this moment.

"I don't care. Surprise me."

He smiled, revealing a magnificent flash of dimples.

"Right," he said. Squinting, he put a hand to his chin as if to consider her challenge carefully, alternating his gaze between her and the bottles. "I don't take you for a Bombay Sapphire girl—too fruity and bright for you." She tried to decode the compliment. One was in there somewhere. "And I feel like Hendrick's is too spicy and floral for your mood."

"My mood?"

"Tense, but contemplative. Too much juniper on your tongue will aggravate you even more."

"I'm not aggravated." The lie tasted bitter on her tongue, more so than any gin could.

"Right," he said. "Tanqueray, on the other hand—"

"Tanq will be fine."

He pulled a green bottle from the shelf. "So you really didn't want to be surprised at all, did you."

"I guess I like to be in control," she said, shrugging her bare shoulders. Control was her sanctuary, her fortress against vulnerability. She'd learned early that losing it meant getting hurt.

He poured a measure of gin over ice and topped her glass up from a mini bottle of tonic water without commenting on her remark, though she could see he was biting his tongue, his dimples sinking deeply into his cheeks. He squeezed the juice from a wedge of lime into her glass then speared it and placed the fizzy concoction before her on a coaster, setting a napkin to the side.

"Cheers."

"Here's to not catching malaria," she said, raising her glass.

Alex closed her eyes and savored the drink's tartness. With ice cubes tinkling against the sides of the glass, the crispness of the drink soothed her palate. She was reminded why G&Ts had been a favorite of those who had visited this country and this continent before her. All at once, the drink was cold and sweet and bitter, bringing a refreshing and satisfying end to another day on the dusty and dangerous savannah. It was survival in a glass. One of tonic water's ingredients—quinine—had antimalarial properties and was responsible for imparting the classic bitterness of the concoction, even if the quantity of quinine in most contemporary tonic waters is insufficient to prevent the disease.

She dragged the lime-tipped spear along the rim of the glass, and then let the wedge slide down through the ice cubes to the bottom of her drink. She gave it a stir and took another sip, its tartness drawing her lips together tightly.

The bartender leaned on the wide counter.

"Well?" he asked.

"It'll do." She made eye contact and smiled. Next to her rifle, it was her deadliest weapon. But tonight, her arsenal felt depleted.

"Brad," he said, introducing himself.

"Alex."

"What brings you to East Africa, Alex?"

She placed her glass down on the coaster and paused before answering. What did bring her here? Escape? Connection? The chance to feel something other than the constant vigilance that defined her life?

"It's not a trick question," he added.

"But it's a tricky one to answer, isn't it? I either say something completely glib and come off sounding superficial, like just another tourist, or I give you a heartfelt response about wanting to be one with nature in the birthplace of humanity deep in the heart of Africa's Great Rift Valley and come off sounding too intellectual."

"Well, not to be pedantic about it," he said, his Aussie accent oozing across the bar, "but we're a little outside that particular geographic feature." It sounded like he said *fee-cha*.

"I was being allegorical. And anyway, we were in the Ngorongoro Crater a couple of days ago."

"That's inside the Rift, alright. Look, Alex, I think you're overthinking it."

It wouldn't be the first time. Overthinking was her specialty, especially when it came to matters of the heart.

"Are you some kind of expert?" she asked.

"In psychology?"

"No, anthropology."

"Sorta." Off her blank stare, he continued. "I'm a senior secondary school teacher—what you Yanks call college. On sabbatical."

"And you just happened to find yourself bartending in the middle of the Serengeti?"

"I'm friends with one of the owners. He's from Oz, too. Asked if I could lend a hand for a few weeks while they make some staffing changes, and lo and behold, here I am."

"Lo and behold." Another sip, then she added, "I'm doing something I've wanted to do my whole life." The words felt hollow. What she'd wanted her whole life wasn't a place, but a feeling. Safety. Belonging. Things that seemed perpetually out of reach.

"No exotic travel in your past then?"

"I didn't say that," she said without elaborating. She didn't think she should mention Syria, Afghanistan, Iraq, and Ukraine at this juncture. Too difficult to explain in a single sentence. Looking toward the patio, she spotted Caleb walking her way. Her heart performed its usual treasonous flutter. "Tanzania is never short on surprises."

"True. I heard there was an incident out on the savannah today."

"Oh?" she said coyly.

"Some kind of shooting. I guess rangers caught up to some poachers." He leaned on the bar. "But don't say anything to anyone—I really shouldn't have mentioned it."

"Mum's the word."

Caleb slid into the stool next to hers. His presence brought with it the familiar scent of his body wash, triggering memories she'd tried to suppress. Helsinki. Paris. The moments when they'd come close—so close—to crossing the line they'd drawn between them.

"What'll it be, mate?" asked Brad.

"I'll have what she's having."

Brad turned away to fix his drink.

"Look," Caleb said, his voice low enough that only she could hear. "We should have told you."

"You think?" She kept her eyes on her drink, afraid of what he might see if she looked at him directly.

"When David brought it up, I thought it was a great idea."

"*David?*"

"Your dad . . . the general . . . whatever."

"And now?" She finally turned to him, searching his face for the truth.

"I can see why you'd be pissed off." His eyes met hers, and for a moment, she saw something there—regret, longing, fear. It mirrored what she felt but would never admit.

"How intuitive of you." Alex didn't go in much for drama. Caleb might have been expecting her to be angry, which she was, but she'd be damned if she'd show it (much) or let their little surprise ruin her holiday. Or reveal how his presence made her pulse quicken despite her better judgment.

Brad set Caleb's G&T before him. "Bottoms up," he said, before walking off to take care of other guests newly arrived at the bar.

Caleb picked up his drink and raised it to her. "Cheers," he said. Then, "I'm sorry."

She hadn't expected that. The simple apology cracked her armor in a way she wasn't prepared for.

She clinked her glass against his before taking a sip, using the moment to compose herself.

"I guess I figured this would be a good opportunity to spend some time together away from Langley," he said. "We've been working together for about a year now—"

"Less," she corrected, though she'd counted every day.

"Well, whatever it is. We've been through a lot together and, you know, there's some unresolved . . ." His voice trailed off, and she could see him struggling with words that wouldn't come.

"Unresolved what?" she prompted when he didn't finish the thought. Her heart hammered against her ribs.

He adjusted himself on the barstool, his discomfort palpable.

"Unresolved what?" she asked again, an unrelenting interrogator. But this time, she wasn't sure she wanted the answer.

"Things have happened between us. And we've never had a chance to sort them out." His fingers tightened around his glass, knuckles whitening.

"Are you talking about *feelings*?" The word hung between them, dangerous and electric.

He took a long sip of his drink, buying time. "Look, I just want us to spend some time together."

"So these things that need to be sorted out, how's that going to happen? Magic?" She was pushing him away again, her default setting when things got too real.

"Hopefully," he whispered into his drink, and the vulnerability in his voice nearly undid her.

"You're a dick." But there was no heat in the insult, just a desperate attempt to maintain distance.

"Look, Alex, you know it's complicated. I'm your boss—"

"That's horseshit, Caleb. We don't exactly fit the mold of the usual boss/worker relationship." Their relationship had never been definable by conventional standards. They'd saved each other's lives, seen each other at their worst, shared moments of intensity that created bonds beyond professional boundaries.

"I know. I'm just saying—"

"What are you saying? Because so far I've heard you say nothing." She wanted him to be brave enough for both of them, to say the words she couldn't bring herself to utter.

It was his decision to come here, so why should she cut him any slack? She watched as he squirmed on the barstool and drew a Kubotan from his pocket—a blunt, six-inch metal rod meant for close-quarters self-defense—its keyring trailing a battered lead slug. He rolled the small weapon across his palm, caressing the deformed slug like a rosary bead. The compact stick was his crutch whenever stress closed in. A part of her sympathized with his discomfort, but mostly she was just vexed. And terrified of what might happen if either of them actually spoke the truth.

"I've tried to show you." His voice was barely audible, his eyes fixed on the Kubotan in his hand.

"How? Do you mean in Helsinki, when you decked the guy I was with?" The memory of that night flashed through her mind—Caleb's face contorted with jealousy, the raw emotion he'd displayed before shuttering it away again.

He was gently tapping his Kubotan against his knee. Maybe she was pushing him too hard. Or maybe not hard enough.

"Not my finest moment, I admit. But yes, and there have been other times." He looked up at her then, his eyes searching hers for understanding.

"When?" She needed to hear him say it, to put words to the moments that had kept her awake at night.

"I came back for you in Paris."

It's true, he did. *But that was the mission,* she wanted to say. But maybe it was more. The way he'd held her after seeing her in the hospital, his hands trembling as he checked her for injuries, even though it was him who had borne the brunt of the explosion, the relief in his eyes that he couldn't hide—those weren't the actions of just a colleague.

"Look, you've had a long flight and I've had a—I've had a day." She was retreating again, building walls as quickly as he threatened to breach them.

"I know, I heard. I wanted to ask you if you were alright." The genuine concern in his voice made her chest ache.

She nodded. "I'm good. Maybe we should just call it a night." She couldn't do this—not here, not now. Maybe not ever.

She could see in his eyes that he wanted to say more. She was equal parts eager to hear him out and relieved to let sleeping dogs lie—for now. Truth was, she was as annoyed with her dad as she was with Caleb, so maybe this wasn't the best time to express her truest feelings. Feelings she had always known were there, raw and untapped, threatening to overwhelm her if she gave them voice.

She finished her drink and placed the empty glass atop the bar, the half-melted ice cubes circling the bottom like her thoughts, endlessly chasing each other without resolution.

"Good night," she said, walking away. "I'll see you tomorrow." The promise hung between them—another day, another chance, another moment when they might finally find the courage to say what needed saying.

Caleb put the Kubotan on top of the bar, his talisman abandoned as if in surrender.

"Night, Alex," he said, nursing his own drink, filled with words unspoken. His eyes followed her as she left.

She found the general still outside, holding court with a smattering of guests when she stepped into the night.

"You're back," he said.

"Only to say good night."

"Look—" he started, but she cut him off.

"Not tonight, Dad." She put a hand to his shoulder and gently kissed his forehead. "See you in the morning."

He squeezed her hand gently as she pulled away. "Okay, Allie. G'night."

Tomorrow, her dad would leave. He'd go back to the Okavango Republic to do whatever it was he was doing there for the US government. She'd get a good night's sleep and be over her frustration with her dad—with both of them—by morning.

There was no point wallowing in anger.

He was her father and she loved him unconditionally. The time they'd spent together these past few years had been too little. They had each acknowledged that. This trip to Africa was a promise she had made to herself to rectify that. It was a vow she intended to keep.

As she walked back to her cabin, she thought of Caleb, still at the bar. Another relationship that needed mending, another connection she both craved and feared. Tomorrow would bring another chance—for both of them. If only one of them could find the courage to take the first step.

CHAPTER 8

THE BAR, MARA SERENGETI LODGE, TANZANIA

Caleb watched Alex walk away, her long brunette hair flowing with each step. And he sighed. The weight of unspoken words hung in the air where she had been standing moments before.

"Another?" Brad asked, gesturing to Caleb's nearly empty glass.

"Yeah, why not." Caleb pushed the glass toward the Australian bartender. "Make it a double this time."

Brad's dimples deepened as he smiled. "Rough night?"

"You could say that." Caleb watched as Brad prepared his drink with practiced efficiency. "Women, am I right?"

"That one seems particularly complicated," Brad observed, nodding in the direction Alex had disappeared. "Known her long?"

Caleb accepted the fresh drink, taking a long sip before answering. "About a year now. Feels like a lifetime."

"Met on safari?"

"No." Caleb chuckled. "Nothing that simple. We met in the Netherlands. Work thing."

Brad moved away to serve another guest, leaving Caleb alone with his thoughts and the memory of their first meeting. He closed his eyes, letting the gin's botanicals transport him back to that rainy afternoon in The Hague.

The briefing room had been crowded with personnel from multiple agencies—FBI, Interpol, Dutch National Police, and Dutch intelligence. Caleb had been running point in the background—in the shadows—on the operation to intercept stolen nuclear material being moved through Europe. The intelligence was solid, but the team was a hodgepodge of specialists thrown together on short notice to stop the transfer of the deadly material.

That's when she walked in.

Special Agent Alexandra Martel, FBI, on loan to Interpol. She'd been wearing a dark blue tactical shirt and cargo pants, her badge clipped to her belt, her brunette hair pulled back in a tight ponytail. But it was her eyes that had caught his attention—a striking green that seemed to take in everything at once, assessing, calculating.

He remembered how she'd flipped through the briefing materials with quick, efficient movements, asking pointed questions that revealed a sharp tactical mind. Her service record was impressive—Army combat medic with a Silver Star and a Purple Heart. Ranger Regiment, then ISA. The FBI had recruited her after her military service, and now she was working with Interpol on special assignment.

They hadn't exchanged a word until the op went sideways and bullets were flying as they raced to hot-load into a Huey helicopter to get after the escaping bogeys.

Brad returned, breaking Caleb's reverie. "Refill?"

Caleb glanced at his empty glass, surprised he'd finished it so quickly. "I'm good for now, thanks."

"So what's the story with you two?" Brad asked, leaning against the bar. "There's clearly something there."

Caleb laughed softly. "That obvious, huh?"

"Mate, I divide my time between bartending and teaching college, so I can spot unresolved tension from a mile away."

"It's complicated," Caleb said, running a hand through his hair. "We work together."

"Ah, the classic workplace romance conundrum."

"Romance would be overstating it. We've just . . . had moments."

The memory of Arnhem surfaced vividly—the two of them in the Huey, racing over the ancient Dutch city as they pursued a van containing enough nuclear material to devastate a major metropolitan area. The speed and traffic had made Alex's job nearly impossible. Not to mention that their helicopter was going to crash at any moment.

I can't get a clean shot! she'd shouted over the helicopter's roar, her rifle steady despite the turbulence.

We're running out of time! Caleb had yelled back. *They're heading for the bridge!*

The van had swerved through traffic, the driver skilled and desperate. Caleb had watched as Alex's expression changed—her eyes narrowing, her breathing slowing. The helicopter had pitched in the wind, but she'd remained steady, her focus absolute.

Got him, she'd whispered, and squeezed the trigger.

The shot had been impossible—from a moving helicopter, at a moving target. But the van had swerved violently, then crashed through the guardrail into the Nederrijn River below.

In that moment, watching her work, Caleb had felt something shift inside him. It wasn't just professional admiration. It was something more primal, more personal.

"You're thinking about her again," Brad observed, interrupting Caleb's thoughts.

"How can you tell?"

"Your face went all soft. Then determined. Then soft again."

Caleb laughed. "You should work for the CIA."

"Nah, I like my job. I get to psychoanalyze people without the risk of getting shot at."

After Arnhem, they'd worked together across Europe and the Middle East. London had been a blur of foot pursuits and meetings gone bad. In Adana, they'd narrowly escaped being killed in an ambush. He couldn't remember who'd saved who after a fight nearly to the death and a car chase that still featured in his nightmares.

And then there was Paris. Paris had been different. No one could ever forget Paris.

"So what's stopping you?" Brad asked, pulling Caleb back to the present. "From telling her how you feel, I mean."

"I'm her boss now."

"Ah."

"Yeah. She joined my team about a year ago. Lots of action, not much downtime."

Brad whistled low. "Sounds intense."

"It is. And she's . . . exceptional at what she does. World-class. She's saved my ass more times than I can count."

"Wow, who knew?"

"Right?"

"And you don't want to mess that up."

"Something like that." Caleb sighed. "Plus, she lost her husband a few years back. Army guy killed in action—helluva guy from what I hear. I don't know if she's ready to move on. And I don't want to push her."

Brad nodded thoughtfully. "Fair enough. But if she's as tough as you say she is, she'll let you know if you're about to breach that barrier. From what I saw tonight, there's definitely something there on her side, too."

"You think?"

"Mate, the way she looked at you when she thought you weren't watching? That wasn't just professional courtesy."

Caleb felt a flicker of hope, quickly tempered by reality. "Even if that's true, the timing's all wrong. Her father's just been called away unexpectedly, she's pissed at both of us for springing this surprise on her, and we're stuck together on safari for the next week."

"Sounds like the perfect opportunity to me," Brad said with a grin. "Romantic sunsets, starlit nights, no distractions . . ."

"And lions. Don't forget the lions."

"Nothing says romance like the threat of being eaten alive."

They both laughed, and Caleb felt some of the tension ease from his shoulders.

"One more for the road?" Brad asked, already reaching for the Tanqueray.

"Why not?"

As Brad prepared his drink, Caleb's thoughts drifted back to Alex. He remembered the way she'd looked today, out on the patio. Yeah, she'd been surprised to see him, but there really was something more. At that moment, she hadn't been Special Agent Martel or the legendary sniper known as Shooter. She'd just been Alex—passionate, alive, beautiful.

That was the woman he'd fallen for, beneath all the layers of tactical gear and professional distance. The woman whose eyes changed from emerald to stormy seas depending on her mood. The woman who could take out a target at a thousand yards but still got excited about seeing leopards in the wild, according to her father, the general.

Brad set the fresh drink in front of him. "To new beginnings," he said, raising his water glass in a toast.

Caleb lifted his gin and tonic. "To new beginnings," he echoed, hoping it wasn't just wishful thinking.

Tomorrow, he decided, he would try again. No more dancing around what they both felt. Life was too short, their work too dangerous to waste time on fear and hesitation.

As he sipped his drink, he rehearsed what he might say to her in the morning. Whatever happened next, at least he wouldn't have to wonder what could have been. And whatever came next—with Alex, with this safari, with their work—he was ready to face it head-on.

Just like she would.

* * *

As she walked away from the pavilion, Alex took the curving path toward her cabin, the dull orange flame of the tiki torches casting faint light into the darkness beyond. By the rules of the Mara Serengeti Lodge, she should have waited for an escort, but she decided that was a waste of someone's time. Her cabin wasn't far, and tonight, she needed solitude.

The deeper she ventured into the array of huts and cabins, the more the African night enveloped her. Every point of light along her path resembled the hungry eyes of a lion or the glistening drool on a hyena's chin. But unlike the unresolved feelings she'd left behind at the bar, these fears she knew how to handle.

She hadn't been allowed to step outside the perimeter during her postings in Afghanistan, Iraq, or Syria either, but like many operators, she had done so anyway, usually to go for a run after blistering days gave way to bracing nights. Tonight was no different—she refused to be intimidated by the ghosts in the darkness of Africa any more than she had been by the unseen threats on every deployment around the globe.

What truly frightened her wasn't out here in the night. It was back there, sitting at that bar, rolling a Kubotan between his fingers. It was the way her heart quickened when he said, *I came back for you in Paris*. It was the possibility that tomorrow might bring a conversation neither of them was ready to have.

Soon enough, she reached her cabin door and stepped inside, shutting it quickly—not against what lurked in the night, but to guard against the feelings that threatened to overwhelm her defenses. Some dangers couldn't be evaded just by crossing back over the wire.

CHAPTER 9

MARA SERENGETI LODGE, TANZANIA

Alex awoke in her hut, blinking as she tried to focus beyond the gauzelike fabric suspended from the ceiling around her bed. Dawn broke outside her windows, casting a murky light that painted her stucco walls in hues of pink and orange. Her accommodations were luxurious, but if she continued on the safari without her dad, more rustic camping awaited her and Caleb in a few days. She rationalized that she had spent weeks and months sleeping barely above the dirt in Army tents for years, so she deserved to indulge in a bit of luxury for a few nights before roughing it out on the savannah.

After yesterday's gunfight with the poachers and the discord between her and her dad—and her and Caleb afterward—it had been hard to fall asleep. Her insomnia had resulted from all that turmoil, and she resolved to put it behind her and focus on making the most of the rest of the trip. It was disappointing that her dad was leaving today, but she decided to man up, swallow her pride, and forgive him with a hug when she saw him. That would be soon, over breakfast.

She checked her bedside clock: 6:05. James, their safari driver and guide, would be waiting for them—her and Caleb—at seven o'clock sharp in front of the main entrance. That left less than an hour for her to square things with her dad before his ride to the airstrip, then shower, get dressed in her safari gear for the day, and grab a quick bite of breakfast and some coffee.

Today was a new day with a new outlook, and she was eager to spend private time with Caleb. On a personal level, they might not have been completely aligned regarding where they stood with each other, but if they could endure the duration of the safari, they would have six days to sort it out. That should be plenty of time. Alex had experienced relationships that started and ended in less time than that.

She threw on a pair of stretchy athletic pants, a T-shirt, and sneakers before heading to the main pavilion. Unlike last night, when she walked back to her room alone, staff members were positioned along the paths. Although no one explicitly stated it, she suspected they were there to thwart the efforts of unruly vervet monkeys, or hungry lions and hyenas. Despite their serious assignments, everyone she encountered along the way greeted her with a cheerful *"Jambo, jambo!"* Hello, hello!

She entered the building and looked around the lobby for her dad. Not spotting him, she wandered over to the restaurant and peeked inside to see if he had sat down for a meal before his flight. She asked one of the servers, but the server hadn't seen him since last night, so Alex went back to the lobby.

"Miss Alex," called a voice from behind her. She turned and saw a tall Black man behind the reception counter smiling at her, holding out an envelope.

"Good morning," Alex said, reaching her hand out to take it from him.

"The general left you this note before he left."

"Left?"

"Yes, miss. Your father's ride came for him an hour ago."

"But I thought he wasn't leaving until later. Until we . . . ," she trailed off.

"I only know that he left this with me under strict orders to give it to you before you headed out for the day."

She thanked him and went to sit in one of the chairs that faced out the window as she pulled a folded piece of paper from the envelope. Crossing her legs, she read:

Allie,

My ride came early. I didn't want to wake you.

I'm sorry I messed things up by asking Caleb to join us. I didn't mean to step on your toes, baby girl, but you know us dads—we always think we know best.

Enjoy the rest of your trip. Sorry I'm going to miss it (and you)! We'll talk in a couple of days.

PS: Don't be too hard on Caleb.

Love you lots,

Dad xo

Her chest tightened as she read the note, clutching a hand to her breast. She didn't like leaving things unresolved. She might not have been the best at voicing her feelings, but she didn't believe in keeping people guessing about whether there was a lingering problem. She tried to recall the last words she had said to him before she excused herself from the table. Had she been dismissive, even shut him down, before he tried to explain the situation to her?

Guilty. *Don't* Allie *me, Dad,* she remembered saying. She'd cut him off.

Why do I always have to be such a hard-ass?

She didn't allow him to express the words he had been wanting to say. Her anger and ego had interfered. Again. Just as her late husband Kyle had often reminded her.

Pride is your wilderness, he'd say. *Stop being such a stone angel, Alex.*

And he was right. Kyle hadn't been the only one in her life who'd told her more or less the same thing, that it was good to be proud but that pride could cloud one's judgment, as it frequently had hers. But he was the only one to make her actually see it and recognize those things she did that stood in the way of her becoming what her mom had always harped on was her best self.

Damn.

At least she had stopped by and kissed him good night before heading to her cabin. She would talk it out with him in a couple of days. She had already forgiven him. All he wanted—all he had ever truly wanted—was for her to be happy. He had been there time and time again to see to it that she was happy or to subtly guide her when her plans led her astray. Even when she became a grown woman—*when exactly had that happened?*—living on a different continent, he never abdicated his parental role as her father, no matter how mad she got when she felt he had interfered.

"You going on safari dressed like that?"

She looked up. Indiana Jones was standing in front of her. Well, Caleb wearing beige denim pants and a white cotton shirt unbuttoned an extra hole at the top, anyway. On his head was what she was sure was an Aussie Outback hat. All that was missing was the whip.

"What, no. You borrow that from the bartender?"

"What?" he asked, missing the joke.

"Nothing. I'll meet you back here in fifteen minutes. Dad's already gone. I want to shower before we eat."

CHAPTER 10

General David Martel stared into the predawn darkness outside the passenger window of the Land Cruiser, the vehicle's headlights carving twin tunnels of light through the gloom. They'd been on the road for half an hour already, the savannah coming alive around them—rustling grasses, distant animal calls, the occasional flash of eyes beside the road reflecting their lights. He checked his watch: 5:37 AM. The airstrip was less than fifteen minutes away.

"You are quiet this morning, General," said Mbeki, his driver. The man's hands rested comfortably on the wheel of the right-hand-drive vehicle, navigating the rutted dirt road with practiced ease.

"Just thinking," Martel replied. "I hate leaving things unresolved with my daughter."

Mbeki nodded. "Children forgive. It is what they do."

"She's hardly a child anymore."

"To fathers, they are always children." Mbeki smiled, his teeth gleaming in the dashboard light. "My eldest is thirty-two, but when I look at him, I still see the boy who needed me to tie his shoes."

Martel smiled despite himself. The man was right. No matter how accomplished Alex became—combat medic, Silver Star recipient, CIA operative—he still saw the little girl who'd once asked him to check under her bed for monsters. Now she hunted real ones for a living.

The radio crackled with static, then fell silent. Mbeki frowned, tapping it with his finger.

"Problem?" Martel asked.

"Just interference. Common out here." But something in Mbeki's tone suggested otherwise. His eyes flicked to the rearview mirror more frequently now, scanning the road behind them.

Martel's instincts, honed by decades of military service, began to prickle. He casually checked the side mirror. Nothing but darkness. Still, the sensation persisted—that familiar tightening in his gut that had saved his life more times than he could count.

"How much farther?" he asked, his hand unconsciously moving to the Ka-Bar knife on his belt. The worn leather sheath bore the insignia of the 1st Armored Division—IRON SOLDIERS!—a reminder of his days commanding tanks during Operation Desert Storm.

"Ten minutes, perhaps less."

The road curved ahead, and as they rounded the bend, Mbeki slammed on the brakes. The Land Cruiser skidded on the loose dirt, stopping just short of a pickup truck angled across the road. A spotlight aimed from the truck bed blazed directly into their windshield, momentarily blinding them.

"Reverse!" Martel barked, his military command voice taking over. "Now!"

Mbeki threw the vehicle into reverse, but before he could accelerate, the roar of engines erupted behind them. Headlights suddenly blazed to life—vehicles that had been ghosting silently in their wake, concealed by the crimson veil that rose from the Serengeti's iron-rich soil. Martel spun in his seat to see three more pickups blocking their retreat, their headlights illuminating the interior of the Land Cruiser like a stage.

"Shit," he muttered.

A fifth vehicle appeared—a technical with a mounted machine gun, its barrel aimed directly at them. Men with AK-47s jumped from the trucks, spreading out in ragged, but effective, formation.

"What do we do?" Mbeki whispered, his knuckles white on the steering wheel.

Martel assessed their options with cold precision. No weapons except his knife. No cover. No chance of outrunning them. "We stay calm," he said. "Let me do the talking."

A tall figure emerged from behind the lead truck's headlights, his silhouette elongated by the angle of the light. Six feet three at least, with broad shoulders and the lean, predatory stance of a man accustomed to violence. The man cut across the beam of the Land Cruiser's headlights, and Martel could make out his features, including three prominent lines on his cheek—not ritualistic markings as he first thought, but scars that resembled claw marks, as if he'd once faced down a wild beast.

The man stopped a few paces from the Land Cruiser, his face impassive. He made a gesture with his hand, and immediately, armed men surrounded the vehicle.

"General Martel," the scarred man called out, his voice carrying a musical lilt despite its menacing tone. "Step out of the vehicle."

Martel's mind raced. How did they know who he was? This wasn't random. This was targeted. Planned.

"I said, step out!" The man's voice hardened.

"Stay inside," Martel told Mbeki. "Do as he says. Keep your hands visible."

Mbeki nodded, his breathing shallow and rapid. Sweat beaded on his forehead despite the cool morning air.

Martel opened his door slowly. He stepped out onto the red dirt road, keeping his movements deliberate and nonthreatening. The scarred man watched him with the patient focus of a predator.

"I am Lemarti," he said simply.

"What do you want?" Martel asked, his voice steady.

Lemarti's lips curved into what might have been a smile on another man. On him, it looked like the baring of teeth. "You know what I want, General."

Before Martel could respond, a burly man with a pockmarked face and a baseball hat atop his head stepped forward from Lemarti's side. His eyes gleamed with an eagerness that made Martel's skin crawl.

"This is taking too long," the man growled in heavily accented English.

"Patience, Desmond," Lemarti said, never taking his eyes off Martel.

Desmond spat on the ground. "We should just take him and go."

Mbeki chose that moment to speak, his hands raised and trembling above his head. "Please," he pleaded. "I am just a driver. I have children—"

The burst of automatic fire was deafening in the predawn stillness. Desmond had swung his AK-47 toward Mbeki with practiced ease, the muzzle flash illuminating his face in staccato bursts of orange light. The bullets shattered the windshield and tore through Mbeki's body, the impact throwing him back against the seat.

Warm droplets spattered across Martel's face and neck—Mbeki's blood, still hot from his body. The metallic scent of it filled his nostrils, triggering memories of other battlefields, other deaths.

"Goddammit!" Martel lunged toward Desmond, military training overriding self-preservation. He'd made it two steps before hands seized him from behind, wrenching his arms back painfully.

Lemarti's expression hadn't changed, but something in his eyes darkened. He nodded once to Desmond. It was not encouragement, but neither was it reproach.

Desmond shrugged.

Martel struggled against his captors, rage burning through his veins. "He was unarmed, you son of a bitch!"

Desmond stepped forward and drove his fist into Martel's stomach. The blow forced the air from his lungs, and he doubled over, gasping.

"Bind him," Lemarti ordered.

Rough hands pulled Martel upright. Someone yanked his arms to the front while another secured his wrists with rope that bit into his skin. Yet another man spotted the Ka-Bar on his belt and tore it away, examining the weathered sheath briefly before tossing it contemptuously onto the floor of the Land Cruiser.

Martel wanted to lash out, to strike the man for disrespecting the soldier's knife he had carried for decades—longer than the impudent man had even been alive. It deserved more respect than he had shown it.

Desmond must have read his disdain and struck him again, this time across the face. Martel tasted blood.

Lemarti stepped closer, studying Martel with clinical detachment. "The American general," he said softly. "So far from home. So valuable to so many."

Martel met his gaze unflinchingly. "Whatever you're being paid, it's not enough."

A flicker of something—amusement, perhaps—crossed Lemarti's face. "Today, this is not about money, General. This is about blood."

He nodded to his men, who dragged Martel toward a cargo truck. The vehicle's bed was piled high with vegetables—cassava, yams, tomatoes—a clever disguise for whatever lay inside.

"Move," Desmond growled, shoving Martel forward.

They forced him to climb awkwardly into the back of the truck, pushing him past the produce to a false wall behind the passenger compartment. One of the men slid the panel aside, revealing a metal dog crate barely large enough for a man.

"You can't be serious," Martel said.

Desmond's answer was another blow, this one to his kidney. Pain exploded through Martel's side, and he fell to his knees.

"Inside," Desmond ordered.

With his hands bound, Martel had no choice but to crawl forward on his knees, awkwardly maneuvering into the cramped space. The metal bars pressed against his shoulders, forcing him to hunch forward uncomfortably until he could turn onto his back.

Lemarti appeared at the entrance to the crate, his tall frame silhouetted against the lightening sky. Dawn was breaking over the Serengeti, painting the horizon in shades of pink and gold that seemed obscenely beautiful against the violence of the moment.

"You will be my guest, General," Lemarti said, his voice almost gentle. "Until your fate is finalized."

Martel said nothing, conserving his strength. His mind was already calculating distances, time frames, possibilities. Alex would realize something was wrong when he didn't call. She would come looking. And God help these men when she found them.

Lemarti seemed to read his thoughts. "Your daughter," he said. "The warrior woman. She killed my brother."

A cold weight settled in Martel's stomach. This wasn't random. This might not even be about his work in Okavango. This was about yesterday—about Alex.

"She will come for you," Lemarti continued. "And when she does . . ." He left the threat unspoken, sliding the panel closed with a finality that echoed in the confined space.

Darkness enveloped Martel as the truck's engine roared to life. Through the thin slats in the crate, he could see nothing but shadows and the faintest hint of dawn's light. The vehicle lurched forward, beginning its journey to wherever Lemarti had established his base.

Martel closed his eyes, focusing on his breathing. In. Out. Steady. He'd been in worse situations. He'd survived desert warfare, insurgent attacks, political minefields. He would survive this, too.

But as the truck bounced along the rutted road, one thought kept circling in his mind: Alex was coming. And these men had no idea what they'd just unleashed.

CHAPTER 11

MARA SERENGETI LODGE, TANZANIA

The morning sun poured into the lodge's lobby. It was so bright that Alex donned a pair of sunglasses as she strode to the restaurant to meet Caleb for breakfast in the dining pavilion. This morning, she had prioritized comfort over style, wearing khaki cargo pants and a lightweight blue button-down shirt to stay cool in the African heat. Her hair was pulled back in a simple ponytail. She had skipped makeup in favor of high-SPF sunscreen.

The events of yesterday—the gunfight with the poachers, her father's sudden departure announcement, and Caleb's unexpected arrival—left her with a restless night. But morning in Africa had a way of washing away the darkness. Her mood was suddenly buoyed by the sound of the trumpeting of a herd of elephants somewhere in the distance.

She spotted Caleb already seated at a table on the pavilion's edge, where the thatched roof opened to the sky. He was studying a map laid out on the table, a steaming mug of coffee by his elbow. The morning light highlighted the silver at his temples, and for a moment, she allowed herself to appreciate the sight of him—focused, capable, and undeniably handsome in his element.

He looked up as she approached, his face breaking into a smile that reached his eyes. "Morning, Shooter."

"Morning," she replied, sliding into the chair opposite him. "So it's just us, then."

"And about ten thousand wildebeest, according to James." He folded the map, tucking it into his shirt pocket. "Sleep okay?"

"Like a baby—if that baby had insomnia and kept thinking about getting shot at."

His expression sobered. "About yesterday—"

"Let's not," she cut him off. "It's a new day. Clean slate."

A server approached their table, his smile bright against his dark skin. "*Habari za asubuhi*," he greeted them. *Good morning!*

"*Nzuri, asante*," Caleb replied without hesitation. *Fine, thank you*, flowing naturally from his lips.

Alex raised an eyebrow. "Show-off."

"Just being polite," he said with a grin. "Besides, I've been brushing up. Figured it might come in handy. That is, if I need to order breakfast along the way."

The server—whose name tag read Emmanuel—beamed at Caleb's effort. "Very good, sir! Would you like to order your breakfast in Swahili as well?"

"Might need some help with that," Caleb admitted.

"I'll teach you," Emmanuel offered. "For coffee, you say *kahawa*. For tea, *chai*."

"*Kahawa, tafadhali*," Alex said, the words *coffee, please* feeling foreign but satisfying on her tongue.

Emmanuel's smile widened. "Excellent pronunciation, madam! And how would you like your eggs?"

"Is there any chance of a Western omelet?" she asked. "With peppers and onions?"

"Of course."

"And some of that amazing fresh fruit," she added.

"*Matunda*," Emmanuel supplied. "Fruit fresh from our gardens this morning."

Caleb leaned forward. "I'll have eggs, too—scrambled. And is that *mandazi* I smell baking?"

"Yes, sir! Our chef makes them fresh each morning. *Mandazi na mayai ya kuchanganywa?*" *Bread and scrambled eggs?*

"Perfect," Caleb said. "*Asante sana.*"

As Emmanuel departed to place their orders, Alex studied Caleb with renewed interest. "Mandazi?"

"Tanzanian doughnuts, basically. Slightly sweet, fried bread. They're addictive."

"How do you know so much about local cuisine?"

He shrugged. "I did some homework before coming. Figured if I was going to crash your vacation, I should at least be prepared."

The mention of his surprise arrival hung between them for a moment, but Alex chose not to pursue it. Instead, she gestured toward the map in his pocket. "Planning our route for today?"

"James suggested we head toward the Mara River. Apparently, there's a crossing happening—part of the great migration."

"Sounds incredible."

"But he said he has another plan for us along the way."

"Can't wait." She beamed.

Emmanuel returned with their coffee, setting down two steaming mugs along with a small pitcher of warm milk. "*Kahawa,*" he announced proudly.

"*Asante,*" they replied in unison.

"Your breakfast will be ready soon," he assured them before moving to another table.

Alex wrapped her hands around the warm mug, inhaling the rich aroma. "This might be the best coffee I've ever had."

"It's local," Caleb said. "Grown on the slopes of Kilimanjaro."

She took a sip, closing her eyes briefly to savor the flavor. "So, about yesterday . . ."

"I thought we weren't talking about that."

"Not the shooting. The other thing."

Caleb set down his mug, his expression cautious. "Which other thing would that be? My surprise arrival or our conversation at the bar?"

"Both, I guess." She traced the rim of her mug with her finger. "I was harsh last night. You flew halfway around the world to join this safari, and I wasn't exactly welcoming."

"You were surprised. I get it."

"Still. It was . . . nice of you to come."

He studied her face, as if searching for the catch. "That almost sounded like a compliment, Martel."

"Don't get used to it," she replied, but there was no edge to her words.

Their breakfast arrived, saving her from having to elaborate. Emmanuel set down a plate with a fluffy Western omelet before Alex, the eggs perfectly cooked with colorful peppers and onions folded inside. Beside it sat a bowl of fresh fruit—mango, papaya, and pineapple glistening in the morning light.

Caleb's plate held scrambled eggs and several golden-brown *mandazi*, their exteriors crisp and dusted with sugar, their interiors soft and slightly chewy.

"*Chakula chenu*," Emmanuel announced. "Your food. Enjoy!"

"This looks amazing," Alex said, cutting into her omelet. The first bite was a revelation—light, flavorful, with just the right amount of seasoning.

Caleb tore a *mandazi* in half, steam escaping from its center. "Try this," he said, offering her a piece.

She accepted it, their fingers brushing briefly. The bread was warm and slightly sweet, with hints of cardamom and coconut.

"Oh my God," she mumbled around the bite. "That's dangerous."

"Told you." He grinned, taking a bite of his eggs. "So, are we good?"

She considered the question as she speared a piece of mango with her fork. Were they good? The tension from last night had dissipated somewhat, but the underlying current remained—that unspoken thing between them that neither seemed ready to address directly.

"We're good," she decided. "Professional colleagues enjoying a safari together."

Something flickered in his eyes—disappointment, perhaps—but he nodded. "Professional colleagues it is."

They ate in companionable silence for a few minutes, the sounds of the lodge coming to life around them—other guests chatting, staff moving efficiently between tables, the distant calls of birds greeting the day.

"I heard from James that the ranger you helped yesterday is stable," Caleb said eventually. "They airlifted him to a hospital in Nairobi."

"That's good news." She felt a weight lift from her shoulders. "That tourniquet was pretty makeshift."

"Your dad said you were impressive out there. Not that I'm surprised."

She shrugged, uncomfortable with the praise. "Just muscle memory from my medic days."

"And the shooting?"

"Also muscle memory." She met his gaze steadily. "I did what needed doing."

He nodded, understanding in his eyes. They'd both been in situations where split-second decisions meant the difference between life and death. It created a bond that few outside their world could comprehend.

"James thinks they weren't ordinary poachers," Caleb said, lowering his voice. "Too well-equipped, too organized."

"I got that impression, too."

"Mercenaries, maybe?"

"Maybe." She took another bite of her omelet, considering the possibilities. "Or something else entirely."

Emmanuel approached their table again, this time with a pot of coffee. "Refill your *kahawa*?"

"*Ndio, tafadhali*," Alex replied, pleased when he beamed at her correct usage of *yes, please*.

"You learn very quickly," he said as he poured. "Both of you."

"She's always been a quick study," Caleb said, his eyes never leaving her face. "Picks up languages like most people pick up souvenirs."

"It's a useful skill in our line of work," she replied, then immediately regretted the slip.

Emmanuel, however, simply nodded. "What work do you do, if I may ask?"

"Security consulting," she answered smoothly. "International risk assessment."

"Ah, very important work." Emmanuel seemed satisfied with the explanation. "James is waiting out front. He says to tell you he will be ready whenever you finish breakfast."

"*Asante*," Alex said. "We won't be long."

As Emmanuel moved away, Caleb leaned forward. "Security consulting?"

"It's not entirely a lie," she said with a half smile. "We do assess risks."

"And occasionally shoot at them."

She laughed, the sound surprising her with its genuineness. It felt good to laugh with him, to share this moment of normalcy in their decidedly abnormal lives.

"We should get going," she said, finishing the last of her fruit. "James is waiting, and I want to see this river crossing."

Caleb nodded, polishing off his final *mandazi*. "Ready when you are, Shooter."

As they rose from the table, the morning sun now fully above the horizon, Alex felt something shift between them—not resolution, exactly, but a truce. For now, that would have to be enough.

The Serengeti awaited, vast and wild and full of possibilities. Whatever lay ahead—for the day, for the safari, for them—she was ready to face it. With Caleb beside her, she realized with a start, she felt more than ready. She felt alive.

CHAPTER 12

SERENGETI NATIONAL PARK, TANZANIA

When they emerged from the lodge, James was waiting at the back of the Land Cruiser on the wide circular driveway, standing beside other safari vehicles and drivers. He was a big man whom Alex had grown fond of since he first picked her and her dad up from Kilimanjaro International Airport in Arusha a few days ago. Affable and funny, he amazed Alex with his encyclopedic knowledge of African flora and fauna. His mastery of Tanzania's animal kingdom was impressive. His pride in his country's riches was evident in how he spoke of not just the wildlife, but also its people, from the Maasai to the Chagga, from whom he descended.

"*Jambo*, Alex," he said, a happy-to-be-alive smile brightening his face as it did every morning.

"Good morning, James. This is my friend Caleb. He will be with us till the end of our time here."

"*Habari za asubuhi,* Caleb. We have been expecting you." *Good morning.*

"*Jambo,*" Caleb said.

Alex studied James's face. "You knew, too?" she asked.

"I'm sorry, Alex. Your father asked me to say nothing. Your father is a very persuasive man. Where is the general?" he asked, looking toward the building for any sign of him.

She briefly explained that he was called away for work.

"I'm sorry to hear that. We will miss him, yes?"

She grunted in response and walked around to the side of the

4x4, climbing into the open door and taking a seat. Caleb climbed in and sat across the aisle from her. James finished stowing their lunch into the small electric refrigerator in the back, then hopped into the driver's seat.

"Let's go!" he said, dropping the truck into gear and driving off. "Today will be a glorious day. Let's go find some big cats!" he announced.

The Land Cruiser bumped along the dusty track as the first rays of sunlight painted the Serengeti in hues of amber and gold. James had them on the road by 7 AM sharp, his promise of finding big cats still hanging in the morning air. Alex sat forward in her seat, her camera ready, eyes taking in the view out to the horizon.

"Serengeti means 'endless plains' in Maasai," James said, his deep voice carrying over the rumble of the engine. "And today, we will see why."

Caleb nodded, his eyes narrowed against the morning sun. "How many animals are we likely to see today?"

James's laughter filled the vehicle. "My friend, I will try my level best to show you everything Tanzania has to offer."

They were deep into their first hour of driving across the savannah and had spotted zebra and wildebeest—vast herds of them—the males bleating and calling to warn off other males as they claimed groups of females as their own. And though the herd would at times settle into a pace suitable for its members' grazing, the males were constantly on the move, racing around the harems they collected, battling any would-be suitor that came along. Battles were fought, horns and skulls clashing in combat, an age-old display of strength and will.

But Alex was eager to see more from the predator side of the equation. Sure, all animals were God's creations. Whatever. But she hoped to catch a glimpse of the apex predators—the lions, cheetahs, and leopards—that called the savannah their home and kept the populations of the lesser beasts in check. Right or wrong, so went her thinking.

"When will we see the cats, James?" she asked, as if he had the itinerary for each species on the plain.

"Africa requires patience, Alex," was his reply.

"If Africa is expecting patience from this woman," Caleb said, "then Africa will wait a long time."

"Do you see the irony of your words, Mr. Caleb?"

Alex was sure he did. Caleb had a knack for coming off folksy, which some people equated with being less finely attuned to the world around them or, in plainer speak, dumb. With Caleb, nothing could be further from the truth. Even though Alex herself had occasionally gotten caught up in that illusion, he had repeatedly proved to be one of the brightest and most cunning people she knew—always switched on, his situational awareness constantly dialed in.

"Fear not, James," she said when Caleb didn't answer. "He's a lot brighter than he looks!"

James spun around to look at her, then laughed again. "You play dangerous games, Miss Alex," he said, wagging a finger at her.

"She sure does," agreed Caleb, his eyes meeting hers with a warmth that hadn't been there before.

The morning unfolded before them like pages in a storybook. By 8 AM, they had already spotted a tower of giraffes—twelve of them—gracefully moving across the savannah, their long necks swaying with each deliberate step.

"Look at them," Alex whispered, lifting her camera. The telephoto lens captured a mother and baby, their spotted patterns nearly identical. "They're so elegant."

The animals were so accustomed to the safari vehicles that it was clear they weren't regarded as a threat. They must have passed within fifty or sixty feet of some Maasai giraffe, a species with remarkable markings. Alex became enamored with their doe-like eyes, so gentle and kind-looking, rimmed by lashes any woman would kill for.

"A group standing is called a tower," James explained. "When they run, it's called a journey."

"Why's that?" Caleb asked, leaning slightly closer to Alex as he peered through the roof opening.

James shrugged with a smile. "That is just what it is called."

She would have found it difficult to articulate the joy she felt at that moment, faced with the spectacle before her. She was amazed at how quickly one's perspective could change. Just a couple of days ago, she had been ecstatic seeing all the giraffes, their towering majesty paired with the most adorable eyes and cute ears. Now, she barely noticed them, sometimes missing them entirely as they blended into the landscape. It was astonishing how these and other great creatures of Africa could go unseen if you weren't actively looking for them. Here, just as in life back home, one could wander right past something of incredible danger or beauty unless one remained aware of one's surroundings. Situational awareness presented in many forms.

The Land Cruiser rounded a bend in the track, and James suddenly slowed, pointing to their right. "Troublemaker," he said quietly.

A massive bull elephant stood alone, his tusks nearly touching the ground and gleaming in the morning light, while his ears flapped lazily against the rising heat.

"Why is he alone?" Alex asked, already framing the shot.

"He has been pushed out of the herd," James explained. "Too aggressive. Now he wanders alone, never to mate again."

"That's sad," Alex said, lowering her camera.

"It is the way of nature," James replied. "Some rules cannot be broken. He used to have his own harem," he continued. "Now he never gets to mate with any females. He is too big and mean, and they want nothing to do with him."

"Well, that sounds pretty reasonable to me," she said.

"I don't know," said Caleb. "I kind of sympathize with the old guy."

"Explains why you're still single."

James chuckled again, and off they drove, leaving the troublemaker behind. She looked at Caleb, who was looking back at her, seemingly trying to figure something out. She smiled, and his face lit up in a way that made her stomach flutter unexpectedly.

By 9:30, the heat had begun to build, but the wildlife sightings only increased. A herd of wildebeest crossed their path, moving in single file to preserve the grass. James explained the grazing succession—zebras first taking the tall grass, wildebeest following for the medium growth, and gazelles and buffalo coming last for the shortest blades.

"It's like they have an agreement," Caleb said, watching the organized chaos of the herds.

"They do." James nodded. "One made over millions of years."

Alex found herself lost in the rhythm of the savannah—the constant movement, the interplay of predator and prey, the delicate balance that existed long before humans arrived with their cameras and Land Cruisers.

At 10:15, James brought the vehicle to an abrupt halt.

"There," he whispered, pointing to a kopje—a rocky outcropping—about two hundred yards away. "Look carefully."

Alex and Caleb stood, poking their heads through the roof opening. At first, Alex saw nothing but grass and stone. Then, movement—a tawny shape slinking through the tall grass.

"Lion," she breathed.

"Lioness," James corrected. "And look—cubs."

As if on cue, two small shapes emerged from behind their mother, tumbling over each other in play before the mother called them back with a low growl.

"Part of the Seronera pride," James said proudly. "The super pride has more than two dozen members, with six adult males."

"Will we see more?" Alex asked, unable to tear her eyes away.

"I will do my level best," James replied, his standard answer that somehow always delivered.

They watched the lions for twenty minutes before James suggested they move on. "There is much more to see," he promised.

By 11 AM, they had counted four more lionesses, a male lion with an impressive mane lounging beneath an acacia tree, three cheetahs in the distance, and countless zebra, impala, and Thomson's gazelles. The morning's tally was already beyond Alex's wildest expectations.

As they stopped for a midmorning break, Alex stepped down from the Land Cruiser, stretching her legs while staying close to the vehicle as James had instructed. The vastness of the Serengeti stretched before her—a living, breathing ecosystem that had existed for millennia.

"It's like nothing I've ever seen," she said to Caleb, who stood beside her, sipping water from his canteen.

"Better than Wyoming?" he asked with a half smile.

"Different," she replied. "The Tetons are majestic in their own way. But this . . ." She gestured to the plains before them. "This feels like going back in time."

Caleb's eyes lingered on her face longer than necessary, and Alex felt a warmth spread through her that had nothing to do with the African sun.

James approached, offering them each a piece of fruit. "The animals have been here long before us," he said. "And if we are wise, they will be here long after."

Alex nodded, understanding the weight of his words. In that moment, standing in the heart of the Serengeti with the morning sun high overhead and the sounds of Africa surrounding her, she felt something shift inside—a connection to something larger, older, and infinitely more important than herself.

"Ready?" James asked, already moving back to the driver's seat. "Let's see if we can find the rest of the super pride."

Alex took one more look at the landscape, committing it to memory in a way no photograph ever could. She glanced at Caleb, who was watching her with an expression that spoke of more than just shared adventure.

"Ready," she said, and climbed back into the Land Cruiser, eager for what the rest of the day would bring.

Standing above the roofline, Alex watched while the landscape drifted by as James drove slowly and scouted for the rest of the pride.

The scene before her looked as if it had been plucked from a Monet landscape, aglow with flowers of purple and violet and hues of seemingly every color of the rainbow that dotted a savannah as lush as any meadow in the artist's home in Giverny. Except this was Africa, and unlike the Normandy region of France, this part of the world remained wild and untamed, its creeks and watering holes full, its grasslands verdant and lush. It wasn't hard to understand how a few lions could be hidden in plain sight.

Caleb heard it first.

"What's that?" he asked, his head turning to home in on the sound.

A second later, she heard it, too—a low hum that grew into a deep rumble before evolving into a rapid thrumming. It wasn't the sound of any beast, but something more familiar. As it drew closer, it drowned out the buzzing insects and birdsong that had filled the warm, fragrant air just seconds before. She searched for its source and finally spotted a dark shape along the horizon that, as it neared, took on the unmistakable form of a military helicopter.

CHAPTER 13

SERENGETI NATIONAL PARK, TANZANIA

Even nose-on, Alex couldn't mistake the distinctive shape of a Sikorsky UH-60 Black Hawk. And it was heading straight for them. Stub wings were affixed to its fuselage, each fitted with massive external fuel tanks that added range to the already impressive machine.

What the hell? thought Alex. "James, stop the car."

"What is it, Alex?" he asked, halting the Land Cruiser.

"Not sure yet," she replied.

"Is that what I think it is?" asked Caleb.

"Yes, and why is a Black Hawk on an intercept course with our current position?"

He grunted.

Alex raised her camera and zoomed in on the approaching helo. It was within a few hundred meters. It banked out, then turned back to approach their position in an arc. They were abreast of it now as the pilot drew closer, maneuvering the large aircraft into a hover, maybe a hundred and fifty feet away. The side door slid open and pinned to the rear, revealing a crewman crouched in the open space. The Black Hawk settled onto the savannah amidst a vast cloud of dirt and sand kicked up by its main rotor.

"Alex," said James. "What should I do?"

"Just sit tight, James. Hold here. And unless you want your jeep to fill with sand, we'll close the roof. Roll your windows up."

"Are we in danger?"

"I'm sure everything's fine!"

In truth, she didn't have a clue, but since there weren't any crew-served weapons or door guns aimed at them from inside the aircraft, she felt fairly certain they were safe. It wasn't likely these were the poachers returning to seek their revenge. Still, one could never be too sure.

Two crew members jumped out, carbines at the ready, and positioned themselves on either side of the door's opening before the helicopter had fully settled on its gear. Each wore a familiar style of paramilitary contractor clothing—beige cargo pants and black golf shirts—and both held what looked like a short-barreled M4A1 rifle.

A moment later, a third person—a woman—hopped out, her rifle slung in front. Even from a hundred feet away, she looked all business as she strode in their direction, the men flanking her.

Alex turned to James. "Wait here. If there's any shooting, get the hell out of here."

"I cannot leave you here—"

"We can take care of ourselves. And if we can't, there'll be nothing you can do about it, so hightail it back to the lodge and radio for help on the way."

"I will not be able to outrun that helicopter." Off her look, he relented. "Okay, Miss Alex, but if these people don't kill me, your father surely will for abandoning you."

"He won't and you won't be abandoning us," she said, swinging open the side door of the Land Cruiser.

Caleb was at her side as they advanced toward the Black Hawk, the landscape beyond shimmering through the hot exhaust that streamed from two turboshaft engines. The growl they emitted was only somewhat less than the roll of distant thunder.

"Do you know anything about this?" she half yelled to Caleb over the din of the engines.

"Not a thing." She interrogated him with her eyes. "I swear, Alex. I'm like Jon Snow here—I know nothing."

The woman wore the same outfit as the men—paramilitary chic—and it looked good on her. She might have had an inch on Alex, but not more than that. Her hair was long, jet-black with auburn highlights that shimmered in the morning light. From the rotor wash off the Black Hawk, Alex could see she had a braided ponytail that probably reached the middle of her back. She was striking with deep brown skin and high cheekbones. She fit right in against the backdrop of the Serengeti, like a Nubian queen. Okay, so Alex's geographic landmarks were off, but whatever. She thought the woman was stunning, doubly so the way she cradled her rifle like a pro.

If anything unpleasant was going to happen, Alex decided it would have happened by now. Still, she remained wary as they approached the helicopter and its dismounted personnel walking toward them, wishing she had a carbine of her own. They stopped short and waited for the woman and her companions to close the distance between them.

"Alex, I'm Harley," said the woman, now standing six feet in front of her.

On the rare occasions Alex was caught off guard, her default dialogue mode was sarcasm. "I'm not the least bit surprised," she said.

In the background, the Black Hawk's rotors were winding down, and the volume of noise and dust being kicked up by the blades lessened correspondingly.

The men flanked the woman, scanning to the sides and behind, as if expecting an armed troop of hyenas to come charging out of the grass.

"We need to take you in," continued Harley.

"*We* who? Am I being detained?"

"No, ma'am. We're with the State Department. I've been ordered to bring you to safety."

State Department? Not likely, thought Alex. "Even if you *were* special agents with the Diplomatic Security Service, I don't see the need. We're on a photo safari. You see anyone here with guns other than the three of you?" Harley raised an eyebrow but stood her ground, apparently neither angered nor rebuffed by the comment. "Is this about yesterday? Are you worried about blowback from the poachers?" Harley still said nothing. "Listen, I'm on vacation. Speaking of which, how'd you find me? Are you tracking my phone?" She pulled out her mobile and glanced at it as if she'd be able to see a *you are being tracked* dialogue box on its screen. "Well?"

"Not yours." Harley waited a beat.

"Shit, you're tracking *his* phone," Alex said, nodding her head toward Caleb.

Harley gave an almost imperceptible nod. "We keep tabs on our chiefs."

Caleb chimed in. "They're not DSS, Alex," he said. "They're Agency."

"Is that true?" Alex asked. "You're CIA?"

"Look," said Harley finally. "We can stand out here and hope that pride of lions over there doesn't come kill us—"

"Wait," Caleb said. His face lit up. "You saw the super pride?"

"The what?" Harley asked. "Look, Alex—both of you—get on the helo."

Harley looked at Caleb. He didn't budge. She spun her rifle so it was slung behind her, then reached for her side. Her two companions remained stoic, neither threatening nor friendly. Just . . . *there*. Alex fully expected a sidearm to pop into view, but instead, Harley drew a satellite phone from her hip and punched a button. She turned away and walked a few steps back toward the helicopter. Even with the Black Hawk's engines shut down, Alex couldn't make out what she was saying.

Harley turned back around and held the phone out to Caleb.

"Someone wants to talk to you," she said.

"Me?" He reluctantly accepted the portable handset from her. "Hello?" He straightened up. "Yes, ma'am . . . Shit . . . Yes, ma'am." He handed the phone back to Harley.

"Yes, ma'am," she said. "I'm sure it did. Thank you."

With that, she signed off. Caleb placed his hand gently against the center of Alex's back and whispered in her ear, "You go climb aboard. I'll explain to James what's happening and ask him to drop our gear off with lodge staff. We can pick it up later."

"I wish someone would explain it to me," she said.

"Alex, it's time to go," he said. "Get on the helicopter."

CHAPTER 14

"What aren't you telling me?"

Alex didn't enjoy being coerced into any decision that wasn't 100 percent of her own making. And she sure wasn't thrilled with the notion of being herded onto the Black Hawk without knowing the reason. Did she have trust issues? Probably. Were they well-founded? Maybe, but in this instance, the jury was still out.

Harley held up a finger. She was either saying, *Wait one minute,* or she was pointing up to the sky to tell her she would learn more once they were aloft. As if there was a possibility that once Alex knew, she would demand to be let off the chopper. Caleb was strapped into the seat across from hers.

"Okay, we're airborne," she said into her helmet comm unit once the helicopter's gear had cleared the loamy sand. "You mind telling me now what this is all about? I'm off the clock for another week."

Harley sat next to Caleb. The look on her face was one Alex knew well. She bore the same expression Alex had perfected over years of operations on a previous assignment with the unit called Intelligence Support Activity, or ISA. It was the look of an interrogator or cop who, when guarding against an attempt by some malfeasant to crack the warrior facade and climb into their head, would put the shields up. It was a technique used to mask ugly truths.

"That was Mustang," Caleb said, his voice reverberating in stereo inside her skull.

Her eyes widened. Mustang was the code name of CIA deputy director Kadeisha Thomas. Besides being the Central Intelligence Agency's second-in-command, she also directly oversaw Caleb's

Special Activities Center direct action team, making her Alex's supreme boss as well. Thomas was a hands-on, mission-focused leader who didn't mess around or tolerate bullshit.

"What aren't you telling me?" Then it hit her. Her heart rate briefly matched the RPMs of the Black Hawk's thrumming rotors. "The general—what's happened to my father?"

Caleb raised his hands in a calming manner, which only increased her agitation. She took a slow, deep breath and, in a low voice, asked, "What has happened to General Martel?"

"They don't exactly know—" began Caleb.

"So help me God, Caleb—"

"He's been taken," Harley jumped in.

The Black Hawk's cabin went eerily quiet, muffled by her noise-canceling headphones and the sound of blood coursing through her ears. Conversely, the comfort of the leatherette pads stuffed with slow-recovery foam made her feel like her head would explode. She closed her eyes and bore down, tightening her core and breathing slowly, willing her heart rate to fall in line.

"Harley, tell me what you know."

"He was on his way to the airport when his truck was ambushed."

"Is he dead?" She could scarcely get the words out.

Harley hesitated barely a second, so Alex repeated the question. "*Is. He. Dead?*"

"His driver was killed in the attack, but there were no signs that the general was," Harley said, reaching into a duffel bag at her feet. "We found this on the floor in the front seat where he was sitting."

Harley reached across the space between them holding a sheathed Ka-Bar knife. Iron Soldiers!, the motto of the 1st Armored Division, was boldly branded on its worn leather sheath.

"It's my father's."

A tear streaked down her cheek and dropped to her pant leg before she could intercept it. She wiped her eyes anyway as she felt the heft of the knife cradled in her lap. She remembered him pulling it out proudly yesterday as if it were the only tool he would need to deal with whatever threat they were about to encounter when they went off to engage the poachers. And in his younger days, that might have been true. He had been a tank commander and led an armored division during the first Gulf War. But he had kept things from her about his time in Iraq and Kuwait and in subsequent deployments for his country—secrets that suggested a darkness that she knew cast shadows on his soul, as her mother had told her more than once.

She considered yesterday's events. "Wait," she said. "The gunfight—those poachers—is this them seeking revenge?"

Harley shook her head.

"What?" asked Alex. "This isn't revenge, or they weren't poachers?"

Harley was looking at her with a blank expression.

"Was yesterday an attempt to grab my father?" She was thinking aloud, not really asking the question of anyone but herself. Words weren't needed. Awareness dawned on her.

"Fuck," she said, barely loud enough for the voice-activated microphone to pick up.

She gazed at the Ka-Bar. The handle was made of bands of leather washers that were compressed over the steel tang. Her father's had taken on a dark patina over the decades, aging into a deep brown. Dark crimson spots dotted it in places. *Blood?* she wondered, rubbing at the marks with her thumb. She unsnapped the handle and drew the parkerized fixed-blade knife from its scabbard, like a samurai drawing his katana—with reverence. The seven-inch clip-point blade was sharpened to a razor's edge. The black finish held marks indicating it had been put to good use as befitting a military knife. Alex remembered watching as a child while the general sharpened it by hand on whetstones of varying grit—a child entranced by the ritualistic actions of her father.

She thought of the events from the day before and reprimanded herself for not knowing, or at least not suspecting, that it wasn't poachers they had encountered. There had been clues, like why hadn't they run away sooner? Caleb must have read her thoughts, a skill he was getting better at.

"You can't blame yourself," he said.

"Why not?"

"How could you have known? And what would you have done differently if you had?"

"You can't be serious, Caleb. It would have changed everything. We could have made him a harder target to snatch—altered his plans, put a protection detail on him, called in the team to safeguard him, brought in reinforcements—anything but let him drive to an airport by himself in the middle of Africa with only an unarmed driver as an escort. We could have protected him. *I* could have protected him."

She knew he knew. He always knew. He was trying to spare her from self-recrimination. He was nodding. She liked to make fun of him, to pretend that, unlike the blade she held in her hand, he wasn't the sharpest tool in the box. It was their thing, their schtick. But Caleb's situational awareness was never idle. His mind was always focused. He was sharper than any Ka-Bar, any katana.

"Tell me we're not going all the way to Dar," he said.

The United States diplomatic mission to Tanzania and its embassy were housed in a compound off Old Bagamoyo Road in Dar es Salaam. It had been rebuilt stronger and more secure since the bombings orchestrated by Osama bin Laden in August 1998 that destroyed American embassies in Nairobi, Kenya, and Dar es Salaam, Tanzania, taking the lives of more than two hundred and twenty people.

She shook her head. "We have a shop in Arusha." She looked at her watch. "We'll be there in—"

"Arusha?" Alex asked. "We're not going to Arusha."

"Actually, we are," said Harley.

"Is that where my father was when they took him?"

"No, he—"

"Then we're not going there."

"Alex—"

"From what location was the retired four-star general kidnapped?" she asked, emphasizing the importance of the man to America and not just to her. This wasn't strictly personal, though it was.

Harley hesitated, weighing her options.

"Well?" Alex asked.

Harley looked at Caleb, who shrugged his shoulders, as if to say to her, *You're on your own, girl.*

"Where, Harley?"

"Seronera. Just down the road from the airstrip."

"Then take me there."

"We can't do that, Alex."

Alex's eyes darted from Harley to Caleb and back.

"The hell you can't," she said. "I want to see the scene for myself."

"Alex," said Harley. "There's no point in us going to where your father was grabbed. There's a team processing that scene as we speak. We should be at the op center. That's where you can do the most good."

Alex pondered that for a moment, just long enough to dismiss it.

"Is that what Mustang said?" she asked.

"What?"

"Were those Deputy Director Thomas's orders?"

"Well, not in so many words."

"Jesus, Harley. Then tell the pilots to take us to Seronera."

Harley was thinking about it. "But then meet me halfway, Martel. I'll take you to the scene, and notwithstanding your current objections, you agree to come with me to the shop in Arusha after. You can play CSI for a while, but we need you out of harm's way."

"So that's what this is about? Someone's worried that I'll be next?"

"It occurred to the deputy director and me that that's a distinct possibility after you messed up their plans yesterday."

"She has a habit of pissing people off like that," Caleb said.

"I have no doubt. But there are other reasons to get you and your partner there."

"Like?"

"Boss lady said you have a mind for military strategy."

"Not just military strategy," corrected Caleb. "The art of war."

"He means my strengths are more along the lines of tactics than strategy. Strategy is *his* domain," she said, nodding toward Caleb.

"She's more of a boots-on-the-ground, kick-you-in-the-nuts kind of tactician," Caleb said. "No offense, ma'am."

"None taken. I'm getting that impression. Call it what you will, Alex, we could use some of it. A fresh perspective is always good, if you're up to it."

"Done," she agreed. "But only after I get a look at the scene. And I won't be confined to the op center for safekeeping. I'm taking an active role in rescuing the general."

Harley looked at Caleb, who gave her a barely perceptible nod. But clearly, she got the message. She switched talk groups on her comms set and gave the new waypoint to the pilots. The Black Hawk banked sharply left, and Alex felt their air speed increasing.

Better, she thought.

CHAPTER 15

SERONERA, SERENGETI NATIONAL PARK, TANZANIA

The Black Hawk flew NOE, or nap-of-the-earth, as it proceeded to the location from which General David Martel had been abducted. Alex didn't know if the very low-altitude approach was due to ongoing threats or some other reason, but it offered her a great view of the surrounding land. She watched through the window as tens of thousands of wildebeest, zebra, and a massive herd of Cape buffalo scattered across the land away from their flight path. It was an exhilarating sight, but the wonder of the moment was overshadowed by the dread she felt for her father.

Where are you, Dad? What's happening to you? The world was filled with asshats who would love to get their hands on him and, more important, the knowledge he held in his head.

They flew over a cluster of vehicles staged around a stretch of road south of the Seronera Airstrip. Alex immediately sensed that this was the spot where her father had been abducted. She could deduce which agencies were on scene by the brands and models of vehicles she spotted during their flyover. For example, the State Department and its Diplomatic Security Service favored Chevy Tahoes, of which she counted four. The only real surprise was how swiftly resources had been mustered. Optimistically, it was a six- to seven-hour drive from Arusha, the nearest major city, to Seronera via Highway B144. Hardly that much time had passed since the general went missing. But then, the general was not just any American tourist lost in the savannah. He was a genuine source of classified information that could enrich private interests, destabilize governments, or put American programs, teams, and resources in peril.

She wanted to know what had happened, and she didn't care one bit about the ideology or motivations of his abductors. She was singularly focused on one objective—getting her dad back, alive and well. Everything else would be and must be subordinate to that. She would ensure she kept that idea at the forefront of her mind, as her conviction to do so was bound to conflict with the objectives of various other agencies and players.

She had always considered herself, for better or worse, an independent operator, a singleton. She had signed on as a special agent and a member of CIA's global special response staff and was, therefore, undeniably part of a tip-of-the-spear Ground Branch direct action team. But she would be just as happy—maybe even more so—to carry out and execute lethal action missions on her own, with minimal support if necessary. Her analytical skills were strong, and she was well-versed in the art of war, as Caleb had phrased it. She recognized the destabilizing effect her unique skill set could have on the morale of an enemy combatant force. She was a force multiplier all by herself.

Caleb, however, was wired differently. He possessed a sharp intellect, compelling leadership skills, and strength of character. He had demonstrated as much during her abbreviated CIA boot camp, shortened by the agency's need for her to run a critical operation with his team in a region on the other side of the globe that was quickly devolving into a war zone.

At the Farm—the CIA's covert training facility at Camp Peary in Virginia—he had been one of her instructors. He possessed an uncanny ability to visualize the mission briefing system he had devised as the interconnected whole that it was, rather than as individual stages of an operation. It was similar to how a chess master saw the entire game unfolding after just a few opening moves.

Harley was talking on her secure mobile. When she clicked off, she said, "That was my senior analyst in Arusha. We'll get a briefing from the team leader on the ground."

"Then what?" Caleb asked.

Before Harley could answer, Alex said, "Then we'll do whatever it takes to get my father back."

* * *

PFA COMPOUND, BUTEMBA, TANZANIA

After several hours, the caravan returned safely to the rebel camp. Among them, a cargo truck loaded with produce for the village drove into the center of the compound. Concealed between the truck's cab and its cargo was a false wall hiding a secret compartment. This compartment contained a wire crate meant for a medium-sized dog. But it wasn't a dog inside.

Lemarti climbed out of the lead truck and walked toward the prefab building. Those who had stayed behind gathered in a semicircle and sat on the ground nearby. Militiamen, women, and children—some bearing arms and others clutching their mothers' garments—came together to witness the triumphant return of their leader.

Although the road was rough in some sections, it had been an uneventful journey. Lemarti rubbed his back as he walked. The few police patrols they passed by didn't pay them any attention. Even if they had known about the general's abduction, they still would have left Lemarti and his crew unmolested, free to travel the roads with impunity. This was partly because of the voluntary road tolls his militia paid weekly to the local police commission to ensure the safe passage of his men and equipment, and partly because the police officers understood the nature of the militia and their brutality, preferring to live another day.

A woman brought him a wooden bowl, out of which steam rose from a large piece of rib steak still on the bone, nestled alongside yellow sweet potato and a chunk of deep brown bread. She was pretty and wore a lime-green, high-waisted, long, flowy skirt with a long-sleeve black top and a distinctive red-and-yellow kanga cloth wrapped around her shoulders. He flashed her a smile of yellowed teeth and seized the meat. Using the bone for a handle, he took large bites and sat in his chair on the threshold of the opened garage door, a king upon his throne among his subjects.

When he was sated, he handed the bowl with the rest of its contents to the child sidled up next to him. The boy took it and sat on the cold concrete, chewing strings of pink meat off the rib bone, the Chinese-made rifle in his lap acting as a table for the bowl of food to balance on.

Meanwhile, men removed crates of maize, cassava, rice, mangoes, and pineapples from the cargo truck and carried them to a storage shed next to a cookhouse behind the Nissen hut. Four men climbed into the back of the truck while two others stood guard behind it. The camp grew still with anticipation as the sound of a metal crate scraping along the floor of the truck filled the air.

*　*　*

David Martel felt the truck slow and veer off the road. His hands were bound in front of him, and as the vehicle abruptly changed direction and hit a bump on the gravel, he tipped over again, his shoulder striking the side of the wire dog crate that confined him. The air was gray and dank, with only minimal light creeping through the cracks in the compartment's seams. Judging by the voices outside the vehicle, he guessed they had to be at the end of the hours-long journey.

Whatever's going to happen will happen soon, he thought as the truck came to a stop. On the other hand, his life had been spared thus far, so maybe there were no plans to kill him right away, and he could survive long enough to hatch a plan and make his escape. Out of necessity, rescue was the furthest thing from his mind. Someone had to find him for that to happen, and there was no point in putting his fate in anybody else's hands. On the other hand, among life's certainties was that Alex would turn the African continent on its head and shake it hard to find him and set him free.

He considered his situation. The men who had seized him and executed his driver had known of his phone call last night and his departure plans this morning. Perhaps they had staged the crisis at his work themselves or faked it outright and coerced a worker at the plant to summon him back to the Okavango Republic under false pretenses. It wasn't hard to imagine how they might do that, and Martel now wondered if the man he had spoken to last night, a Pentagon contractor and colleague who had told him about the problems with the project, was still alive.

Probably not, he decided regretfully.

The man he had spoken to was a good guy and one of the brightest on the task force. He had repeatedly warned the higher-ups—more like he complained endlessly—that locating a top-secret military project in the heart of Africa—even in a country as seemingly stable as the Okavango Republic—was foolhardy at best. Criminally stupid was a better description, he had said.

Whatever happened next, the general needed to keep his wits about him. He was parched and feeling the effects of heat exhaustion from the limited ventilation inside the truck's hidden compartment. He felt dizzy and nauseous as well, convinced he was suffering from carbon monoxide poisoning caused by the truck's exhaust fumes being drawn in through the rear as they drove. This was a common occurrence in human trafficking and kidnappings, with abductors and others oblivious to the risks associated with exhaust pipes exiting at the back of vehicles. Fumes were carried into the truck by the simple principles of physics governing the movement of turbulent air behind a moving vehicle. This turbulent air was filled with the poisonous by-products of combustion that drifted with eddy currents and seeped inside.

He would have liked to still be in possession of his Ka-Bar, but one of the rebels had found it on him after pulling him from the truck and ripped the knife roughly from his belt, throwing it back inside. Then he'd shoved the general to the ground and kicked him repeatedly before he and the other thugs bound his hands in front.

The general was surprised that the man hadn't taken the military knife as a trophy—it would have made a fine one. Knife or no knife, he would bide his time until he could fight his way to freedom and kill anyone who stood in his path.

It was the American way.

CHAPTER 16

MUTAPA, OKAVANGO REPUBLIC

Artemi Tarasenko stared to the east from his second-story office window. The city sprawled flat and dusty before him, paved roads flowing like slow-moving lava in all directions around any obstacle that dared rise above the same contour line occupied by the town on a topographical map. Throngs of people intermingled with cars migrating along the blacktop in an endless stream, bound for the prosperous markets and businesses of central Mutapa, the capital city of the OR.

The smell of burning black ironwood and roasting Arabica coffee beans rose from the plant beneath him. He lifted his cup and sipped the hot liquid within. *Bold, rich, aromatic with mild berry, floral notes, and a hint of cocoa. Perfect!* he thought.

The art of coffee roasting, particularly the method his company employed using a common source of wood like the black ironwood tree from nearby forests, came naturally to him. He had transformed a hobby—a true passion that he had honed back home in the unlikely setting of the Irkutsk Oblast in southern Siberia along the shores of Lake Baikal—into a profitable venture. Here, in the heart of Africa, his Leopard Bean Collective—a coffee business that served as both a roastery and a warehouse for storing and sorting beans grown and cultivated on local farms—turned out to be an excellent cover for the logistics and administrative aspects of his other business endeavor. The coffee operation effectively masked the movement of personnel and equipment throughout the region while generating tangible revenue, which he, as its sole proprietor, pocketed as a healthy side income.

His assistant entered the office, breaking his thoughts.

"Mr. Tarasenko, sir, the team is ready. They await your arrival."

"Hmm? Yes, of course. I will be right down."

While a boost to his ego, the rising profits of the business were merely a facade he hid behind. The real profits of his operation stemmed from that other enterprise, the one sanctioned by the Russian president himself, the one that functioned in this region of sub-Saharan Africa, paving the way for greater involvement through which he could bring Russian military might to bear to counter Chinese inroads with their Belt and Road Initiative, or Indigenous revanchism, or American imperialism in the region.

The real money to be made in Africa stemmed from mining—for gold, of course—but increasingly, for the rare-earth minerals so essential for high-tech applications, renewable energy technologies, and defense systems. Cobalt, lithium, copper, and other rare earth elements were what the superpowers were increasingly in search of. And he who controlled the mining controlled the race. Tarasenko and his advisors had been astute in targeting the fledgling operations that were identified by the mining engineers and geologists, and then muscling in to scoop up mining rights that gave them the advantage in world markets.

Where the minerals flowed, the money flooded in. And like any good crime boss, after he bankrolled his operation and took his profits, he made sure to pay a tribute to the Russian president as a sign of his continued allegiance and, of course, to the Russian state.

Tarasenko relished his role as the commander of the Russian president's unofficial private army, Leopard Group PMC, fully aware of what had happened to the previous leader of such an organization. The former leader of the Wagner Group, Yevgeny Viktorovich Prigozhin, was a boastful man and ultimately paid for his vanity and ego with his life. With him gone and the remnants of his band of warriors and criminals scattered, Tarasenko simply sorted the wheat from the chaff as it settled in the breeze, allowing the waste to be swept into the furnaces of the ongoing war zone in Eastern Europe. Meanwhile, he fortified his army with the best elements of Prigozhin's legacy. In an unusual show of creativity, the Russian press dubbed Tarasenko *the president's new barista*, a fitting title for the man who was altering the coffee habits of Russians back home and had succeeded President Sergachev's former *chef*, as Prigozhin had once been known.

He checked his reflection in the wall mirror, a habit shaped not by vanity but by years of service in his country's military, and smoothed back his dark, wavy hair. Outside his office, he descended the open staircase to the warehouse floor below, blending in with the mercenaries gathered there dressed in black boots, khaki pants, and sand-colored T-shirts. For this operation, there would be no insignia, shoulder patches, flashes, or flags. It was intended to be a routine drive-by of the American compound to the west, which the Americans believed was cleverly disguised as a local machine parts plant, but one that Tarasenko knew concealed their latest war technology, foolishly situated on a continent whose very existence and loyalty were being contested by the world's three superpowers.

Placing the operation so cavalierly on contested soil represented to Tarasenko the epitome of outlandish bravado. But then, he expected no less from the Americans, who were always so full of bluff and bluster, daring the world to confront them. Well, challenge accepted. Today, they would ride past in their cars. The Americans on sentry duty would no doubt identify them and report the incident to their higher-ups. But now that the project manager had been dealt with, it would be interesting to size up their response. David Martel had been the key figure here, and with his removal from the picture, Tarasenko hoped to get a clearer picture of the plant's contingency plans. He had only a pair of watchers on the inside, and they were still too poorly placed to judge day-to-day business continuity or emergency planning. Now, though, he suspected the plant would move into crisis operations, and that should prove revelatory.

Human systems were not unlike coffee production: it was only when one put the bean to the fire that the essence came to the fore.

Tarasenko breezed through the group on his way to the rear doors where the vehicles were waiting. He was feeling invigorated. It was a childish response to the knowledge that he had eliminated a foe, but that bit of self-reflection and personal insight did not disturb him.

"Ready?" he asked his deputy in Russian.

"*Da, nachal'nik.*" *Yes, boss*, replied the man, hurrying to keep up.

It would be a twenty-minute drive to the part of town where the American compound housed Project Aegis. Tarasenko would seize the opportunity to scout the perimeter of the building—taunt the workers, really—then call the man to whom he had assigned the task of eliminating the American general. His contractor was a native of Tanzania and, like so many Indigenous peoples worldwide, had been displaced by newcomers—those who would exploit the richness and beauty of the country while decimating the population of the remaining Maasai in the Ngorongoro region to claim the land for themselves.

But Tarasenko cared not about such matters. Land—indeed, entire nations—belonged to those who could conquer and hold them. Borders were merely artificial lines drawn on paper. Treaties were not meant to be honored if future leaders deemed them unworthy of their approval. A planted flag or a mud hut in a field signified nothing if its owner could not fight to maintain possession of the blood-soiled earth beneath it. Like every despot who came before him or ruled today, that was his operating premise, how he viewed the world.

It was the way it had always been. And it was that way still.

CHAPTER 17

BUTEMBA, ON THE SHORES OF LAKE VICTORIA

David Martel was blinded by the sudden flash of daylight as the gray, rotted plywood covering the hidden compartment in the back of the truck was ripped away. He raised his hands—bound together with rough twine—to shield his eyes. Abruptly, his wire-crate prison was yanked and pulled from its confines by men who looked as though they felt no emotional or moral discomfort with their task. He was merely another burden that was theirs to unload from the truck, like the produce he knew had been packed in behind him. With one more shift of the crate, he fell again onto his back.

There were loud shouts and voices from outside the truck, all in a language he didn't understand, though he believed it to be Swahili, like the one James, their safari guide, spoke. Even a man like David Martel couldn't help but feel a cold chill of fear run down his spine. His eyes gradually adjusted to the light, and he saw four men casting dark shadows. They dragged the crate to the back of the truck, but instead of lifting it, they tipped his cage off the tailgate, and he plunged onto the muddy ground three feet below.

Pain jolted his back and shoulders. He was relieved he hadn't landed directly on his face or hands—that could have been debilitating. As it stood, he saw stars twinkling before his eyes from the force of the impact and the pain that shot through him. A crowd of onlookers encircled him in a ragged loop. Some kicked the cage, some spat on him, but everyone, it seemed, shouted and voiced their unvarnished hatred for him—a man they did not know.

The four men dragged his crate through the mud toward a steel outbuilding. He recognized it as a type common throughout much of Africa, fabricated from cheap materials and forming a timeless and efficient design.

The crowd parted before him. His captors positioned his steel cage so that he faced the open door of the building and the man seated inside. Martel looked around. The men around him were armed with AK-47 rifles—probably Chinese knockoffs of the ubiquitous Russian-made Kalashnikov rifles. The man looked confident and cocky. Beside him on the ground was a boy, maybe twelve or fourteen years old. He, too, had a rifle in his lap which, in his case, braced a wooden bowl of food. The boy eyed him without emotion nor even, it seemed, the faintest suggestion of curiosity. The general, though, was very curious, despite his own hunger and thirst.

Who are you? he thought as the boy continued to gnaw on a bone.

The man stood up. He was tall and lanky, and Martel recognized him as one of those who had abducted him. In fact, he was the man who had stood by as his driver was shot without mercy even as he pleaded for his life. He strode over, bronze-tinted aviators shading his eyes from the afternoon sun, and glared down at him trapped inside this crate designed to hold dogs or other livestock.

"Welcome to my village!" he said cheerily. Then, in what Martel judged to be Swahili, he barked an order at the others. One of the men bent down and unlatched the door on the crate. It swung open. "Well?" he said. "What are you waiting for?" The smile disappeared. "Get out."

With his hands bound in front, Martel supported his weight awkwardly on his elbows and knees, struggling to crawl out of the cage. For his slow progress, the men who had pulled him from the truck kicked the crate, knocking him again onto his side as the crowd cheered. Pain shot through every joint, including his lower back and pelvis, courtesy of injuries sustained over four decades in Uncle Sam's Army.

Eventually he emerged, taking a few extra seconds to get fully to his feet while sizing up his surroundings. A pewter-tinged light hung over the compound—sunlight filtered by the smoke from cooking fires and the burning of waste. Dark smoke billowed skyward, and his gut clenched.

Great. More burn pits.

The acrid stench transported him back to Iraq and Afghanistan, where those toxic craters devoured everything from medical waste to spent batteries, spewing poison into the desert air. The military's crude solution had turned their bases into toxic waste sites, the noxious cocktail of dioxins, benzene, and chemical particulates settling in soldiers' lungs like a curse. As a commander, he should have known better—they all should have. Now those black columns of smoke rose in his nightmares, a constant reminder of decisions that had marked his men with invisible scars.

The air was redolent of it and the smell of unwashed humanity, but it was fresher than what he had endured for hours inside the compartment within the truck. Acrid as it was, it was helping to clear his head.

The man before him stood maybe six-three, a Black man with physical characteristics Martel judged to be Maasai. He sneered at the general and turned his back, walking toward the Nissen hut. When the general didn't move, someone nudged him from behind with the barrel of a rifle.

He followed the man through the opening of the hut. Beyond the threshold, the man sat in an aging executive office chair, leaning back against the cracked and torn leather until it tilted at an impossibly steep angle, his legs stretched before him. Martel knew better than to speak, waiting instead for a cue he knew would eventually come from his host.

The boy who had been outside gnawing on a bone came in behind them and sat on the floor next to the man. Although his expression was dull and unaffected, his eyes were bright. Martel observed that, despite the presence of the rifle slung behind him, he didn't possess the dead eyes of a killer. He wondered if the boy had, in fact, killed before. But then he tamped down any sympathy he might have felt for the child with vigilance. He knew of and, in some cases, had witnessed too many children, mostly boys, committing acts of profound violence—rape, murder, mutilation—neither disturbed by nor fully comprehending the gravity of the acts they carried out, merely following the examples and urgings of those in power positions.

One of the many lessons Martel learned throughout his career during operations in many African nations, from Somalia to Rwanda, was never to underestimate the capacity of a child to murder another human being in cold blood. Africa was a continent that remained largely at war with itself, an endemic disease unchanged in generations if not centuries. He peered over his shoulder at the mob outside. No fewer than half, and perhaps as many as two-thirds, were children—those he guessed on a cursory glance to be less than eighteen years of age, the threshold set by the UN General Assembly for individuals to participate in armed conflict. This village was a primary school for killers, and the men before him its tenured faculty. He knew the issues were complex, involving both supply-side and demand-side economics. Still, war was war, and even an old soldier—maybe *especially* an old soldier—knew that life or death was strictly a binary proposition.

However it was rationalized by those who exploited children to commit unspeakable acts of violence in conflict zones, the underlying theme was subhuman cruelty and ambivalence toward their suffering, both now and in the future. It was a nihilistic practice that wasn't sustainable, yet it persisted, and children were fighting and dying across Africa by the tens of thousands.

Another man stepped in front of him. Like one of their attackers yesterday, this one, too, wore a baseball cap with the Philadelphia Eagles team logo on it. He drew a long, fixed-blade knife from beneath a tattered shirt. It was the same man who had shot his driver with a burst of gunfire from his automatic weapon, stitching a line of holes from his belly to his neck. It was an unnecessary and excessive act of violence, as his driver posed no threat to the gang of kidnappers.

Martel studied the man's face, hoping to discern his intent. Was he about to be killed, here and now, in front of the group's leader and the crowd of onlookers behind him? He thought it was unlikely, but he couldn't be sure. Like the child's eyes, this man's revealed nothing. Unlike the child's, though, his were cold and lifeless. This was a man who had spilled blood and taken lives. The quandary for every warrior was, when faced with an enemy who, like himself, had killed in battle, how to avoid judging or hating them for it.

The man sneered and abruptly raised the blade against his neck. The move surprised him, but Martel didn't flinch. Though he could feel his heart beating in his throat, his lifeblood literally pulsing on a knife edge, he showed no fear. Instead, he squeezed his lips together and sneered back into the man's dull eyes, pressing forward into his face. It was an imperfect mirror that stared back at him. The man lowered the knife and severed the bindings around Martel's wrists, then backed away, resheathing the blade.

Clearly, he's seen too many gangster movies, Martel thought as he watched him retreat. He brought a newly freed but still numb and tingling hand to his neck and wiped away a slow stream of blood. He watched it trickle over his palm and decided that, one way or another, he would soon kill this man.

In front of him, the man in the chair laughed.

"You are as I expected you would be, General," he said. "Strong and defiant."

Martel didn't reply as he wiped his own blood onto his pants and swatted dust and splatters of mud from his clothes.

The man got out of the chair and sauntered toward him. "We are both soldiers," he said. "But we are not alike. You see, unlike you, this life chose me. But I have found it agreeable and I am good at it."

"What exactly do you think you're good at?" asked the general.

"This," he said, gesturing to the people gathered outside the building.

Martel turned to look outside. Memories of news coverage about a man named Jim Jones and vast quantities of cyanide-laced Flavor Aid amidst the massacred bodies of almost a thousand innocent men, women, and children flooded back to him.

"There's nothing new about a madman in the jungle with an endless supply of devoted followers," he said. "It doesn't make you special. Rare, thankfully, but not particularly noteworthy."

"A madman? That's what you see here, General Martel? I expected more from you."

"You shouldn't have. I'm just a simple man."

The man stood an arm's length away now. Close enough that the general could wrap his hands around his throat and extinguish his life if he was fast enough.

"My men came for you yesterday, but they failed."

"You know what they say, if you want a job done right, do it yourself."

Without prelude, the man punched him hard on the right side of his abdomen. Martel stumbled backward and crumpled to his knees, gasping for breath and feeling sharp stabs of pain spread like a hot knife deep inside, his organs in spasm from the blow.

"So very true," he said. "Then maybe my brother would not be dead."

Martel fell onto his back. He struggled to breathe, his diaphragm feeling as though it were going to explode out of him. The man's words caught him off guard. Their gunfight yesterday was with this gang. It made sense now.

The crowd outside, waiting for something to happen, now cheered and moved in closer. They shuffled restlessly, like a pack of hyenas waiting for their share of carrion. His host spoke emphatically to them, but Martel didn't understand a word he said.

"Get up."

He tried.

"I said, get up." The man kicked him to motivate him.

Martel staggered to his feet, still reeling from the blow to his gut.

"Was it you that killed my brother?"

Shit. That explains a lot.

He continued, "Or was it your daughter, the woman soldier?"

Martel said nothing.

"No matter. Soon she will be dead, too."

Not fucking likely, friend, he thought. *But feel free to misjudge her. She loves that.*

The man turned back to the crowd. After a short exchange, they dispersed. Then he turned to his lieutenant, whom he called Desmond, and issued orders. The man walked over and grabbed him roughly by the arm, dragging him toward an exit with another man following behind with a rifle.

"We will talk again later."

This clearly wasn't a good situation, but Martel was grateful that this might signal he wouldn't be part of a larger spectacle.

Maybe today, at least, he wouldn't lose his head.

CHAPTER 18

SERONERA, SERENGETI NATIONAL PARK, TANZANIA

The Black Hawk settled onto a makeshift landing zone half a klick from the ambush site. As the rotors wound down, Alex caught herself tracing the outline of her father's Ka-Bar knife beneath her shirt. The blade sat cold against her skin, tucked into her waistband—the last tangible piece of him she possessed.

"Watch your six out there," Harley said, shouldering her daypack. "The local authorities are cooperating, but jurisdiction gets complicated when every three-letter agency shows up to the party."

"Noted," Alex replied, releasing her harness. "But I'm not here to make friends."

Harley caught her arm. "That kind of thinking won't help you, Martel. It'd be just as easy to PNG your ass."

"I'm not looking to get declared persona non grata, just to find my father."

"Same difference if you piss off the wrong people." Harley pulled her close enough that the others couldn't hear. "This isn't a Ground Branch op, Alex. It's a kidnapping on foreign soil. Different rules."

The moment her boots hit the red earth, Alex felt a familiar clarity descend—the kind that came with operational focus. She threaded the Ka-Bar through her belt where it belonged. The savannah stretched endlessly around them, deceptively peaceful under the midday sun. Only the cluster of vehicles fifty meters ahead betrayed the violence that had occurred here.

The scene materialized as they approached: a Toyota Land Cruiser angled off the road, its windshield a spiderweb of bullet-riddled glass. Blood had dried black against the beige upholstery. Beyond the vehicle, suits and uniforms created a human perimeter—DSS agents in tactical vests, embassy staff with clipboards, and Tanzanian police in dark blue fatigues.

Alex registered details automatically: brass casings marked with small yellow evidence tents, tire tracks cast in plaster, the distinctive smell of fingerprint powder mingling with the metallic tang of dried blood. The hard-faced man directing the scene wore a bulletproof vest with FBI emblazoned across the chest.

He intercepted them before they reached the vehicle. "Restricted crime scene. Turn around."

Harley stepped forward. "Catherine Harris," she said. "Regional Security Office. My team, my jurisdiction."

"Agent Burke, FBI." His eyes settled on Alex with a flicker of recognition. "We've established joint precedence with State. General Martel fell under our protective scope."

Alex pushed forward. "I'm his daughter, Special Agent Alex Martel. Where is he?"

Burke's expression softened imperceptibly. "Still working on that, Agent Martel."

"Working on it?" The words hung in the air between them. "It's been hours."

"We've got satellite retasking, signals intelligence, and coordination with Tanzanian authorities and neighboring countries. We're working every angle."

Alex moved past him toward the Land Cruiser, ignoring his protests. The smell hit her first—the coppery scent of blood, the acidic sting of gunshot residue, the plastic odor of shattered safety glass. This was where her father had been taken.

She leaned inside through the frame where the window once was, scanning the interior with practiced precision. The driver's seat was saturated with blood and brain matter—execution style, just as Harley had said. The passenger seat was also blood-spattered, the passenger already out of the vehicle when the driver was shot.

"They wanted him alive," she said, more to herself than anyone.

Caleb appeared at her shoulder. "Tactical approach from multiple directions. Professional job."

"Too professional for local poachers," she agreed.

Burke joined them, his initial hostility replaced by professional courtesy. "We've got witnesses describing a convoy of five or six Toyota Hilux trucks and a produce truck heading northwest after the attack. One was a technical vehicle with armed men in the back. Unfortunately, the descriptions match half the NGO security details in the region."

Off her puzzled look, he continued. "Hold that thought, I'll come back to it. Two blocked the road from the front, two from the rear. Our bad guys dismounted with rifles as the fifth carrying the shooters and the group's leader hit the general's truck. All subjects are male, all Black of mixed local ethnicities. Witnesses said the crew was led by a man described as tall and tough. Maasai, they speculated."

"That fits," Harley said.

"Fits what?" Burke asked.

"There's a large rebel group operating in West Serengeti and along the coast of Lake Victoria led by a Maasai warrior."

"I thought the Maasai were peaceful," Alex said.

"Today, maybe. But historically and traditionally, the Maasai were fierce warriors and dominated the Rift Valley. For the most part, they're a seminomadic pastoralist people, but they still maintain warrior traditions and rites of passage."

"Meaning what, exactly?"

"Meaning they train with traditional weapons to protect their communities from predators, but mostly they herd cows, goats, and sheep."

"So how is a Maasai leading this rebel group, and why don't government forces take them out?"

"To your first question, many of the Maasai have been displaced from their lands, even slaughtered. The People's Freedom Army of Tanzania—the rebel militia we're talking about—has, generally speaking, been limiting their activities to cross-border raids into Burundi and Rwanda, with occasional forays into the DRC. They've been only a minor nuisance in-country, so the government's been dealing with them on an incident-by-incident basis."

"How's that working out?" Alex asked, her words dripping with sarcasm.

"So," Caleb said, "they're stirring up shit but not shitting where they eat, is that it?"

"Something like that."

"Do we know where they're headquartered?" Alex asked.

"They have several encampments, but they are also nomadic when it suits them. They can stay on the move under the cover of the land if they have to."

"Then what are we waiting for, Harley? How hard could it be to hit a few camps or track down a wandering band of rebels?"

"It's not that simple—"

"It sure as hell is. Get me a few Green Berets or Rangers—"

"It doesn't work like that, Alex."

"It should."

"And what if you hit one camp only to find out he's been moved to another?"

"Then you hit the other."

"There's more than just soldiers living in those camps; they also house women and children. We can't ensure the surgical precision required to avoid harming noncombatants. And you know how the administration feels about the deaths of innocent civilians—especially children."

"Alex," Caleb said. "We don't have a location on the general yet. If we hit the wrong camp, or even if we hit the right camp, they could kill him before we can rescue him. We need a better plan than to go charging in recklessly. You know that."

Alex knew this all to be true. "Tell me about the produce truck."

"It's how they conceal cargo—they most likely locked him in a compartment in the back. Now, if you'll excuse me, I better get back."

She nodded. As Burke turned away to confer with his team, Caleb drew closer. "You thinking what I'm thinking?"

"That my father's work in Okavango just became very relevant? Yeah." She surveyed the scene once more.

She contained her seething rage and anguish like a volcano's caldera cradled magma, the pressure beneath building toward an inevitable eruption.

"They could be interrogating him right now," she said, her pain yielding to frustration. She felt like she was eleven again.

"We don't know that," said Harley feebly.

"Someone could be trying to extract everything he knows. My father won't give up information lightly. He won't spill secrets until they make him spill secrets."

The expression on Harley's face showed that she knew what Alex was implying. Her lips pressed together in sympathy. "Alex, your father is a trained professional—"

"Which is why we need to go free him now, not tomorrow or next week."

"We'll get him back, Alex," Caleb said. "I promise. We'll bring him home."

She felt the weight of her father's knife against her hip—a promise made in steel. Whatever came next, blood would answer for blood.

CHAPTER 19

CIA OPERATIONS CENTER (BLACKBIRD), ARUSHA, TANZANIA

At the scene of the abduction, the lead investigator from the FBI guided Alex through a summary of their evidence collection and processing, along with an overview of the next steps for the proposed investigation. Meanwhile, an evidence response team gathered anything—bullet casings, footprint casts, blood samples—that they considered potentially relevant to the investigation. Finally, when she was satisfied that everything possible was being done to find her father, Alex, her companions, and their security detail climbed back aboard the Black Hawk.

Less than ninety minutes later, the helicopter landed and was towed into a hangar next to the main terminal of Kilimanjaro International Airport, located at the eastern edge of Arusha. As Alex disembarked, she lifted her nose into the air, her nostrils flaring like a predator in unfamiliar hunting grounds. The city smelled different from what she was used to in the streets of major cities around the world. There, the canyons of towering buildings funneled wind currents through the streets, drawing air from the subterranean labyrinth of subways and service tunnels beneath the great metropolises. Thus, the city was infused with the scent of dust, concrete, and grit from below it.

But here, in the heart of Africa, at an elevation of over 4,500 feet, the air was rich and pungent with the scent of charcoal and roasting coffee—an olfactory mélange more complex than the aromas of New York, London, or Paris. It reminded her of her childhood, of happier times spent with her mom and dad in the family cabin in Wyoming, of cookouts and campfires in the woods, and of the cowboy coffee her dad brewed with skill.

In short, Arusha smelled like a family bonfire.

They crossed the tarmac to waiting vehicles. When it came to in-country operational transportation, the CIA's tastes were more esoteric than those of its federal sister agencies, which favored General Motors brands. The group loaded into two Mercedes G-Wagens and a Land Cruiser and sped across the tarmac, passing through the airport's gates and continuing up a service road. They drove for ten minutes before entering an industrial zone, pulling into the rear loading dock of the complex. Harley swiped her ID card, then placed her palm on a scanner, and the heavy door clicked open.

Inside, the unit looked nothing like what a casual observer might assume from outside its walls and blackened windows. Instead, the poured concrete floor was covered with sound-absorbing carpet, and the room was filled with an array of computers and monitors mounted on the wall. The shop, as Harley had called it, was not exactly a place that sold Maasai trinkets and souvenirs made in China.

"And here I thought we'd be working out of an RV in a local strip mall parking lot," Alex said.

Harley shot her a glance. "I'm not sure how much Caleb shared with you, but overseeing physical and pop-up operations centers worldwide is part of my job portfolio. Welcome to the CIA Operations Center in Arusha, dubbed Blackbird."

It made sense. Having an in-country operations center for intelligence activities was critical for success. A good one could not only provide oversight of operations, but also act as a clearinghouse of information and a resupply center for personnel and materiel.

"Are there a lot of places like this?"

Caleb chimed in. "Anywhere the US has special interests."

"So, everywhere?" she asked.

"Pretty much," said Harley. "Tanzania is generally friendly toward America. They allow us to operate here and have the run of the country for the most part. Our Green Berets and elements from JSOC"—Joint Special Operations Command, the center of US military special operations—"have been assisting the Tanzania People's Defense Force in rooting out ISIS terrorists."

"I thought ISIS was more of a problem in Kenya than here."

"They are, but they've been making more frequent forays into villages along the country's southern border with Mozambique, doing their usual: indiscriminately robbing, raping, and killing civilians."

Alex felt an uptick of hope. "So we should be able to call up AFRICOM and borrow some SEALs or Raiders and get this done." United States Africa Command was one of eleven unified combatant commands of the US Department of Defense.

"Not so fast," said Harley. "A recent interdiction by one of our Special Mission Units went a little off the rails—"

"Define *a little*."

"Civilian casualties, including women and children."

"That's the risk of doing business with guns."

"Alex," Caleb said. "I know you don't mean that."

She shrugged, wishing she shared his confidence in her.

"The Tanzanian president doesn't like when civilians die. It's not even a moral judgment, Alex. He's a pragmatist, and this is an election year. That incident caused a pretty fierce backlash from the media that opposition parties pounced on. And since it's become fashionable to throw American interests out of so many African countries, our president gets a little nervous, too."

"Then there's the Russians," Caleb said.

Harley nodded and said, "You'd think that after the Wagner Group's leader was killed, the action in Africa and elsewhere would have slowed down and we'd be less likely to be in conflict."

"But?"

"But it didn't turn out that way. The Russian president doubled down on his interests. And the void left by Wagner's decline has been filled by a new private military contractor, Artemi Tarasenko and his Leopard Group PMC. We see even more activity from them than before. And there's a simmering battle between the Russians and the Chinese People's Liberation Army for control that's all but open warfare. Contrary to what everyone would like to believe, Africa is still an embattled continent facing pressures from every side, including us."

They moved in behind a large, sweeping console with banks of computer monitors, each, it seemed, actively tracking vehicles or displaying live aerial footage of villages and other large encampments.

"Anything?" Harley asked one of the operators.

"Not yet, ma'am, but we'll find him."

Alex interpreted the commotion in front of her to mean that resources—expensive ones—were being utilized to find her father. It was comforting to see the machinations of the US government on display, though she wouldn't relax entirely from that knowledge alone.

"Control of what, specifically?" she asked, in part to keep her brain engaged, which helped quell her need to be moving, acting. Operating.

"Rare earth minerals, coffee, oil and gas, cigarettes, whatever."

"Cigarettes? Seriously?"

"Yup, as serious as a cluster bomb, Alex. We're way behind the Chinese in commercial ventures here. And business means money in the hands of locals and government coffers. That buys goodwill, and goodwill buys the means to protect the homeland from faraway threats."

Harley tapped the computer operator on the shoulder. The woman ran her fingers over a keyboard and moved a mouse around a pad, clicking and highlighting as she went.

Charts and graphs popped up on-screen, with Harley summarizing the deeds of rebel leaders and commanders of local Russian and Chinese operations. Alex knew Russia had interests in Mali, Niger, and other countries to the north and west, but didn't realize their ambitions stretched this far south and into East Africa. Before her were photos of Leopard Group's leader, Artemi Tarasenko, and deputy, Anton Kovalchuk, along with their various aircraft and other equipment dressed in Leopard Group's colors, their snarling leopard head logo stenciled or painted on everything.

Chinese interests were headed by Colonel Zhang Wei and his aide, Lieutenant Liu Qiang of the Ministry of State Security from their facilities in Dar es Salaam, the Tanzanian capital.

"The more we try to keep our nose out of other people's business," Harley said, "the more ground we lose to these asshats and others like them. It's a battle that's been simmering for decades, but it's been ramping up for the past few years and we're falling behind."

"Nature abhors a vacuum," Alex said.

"It really does. Any hope for an American isolationist agenda would simply blow up in our faces. So we've gone more covert. The war-by-proxy we're engaged in with the other superpowers doesn't always mean an armed conflict. President Moore wants it to appear like we've ended our colonialist pretensions of the past. Only now, that means more and more bad actors think we've abandoned the continent altogether, meaning we've emboldened them by our perceived absence, making it even harder for us to maintain even the slightest hint of a presence in some countries. So, beyond arms and diplomacy, we soft-sell the citizenry with foreign aid—or we used to."

"*Hearts and minds*," Alex said sarcastically.

"Don't mock it. Food, medical aid, cultural event sponsorships, and other provisions go a long way in a lot of these places, especially the farther you get outside the big cities."

They moved to another set of consoles where yet more keyboard warriors were busy interfacing with banks of monitors.

"Sitrep," said Harley.

"We might have located a high-probability target," said the man seated there.

"Show me."

He nodded to the front of the room. An aerial view from a Reaper MQ-9 drone of a lakeside village filled a wall-sized monitor.

"This is Butemba, a village ten kilometers outside Mwanza on the shores of Lake Victoria," he said. "And this," he continued, zooming in on a collection of huts and tents surrounded by bushes and fencing standing within the larger village, "is one of the militia camps we monitor."

"Whose is it?" asked Harley.

"People's Freedom Army of Tanzania—the PFA." He panned the camera with the joystick and zoomed in tighter with the mouse for a closer view of what looked like a rectangular building. It reminded Alex of surveillance videos she had briefed with before deploying on assignments as part of Intelligence Support Activity—called simply the Activity—arguably America's most secretive special mission unit. Then, as the position and angle of the unmanned aerial vehicle—a UAV or, more commonly, the drone—shifted in flight as it orbited the target below, Alex could see it was more of a long, dome-like structure fabricated from steel or aluminum. Smoke lent a blue haze to the images coming in. Cooking fires.

"How do we have access to this video feed?" Alex asked.

The analyst looked at Harley, who nodded.

"Trevor's our lead analyst," she said. "Go ahead, Trevor. They're cleared for the intel."

"The drone pilot and sensor operator have temporarily turned over control of the cameras and sensor array to us. This UAV flies out of an air base in Djibouti," he said. "It was on its way back to base from another tasking but we received approval to redeploy it on station here."

"Lucky us," Alex said.

"Not so much luck as ticking off items in a checklist," Trevor said.

"So what are we looking at, exactly?"

"That's the PFA's headquarters building, their command and control center."

"Pretty fancy name for a rebel camp building. Are they that sophisticated?"

"Well, they don't possess our suite of technical resources," said

Harley, looking around the op center, "but the PFA is a highly effective operator in western Tanzania. And they're good at cultivating relationships with foreign interests—the Russians and the Chinese."

Gray streaks could be seen stretching out from the command and control center.

"What are those?"

"Zoom in," said Harley.

As the image filled the screen, the lines on the ground resolved into shadows. Shadows that stretched from the dome-like structure out to a number of other buildings. And from there, to still other buildings.

"Camouflage netting," Trevor concluded. "They've covered the walking paths between the buildings with the stuff."

Shit. Alex's heart sank.

"They've put those up to block our drones from seeing what's beneath them," he continued.

"Like the general," Alex said.

"Yeah, but . . ." Trevor toggled the view to a multicolored heat matrix.

"That's better!"

"We can make out heat signatures, but we can't get a positive ID on anyone this way unless atmospheric conditions are ideal."

"And?"

"And they're not."

"I'm sorry," said Harley.

"For what? Now we know they have something to hide."

"But not just *this* camp, Alex. They *all* have something to hide."

As they continued to watch the monitor, a man emerged from inside with a rifle slung over his shoulder. Trevor toggled the view to regular optics.

Alex squinted for a better look. "Can you zoom in tighter?" she asked.

He did. The man stood at the front of the building. The image was hazy from smoke wafting around the camp.

"Can you clean it up a little?"

As he worked the controls, Harley asked, "Why? What's caught your eye?"

He took a screenshot and made adjustments that cut through the smoky haze.

"There," Alex said. "That's our camp."

"There *what*?" asked Caleb.

"He's wearing a baseball cap."

"That's it? That's all you got?" Harley asked.

As in the firefight yesterday, the man in the image was wearing an identical cap, its sharp lines and green accents like a beacon in the wilderness.

"One of the men I shot was wearing the same cap."

"An Eagles baseball cap? You want me to commit resources because someone's wearing a hat with an NFL logo on it?"

"I'm telling you, the badgers from our gunfight came from that camp."

"Badgers?" said Harley.

"Asshats. Tangos. Whatever."

"Isn't it a leap to conclude that because one of your . . . *badgers* . . . was wearing the same cap as this dude here, this must be our rebel camp—*the* rebel camp? Bit of a leap, wouldn't you say?"

"But is it a leap?"

"Alex," Caleb said. "That's pretty tenuous. Barely meets the threshold of circumstantial evidence, let alone being enough to convict with."

They continued to watch the screen. *Could this be the camp?* People crowded closer to the man standing outside, seemingly to listen to whatever it was he was saying.

"Be nice if we had audio," Alex said.

"We don't employ that upgrade here," Harley replied.

Here? Alex didn't know if she was kidding or not. She wasn't aware of any UAV technology with the kind of enhanced capability to track conversations from fifty thousand feet.

"Ma'am," said a woman seated next to Trevor. "You should see this."

The trio moved in behind her, peering at her monitor.

"We're flying a multicam drone over that camp. This," she said, putting the image up on the bank of monitors at the front of the room, "is an alternate video feed from the same UAV."

An image of a group of pickup trucks and a cargo truck dominated the screen. As the drone circled the militia encampment, the angle on the vehicle changed. The operator froze an image and zoomed in on the larger truck.

"What are we looking at?" asked Harley.

Caleb leaned forward. "Fuck me gently," he said, tracing a finger over the image. "Looks like that truck was made for carrying fruits and vegetables."

CHAPTER 20

PFA COMPOUND, BUTEMBA, TANZANIA

David Martel leaned against the wall inside the shack his abductors had stuck him in. Gray light spilled in through a space between the ceiling and the wall. Still feeling the twinges of pain in his lower back from the cramped enclosure of the dog crate and the rough ride in the truck, he stretched out, straightened his legs, and contracted his core, stifling the spasms that hadn't yet subsided.

Being an aging soldier isn't easy, he thought. *But it beats the alternative. Pain is a privilege only endured by the living.*

He brought his legs under him and stood. A small, barred window—little more than a hole cut in the wall—was shuttered from the outside by a sheet of corrugated steel. Its dull gray patina and streaks of rust stood in contrast to the weathered wooden framing and plywood walls. He stuck his fingers into the gap, trying to force open a space through which he could gather a better sense of his surroundings, but all he accomplished was to cut two of his fingertips.

Great, he thought. *I'll survive long enough to be rescued and then die of a tetanus infection.*

He laughed to himself, aware that the voice in his head was as much Alex's as it was his own. She could be a real pain in the ass and incredibly opinionated, but she came by it honestly. No one had ever accused him or his late wife—Alex's mother—of being timid or docile. Both of them had always held strong opinions that they were eager to share with anyone around them, whether asked or not.

Apple, meet tree.

He sucked the blood off his fingers, then wiped them on his cargo pants. Studying the room, he saw nothing but a table and lone chair against the opposite wall. He picked up the chair and flipped it over. It was an old wooden one, the kind with sturdy legs screwed into the seat.

That could prove handy.

He walked to the door. It was nothing special, maybe MDF or hollow core construction. He tried the handle. Locked. It wouldn't take much to break through the flimsy construction, but until he had a more comprehensive plan of escape, there would be no point busting out. At this moment, he was unbound. But that could change in an instant. Worse, his value and status as a hostage was directly tied to the prospect of using him as leverage or a source of revenue. But he knew of instances where abductors had considered their abductees not worth the trouble of holding on to and killed them rather than trying to control them.

He was a graduate of the Army's three-week Level C SERE training program, so he knew better than to antagonize his kidnappers—at least until a time of his own choosing and when he was better prepared. In fact, he'd been through the program multiple times, although, amusingly, his certificate had lapsed years ago. The concept of SERE—survival, evasion, resistance, and escape—hinged on its first precept: survive. Everything else followed or nothing did.

Survival wasn't just about fieldcraft—trapping food, building shelters, keeping dry and warm—it was also about not antagonizing one's captors, blending in long enough to form a plan, but not waiting too long. Day one was about living until day two while surveilling the environment as well as one could from the vantage point of a prisoner.

What the general had learned so far was that his host—the man who called himself Lemarti—was bold, cocky, and had the loyalty of his soldiers as well as the others in the village. And while he hadn't been the one to execute his driver, he hadn't restrained the man who had, or expressed any disapproval at the overzealousness with which the act had been carried out. Instead, he had smiled, and after Martel had been bound at the wrists, Lemarti had casually draped an arm around the killer's shoulders, a fraternal gesture as encouraging as any squad of cheerleaders on the sidelines.

A leader, maybe. But a callous human being just the same.

As he stood before it, the door swung open and two men barged through. The first was Desmond—Lemarti's aide—the one who had cut Martel's restraints . . . and his neck. He was flanked by another unsmiling human armed with an AK-47. Without warning, the man shoved the general hard, shouting at him.

Martel fell over backward, his head bouncing off the leg of a chair. He jumped up and lunged at the man, but halted at the distinctive sound of a rifle's safety being cycled, likely into fire mode, by the second man.

They laughed. Behind them, the youth he had seen next to Lemarti waited in the doorway, still holding his own AK slung over his shoulder. A woman wearing a long lime-green skirt breezed into the room carrying a tray. She set it down on the table.

"You should eat, and drink plenty of water," she said in accented English.

"You speak English."

"Yes, everyone in my country does."

Martel knew that English was one of the official languages of many African countries, including Tanzania, but the fluency with which it was spoken varied, its prevalence decreasing the farther one traveled outside the bigger towns and cities.

As if to emphasize this point, the man with her began shouting in Swahili and raised a hand as if to strike her. Martel bounded to his feet, instinctively preparing to prevent that from happening, but before he could intervene, the boy at the door leveled his rifle at him.

"Stop!" he shouted in barely passable English.

Pretty quick with that rifle, little one, Martel thought, showing his hands in surrender. "You're fast," he said out loud to the boy, smiling. "It's okay. Look, my hands are up."

The man slapped him hard across the side of his face, hard enough that he saw stars. He, too, shouted at him.

The woman spoke again. "He says he would kill you if Lemarti permitted him. I would believe him if I were you."

"I do. Can you tell the boy to lower his gun?"

She turned and spoke in Swahili, and the boy reluctantly pointed the muzzle to the floor, wearing a scowl on his face that seemed incongruously funny to the general.

"He is still learning English."

Martel kept his hands in the air. "It seemed pretty effective a moment ago." She smiled at his comment. "Does he have a name?"

"He is called Kijana, which means *boy* in Kiswahili."

"Kiswahili?"

"The name of our language that Americans improperly call Swahili."

"Hello, Kijana," he said to the boy.

He didn't answer, but the muzzle of his rifle pointed closer to the floor.

"You please eat and drink now," she said. "And get some rest. You may be traveling soon."

"Traveling where?"

The man named Desmond eyed the two of them before saying something to the woman.

She spoke back to him angrily, then stepped away from the table and tray.

"I must leave."

"Wait. What is your name?"

She hesitated in the threshold of the doorway.

"Adiya," she said before stepping away.

Adiya, the general repeated to himself, hoping that somehow it meant *friend*.

CHAPTER 21

MUTAPA, OKAVANGO REPUBLIC

Among the many manufacturing plants and distribution centers that had emerged along a tree-lined boulevard in Mutapa's commercial sector stood a squat three-story building encircled by a tall steel fence topped with security cameras and equipped with motion and acoustic sensors on the manicured lawn surrounding the structure. A formidable guard booth positioned along the entrance road off the boulevard deterred uninvited guests and curious passersby.

Artemi Tarasenko led the convoy in a Toyota Land Cruiser 300, the civilian equivalent of the ubiquitous model that dominated the safari operator market. While it was certainly capable, the interior luxuries of this model clashed with his austere sensibilities. He would have preferred the scent of oil and grease on the floorboards over the pretentious leather aroma that filled the cab. Tarasenko viewed cars and trucks much like he viewed guns—the simpler, the better. It was the Russian way—or at least it once was—evidenced by the success and lasting legacy of Russian-made Kalashnikov rifles. It's hard to improve on a nearly perfect design.

As they neared the driveway leading to the guard booth, Tarasenko felt a surge of satisfaction. By now, General Martel should be dead—his body cooling somewhere in the Tanzanian wilderness, his control over Project Aegis forever eliminated. The developments would stall long enough for Russia to gain access; and, if not, to sow more chaos and disrupt it again. The Americans would soon discover their security breach, and Tarasenko wanted to be there to witness the first tremors of panic. This drive-by was his victory lap—a calculated taunt to destabilize the Americans at precisely the moment they would be most vulnerable.

"Slow down," he instructed his driver. "I want them to see us clearly."

The driver complied, reducing their speed to a crawl as they approached the American facility. Tarasenko studied the armed detail patrolling the front lawn, with two officers holding leads that connected the men to their K9s. He scrutinized the men—most likely American private military contractors—and concluded that the dogs likely represented the smarter end of the leash.

He realized that their reconnaissance party had been detected. He also understood that the news would reach the CIA's higher-ups. But no one would be certain that he and his team were responsible for the act that eliminated General Martel, and he preferred to keep his adversaries off-balance and wondering. This uncertainty would force them to divert resources, second-guess their security protocols, and waste valuable time investigating multiple suspects—all while Tarasenko's team moved forward with their plans to exploit the vulnerabilities in Project Aegis they had already identified.

As they drove past, he waved to the guard booth, but it was as much a gesture for the video surveillance system as it was for the men on guard duty. *Let them review the footage later,* he thought. *Let them see my confidence. Let them wonder what I know.*

Then he pulled out his cell phone and dialed a number.

"Lemarti!" he said when the line was answered, his voice ebullient.

"Comrade Tarasenko," came the reply.

Comrade Tarasenko? Startled by the formality, he replied, "There is no need for such old-world salutations among friends. I am Artemi."

"Whatever you say, Artemi."

"Am I to understand your mission was successful? Your text message was somewhat vague on the matter, but the job is complete, yes?"

"In a manner of speaking," came Lemarti's reply.

Tarasenko hated the man's voice, unusual accent, and vocal inflection. But more than that, he loathed his unearned cockiness, the self-assuredness that came from commanding a village of peasants and a battalion of undisciplined killers. In fact, Artemi Tarasenko, the progeny of a long history of glorious military tradition, despised most of the people he had met on this continent.

His affect shifted immediately from relaxed to on edge. He sat up, adjusted his seat belt, became more alert. Dropping his voice an octave, he spoke slowly and deliberately. "There is only one acceptable response to my question, Lemarti, and what you provided is not it."

"But it is the only one I have for you."

The man's voice was almost gleeful, no longer that of a partner, but asserting himself as one in command of the situation. Tarasenko felt heat spread across his face, suddenly aware of the African sun beating through the window glass. His moment of triumph was evaporating with each word from Lemarti's mouth.

"Explain," he barked, listening to the sound of Lemarti's rabble militia and villagers in the background, doing whatever the hell it was they did, caught between the jungle and civility. His driver looked over at him, concern etched in his brow.

"I altered the mission, Artemi."

"You what? In what way? Either you killed the general or you did not. Which is it?"

There was the briefest pause before Lemarti answered.

"I did not," he said.

Tarasenko had been a soldier and officer for decades, forged in the fires of combat and bureaucracy. Rising through the ranks, he had aggregated friendships and professional relationships with other officers and government officials before building his own private military contractor enterprise. Eventually, his Leopard Group PMC had become Russia's number-two army-for-hire, until one day, the number-one seed had deposed himself before being permanently deposed.

He drew a deep breath as if he were about to dive into the cold, black waters of Lake Baikal back home in the Siberian wilderness. His carefully orchestrated show of force outside the American facility now seemed like a catastrophic miscalculation. Instead of taunting a grieving enemy, he had just revealed himself to an adversary who would soon discover their prized asset was missing—and would immediately connect Tarasenko to the abduction.

"Lemarti, we had an agreement. A contract, actually, for which you have been handsomely compensated."

"Compensation is nice, Colonel. But as I considered the matter, I grew convinced that I should follow my own plan."

"Which is?"

"There are other interested parties in this matter. Those who will pay to take possession of this property."

"This property, as you call him, is a man we—I—already paid you to dispose of."

"Then, Colonel, as you see, our contract is intact. We are disposing of him—just not how you wanted it done."

"Lemarti, must I remind you of who you are dealing with? I am not a person who is accustomed to being deceived or lied to. And I am most certainly not someone who permits others to unilaterally alter the terms of an agreement that has already been executed. You were paid to kill the general, and to stage it in such a way as to leave doubt regarding the responsible parties. You have already blown part A of our agreement. And you will be found out. Should that happen, its discovery will expose our arrangement."

"Colonel," said Lemarti. "I already have a buyer lined up for our mutual acquaintance. It is a done deal, as the Americans would say."

Tarasenko's blood boiled. His victory drive had become a liability. The Americans would review their security footage and see him—practically announcing his involvement in the general's disappearance. The Chinese would learn of Martel's capture and move to acquire him. And Lemarti, that treacherous jackal, would profit twice from the same operation.

"Then, my friend, you are a dead man."

* * *

CIA OPERATIONS CENTER (BLACKBIRD), ARUSHA, TANZANIA

"Do we have security footage from the airstrip near where General Martel was abducted?"

Alex turned expectantly to the analyst Trevor, whom Harley had asked. He didn't respond directly but instead projected his computer feed onto the main screen at the front of the room. Image thumbnails raced by as he scrubbed through the video.

"There!" Alex exclaimed. "Back up."

Trevor reversed the video as the group watched. He seemed to know what Alex had seen and fast-forwarded through the video again, then slowed to normal speed. A group of pickup trucks drove south past the airport access road. The image was grainy, captured by security cameras mounted atop the airport terminal building, a long way from the dirt road, but it was clear enough. Plumes of red dust kicked up behind them. Five pickup trucks passed the airport, along with one truck meant for hauling produce. Or kidnapped generals.

"Can you put the pictures of the compound up?" Alex asked.

He did.

"Damn," mumbled Harley as the apparent similarity between the vehicles in the rebel compound and the ones that had driven past the airstrip in Seronera became impossible to dismiss.

"Damn is right," Alex said. "How far away is the PFA compound from here?"

"Look, I know what you're thinking, Alex, but we can't just load up the Black Hawk and go raid their camp."

"I know. I think a couple of Little Birds would be better."

Caleb let out a tense chuckle. "Alex, Harley's right. It's not like we have the Night Stalkers"—referring to the 160th Special Operations Aviation Regiment—"sitting around with a couple of their MH-6 Little Birds—"

"Why the hell is everybody so reluctant to go kick some ass and bring the general home?"

"No one is reluctant to kick ass, Alex." Harley's demeanor had turned stern. "It's what we do. I've spent my career butt-kicking just like you. But there's a right way of doing things, and grabbing a couple of attack helicopters and storming across a friendly nation to light up a rebel camp, as fun as that might be, will get people killed. It takes time to plan a rescue op of this magnitude, you know that."

"I'm not asking for a fucking SEAL team, Harley. The three of us plus your security detail and half a dozen SpecOps assaulters who are in-country should do. You already have ISR overhead. We fly in, grab the general, and fly out again. I've done it before."

"We've all done it before," chimed in Caleb. "Doesn't mean that's what we should do here, and you know that. This isn't Iraq or Syria—we're not at war with Tanzania. At least, not until we pull a stunt like that and it goes south. Look, Shooter, you want to get your dad back. We're on the same team with the same objectives. But, like Harley said, there's a right way and a wrong way, and you know what this is and what it isn't."

Alex glared at Caleb, reluctantly accepting the wisdom in what he and Harley were saying. But patience wasn't her strong suit unless she was glassing an area of operations through her rifle scope. And even that was for a defined objective.

Turning, Harley said, "Give me the room. I'm going to update the deputy director. Try not to invade any friendly countries while I'm gone."

They pushed through the door and headed down a hallway, leaving Harley to herself and Mustang, aka Deputy Director Thomas.

"She's right, you know," he said.

Alex didn't reply.

He continued. "We have to—"

But Alex didn't finish listening to whatever he was about to say. She turned left down another hallway and pushed through a doorway near the end that brought her into a large storeroom almost the size of a small hangar. Inside were shelves stocked with gear, rations, and weapons. She looked around, knowing what she could do with all this stuff, but feeling powerless to do anything. She was like a starving woman staring at a steak and seafood buffet while having her hands tied behind her and her mouth gagged.

She felt Caleb's hand on her back and reflexively leaned forward, away from his touch.

"You know I'm on your side, right?"

She didn't answer.

"I want to get your dad back as much as you do."

She presumed this was true, but her inner child wanted to believe no one could want that as much as she did. Maybe that's why she was pushing so hard.

"Alex, never mind the whole security-of-our-nation angle and the danger of everything your dad knows getting into the hands of America's enemies, he's your *dad*, which makes him the second most important person in the world to me right now."

Caleb's fingers rested gently between her shoulder blades, his touch sending tiny bolts of electricity cascading through her body. Instinct urged her to pull away again, but her breath hitched as she melted into the sensation of his touch. Her pulse quickened, and she felt her skin flush, heat spreading through her cheeks at his caress. Her emotions were already heightened; she was on edge, but this . . . this was more.

When she turned to meet his gaze, the world seemed to stop spinning. His hazel eyes captivated her, swirling with amber flames and sparks of firelight that threatened to consume her. The charged silence enveloped them. An ache bloomed deep in her core, a primal yearning that drew her inexorably toward him.

With the tips of his fingers, he lightly brushed her hair back and behind her ear, his hand coming to rest gently on the back of her neck. He drew her in. Their lips met in an achingly tender dance, soft at first, the gentle press of his mouth against hers sending sparks racing up her spine. As passion ignited between them, the depth and rhythm of their kiss deepened, becoming hungry and urgent. Her hands grasped his hips, pulling him flush against her, their pelvises mashing together. A soft moan escaped her throat as she felt him rising against her. His powerful arms encircled her, crushing her to his chest. Her head spun with desire, stealing the very breath from her lungs.

The sound of a squeaking door hinge pierced through her lust-fueled trance and she broke their bond, practically leaping backward. Caleb was left stunned before her, a look of wonderment and surprise painting his face.

"Sir? Ma'am?" a voice called from behind them. It was Trevor, the analyst.

Caleb cleared his throat. "Yes, what is it?" he barked.

"Harley needs to see you both in her office."

Alex turned to face a shelf, half bent forward as if counting boxes or magic wands or unicorns or anything to pretend she hadn't been trading tongues with Caleb when Trevor had walked in.

"We're coming," he replied. Then, rethinking that, "We'll be right there," he said.

The analyst left the storage room and Alex straightened up. Her top had gone askew during their encounter, so she smoothed out her clothes and otherwise tried to make herself look presentable. Then she put a hand over her mouth and took a deep, cleansing breath.

"Holy shit," he said.

"You're telling me," she replied.

"That was—"

"Not another word."

"But—"

"Nope, not now."

His shoulders drooped. "Fine," he said. "Let's go see Harley."

"Uh, I'll go first. You're not going anywhere for a couple of minutes," she teased, staring at the front of his trousers. "Not till you render that safe."

CHAPTER 22

WIND RIVER MOUNTAIN RANGE, WYOMING

Alexandra Martel, age eleven, sat on the wraparound porch of her family's 2,800-square-foot hand-hewn log cabin, gazing out at the lake and granite cliffs in the distance. Above her, Wind River Peak towered over thirteen thousand feet above sea level, piercing the blue sky. A stand of whitebark pines dotted the slopes, forming the tree line that stretched across the ridge.

The tree line marked the upper boundary beyond which no trees could grow, much like her mother's death represented the point beyond which their bond in this life had ended. Their connection would remain forever frozen in the past, with questions of what might have been left to linger forever.

Death, Alex had learned this week, was final.

The screen door behind her creaked open, muffled voices echoing beyond it like whispers from an unfulfilled dream upon awakening. She recognized the footfalls that followed as her father's, weighty yet gentle, slow and ponderous, like a grizzly bear picking its way through an alpine meadow. His cowboy boots and tattered denim cuffs came into view. She paused her rocking and waited.

He draped a blanket around her shoulders and sat beside her on the cushioned rattan sofa while she focused on an eagle circling high above the lake. They sat in silence, the voices inside the house a distant distraction, muffled by the walls Alex had always felt safe behind as if no harm could ever come to her or her family.

"Why'd she have to go?" she asked.

The question could have been specific or abstract. She herself didn't know—was too young to comprehend—whether she had meant why did her mother leave to go on a humanitarian mission with a group of medical doctors, or why did her mother have to die. What she did know was that her mother had left the safety of these walls behind to heed her own call to service and had gone missing in a similarly mountainous region in a faraway land. Alex had wanted to go look for her, but her father had said that there were many people already doing just that, and that they had to be patient while they did their work and conducted their search.

She looked up at her father's face, suddenly more weathered and worn than she remembered it, his mouth closed, his jaw clenched. He reached an arm around her shoulders and drew her to him. He kissed the top of her head, then rested his cheek there, drawing a deep breath as if smelling her hair.

"Promise me you'll come look for me if I ever go missing, Dad."

He pulled away and looked into her eyes. His gaze was intense.

"Allie, I would turn the world upside down to find you. Nothing could stop me."

"Do you mean it?"

"Of course."

"You didn't go look for Mom."

"No, I didn't," he admitted.

"I would look for you, too, Dad. I would search everywhere for you and I'd bring you home. Promise me you'll do that if I get lost or go missing or if my plane crashes like Mom's."

"Allie—"

"Promise!"

His eyes grew damp.

"I promise."

Alex reached to her belt and pulled her father's Ka-Bar knife from its scabbard—the one he carried with him on deployments and allowed her to wear outdoors in the Wyoming wilderness. She remembered hearing stories of the Arapaho and Shoshone chiefs from these very mountains cutting their hands to consecrate their promises with blood. The handle and blade were so big against her hand. She drew the sharp blade across her palm, flinching at the pain of it.

"Alex!" her father bellowed, taken by surprise by her action.

She presented her hand to her father, blood dripping to the deck at their feet.

"Swear it!" she demanded.

His blue eyes pierced hers. She did not see anger there, but fear. The fear of a father disappointing his daughter. He took the knife and laid the blade against his palm, wrapping his fingers closed on it before drawing it slowly toward him. When he opened his hand again, his blood flowed like hers flowed. He clasped her hand in his, their blood intermingling, grasping it harder than he had ever held her hand before.

"Blood of my blood, until my last breath," he said. She stared at him, confused. "Say it."

She held his gaze, her heart pounding in her chest.

"You need to say it, Allie. This is our pledge, our vow. From now until forever, we are bound by blood and the sanctity of our family bond until the very end of life itself. This is our blood oath."

Above them the eagle cried.

"Blood of my blood, until my last breath," he repeated.

"Blood of my blood, until my last breath," she echoed.

"It's an unbreakable oath, Allie. A sacred commitment. Wherever you are, whatever you need, I will never break my vow as long as I live."

She looked at him as intensely as she had ever looked at anyone or anything. Her eyes were fire.

"I will never break my oath, Dad," she said, tears welling up in her eyes. And she meant every word.

Their voices spoke out in unison.

"Blood of my blood, until my last breath."

CHAPTER 23

MUTAPA, OKAVANGO REPUBLIC

Artemi Tarasenko and his crew returned to the Leopard Bean Collective's warehouse, the Leopard Group PMC base of operations in the Okavango Republic. They piled out of their trucks and filed back into the building, Tarasenko making for the stairs to his office. No one had ever openly defied him or broken a contract with him like this before. It had been agreed upon, executed, and paid for.

The warehouse buzzed with activity as workers moved between stations, cleaning weapons, reviewing intelligence reports, and monitoring communications. The aroma of freshly roasted coffee beans—their legitimate business front—mingled with gun oil and sweat. Tarasenko's boots echoed on the metal stairs as he climbed to his office, his face a mask of controlled rage.

It wasn't about the money; no amount could compensate for the loss of one's reputation. By breaking their contract, Lemarti hadn't just unilaterally changed the terms of their agreement; he had fundamentally disrespected him, kicked sand in his face, spat in his drink, and mocked him in public. Nothing could remedy that kind of injury. This was an offense punishable in only one way.

Tarasenko entered his office—a spartan space with a metal desk, three monitors displaying surveillance feeds, and a wall map of Africa dotted with colored pins representing Leopard Group operations. The only personal touch was a small Orthodox icon in the corner, a remnant of his grandmother's influence. He tossed his jacket onto a chair and poured himself a three-finger measure of vodka from a crystal decanter, downing it in one swift motion.

"What are your orders, Artemi?" asked Anton Kovalchuk, Tarasenko's second-in-command.

Kovalchuk was a man in his forties. Bald-headed and more round than athletic, he was solidly built and stoically enduring of discomfort. Tarasenko thought he resembled a taller version of Phil Collins, the British rock musician, but with a Russian accent. He had spent the better part of his life fighting in the ranks of the Russian military in campaigns throughout Syria, Chechnya, and Ukraine before being lured away for the higher pay and marginally longer lifespan of one who worked with Leopard Group.

The two men had first met during the Second Chechen War, where Kovalchuk had saved Tarasenko's life during an ambush outside Grozny. That debt had transformed into a partnership that spanned decades and continents. Where Tarasenko was calculating and strategic, Kovalchuk was practical and unflinching. Together, they had built Leopard Group into a formidable force in the shadowy world of private military contractors.

"Get the men fed and geared up. We will pay this Maasai cow herder a visit."

"Tonight?"

"As soon as they are ready."

Kovalchuk turned to implement his boss's orders.

"Anton, wait. Aim for dawn. We will fly in for first light. But send in an advance team tonight."

Kovalchuk nodded and was gone.

Tarasenko moved to the window overlooking the warehouse floor. Below, his men were already preparing, sensing the coming storm. Some cleaned their weapons with practiced efficiency while others studied satellite imagery of what he presumed was Lemarti's compound and the surrounding African countryside. These weren't ordinary mercenaries—they were former Spetsnaz, GRU operatives, and veterans of Russia's most brutal conflicts. Men who understood that in their line of work, reputation was currency, and preparation was longevity.

Leopard Group PMC was a private military contractor with a decidedly nonmilitary structure. Unlike other Russian PMCs, like Redut and Konvoy, which were directly overseen by Russia's powerful foreign military intelligence agency, the GRU, under the authority of the Ministry of Defense, Leopard Group enjoyed considerably more autonomy and was guided by a civilian leadership structure. In fact, if it weren't for the guns, it would resemble any other testosterone-fueled boys' club. But it did have guns, and it liked to use them.

This autonomy had allowed Tarasenko to build his organization with minimal oversight from Moscow—at least officially. Unofficially, he maintained connections with the highest levels of Russian intelligence and military command. President Sergachev had personally approved their operation in Okavango, recognizing the strategic value of not just disrupting American influence in the region, but of killing the project the Americans had been working on in secret. And since their GRU hacking unit hadn't yet been able to access the program or install malware into its servers, the next best tactic was to kill its leader—or so went the prevailing wisdom.

Kovalchuk returned. "The men are preparing as ordered. The Antonov will be fueled and waiting on the tarmac."

Tarasenko nodded. "It's treachery, pure and simple," he said. Frustration and anger oozed from his pores.

"Yes, sir. We made a deal with a dishonest man, and now he must pay for his deceit with his life."

Kovalchuk waited as Tarasenko made himself a coffee. The machine hissed and gurgled, producing a stream of dark liquid that filled the room with its rich aroma. Tarasenko had insisted on the finest equipment—a small luxury in this remote corner of Africa. He added a splash of vodka to the cup, a habit he'd developed during cold Siberian winters and never abandoned.

"Our primary mission," said Tarasenko, easing himself into the chair behind his desk, "the one we outlined to President Sergachev, was to disrupt the research and development of the military system the Americans had foolishly decided to carry out here."

He pulled up a file on his computer—classified Pentagon documents detailing Project Aegis, an advanced weapons platform being developed under General Martel's supervision. The intelligence had cost them three operatives and millions in bribes, but it had confirmed what Moscow had suspected: the Americans were developing something that could shift the balance of power not just in the region but globally.

Tarasenko leaned back in his chair. Discontent with America had been sweeping across Africa, spreading like a California wildfire from country to country: Mali, Chad, Niger, the Central African Republic. All these nations had been susceptible to the suggestion that they would be better off if they cast off the American yoke. Russia and China both had been quick to fill the void.

The map on his wall told the story—red pins marking Russian-friendly regimes, blue for American allies, white for the Chinese, and yellow for contested territories. Over the past five years, the red had steadily expanded, pushing back the blue, and in some cases even the white, in a strategic game that few in Washington seemed to fully comprehend.

"The general's death is a necessary step," he said. "It will not only sow chaos, it will give the Pentagon reason to pause if they know that American lives are on the line. Those who invest in such programs may think twice about where they put their money."

He pulled up another file—General David Martel's personnel record, complete with family photos, service history, and security clearance details. The general's daughter, Alexandra, featured prominently—a CIA operative with a reputation for effectiveness that rivaled his own. Tarasenko had insisted on knowing everything about his targets, including their weaknesses. Family was always the most exploitable vulnerability.

Kovalchuk added, "And now this glorified farm boy, Lemarti, has calculated that he can profit from his deception. We must use this mongrel to send a message."

"Niccolo Machiavelli said, 'If you need to injure someone, do it in such a way that you do not have to fear their vengeance.' Lemarti will soon be dead." Tarasenko sipped his coffee. "But who else would benefit from knowing what the general knows?"

The coffee burned his tongue, but he welcomed the pain—a small reminder of the physical world while his mind worked through the strategic implications.

"Excuse me, sir?"

"Well, Lemarti wants to sell the general. But who would wish to buy him?"

"I suppose any of the Islamic State splinter groups, sir, would be hungry to get their hands on him for propaganda purposes. One more head chopped off on television. That would send a clear message."

"It would," Tarasenko agreed. "But why waste his knowledge?"

"What?" Kovalchuk wasn't following his boss's train of thought.

"I mean, why buy him only to chop off his head, unless they were going to mine it first."

Tarasenko pulled up satellite imagery of Lemarti's compound—a collection of buildings surrounded by a perimeter fence, nestled in the foothills near Lake Victoria. The compound had expanded significantly in recent months, suggesting Lemarti's operation was growing. Or perhaps preparing for something specific.

Kovalchuk's eyes glossed over. "Mine it?"

"Don't you see? The Islamic State are merely a pack of dogs running rampant over this continent and the one next door in pursuit of their precious Levant. They are thugs without any real strategy other than terror, satisfying the supposed edicts of their prophet and their own depraved bloodlust. But who might actually benefit from getting inside the head of an American general with special operations expertise, one who works on secret programs funded by America's Defense Advanced Research Projects Agency?"

Tarasenko zoomed in on the satellite image, focusing on a building near the center of the compound. Recent thermal imaging showed heightened activity there—guards posted around the clock, regular deliveries of supplies. The perfect place to hold a high-value prisoner.

"DARPA?" Kovalchuk's eyebrows shot skyward.

Tarasenko nodded. Sometimes it was like talking to an imbecile. Kovalchuk was good at tactics, but did not have the intellect for objectives or strategy. "Who might buy the general from a band of Indigenous warrior ruffians while making it look as if it were some other rogue element that snatched him?" Off Kovalchuk's blank expression, he said, "I'll give you a hint—they're Chinese."

He pulled up another file—surveillance photos of Chinese operatives meeting with local officials in Mwanza, Tanzania, just across the border. The time stamp showed the meeting had occurred just three days ago. Too much of a coincidence to ignore.

"*Kitayets?*" Kovalchuk asked, using the pejorative equivalent to the English word *Chinamen*. "Sir, are we now going to also take on the Chinese Ministry of State Security?"

He nodded. "Quite possibly. The point is we must get to the general and kill him as we had planned before the Chinese can get their hands on him, Anton."

The implications hung in the air between them. Taking on the Chinese MSS meant potentially triggering an international incident—one that could draw unwanted attention to Leopard Group's activities in the region. But failing to eliminate the general would be seen as weakness by Moscow, a failure that President Sergachev would not tolerate.

"Yes, sir."

"And before the Americans can mount a successful rescue."

Tarasenko checked his watch—a vintage Raketa that had belonged to his father, a Soviet officer who had died in Afghanistan, yet another graveyard of empires. Time was not on their side. By now, the CIA would be mobilizing assets, and the general's daughter would be moving heaven and earth to find her father.

"I'll see that we are provisioned for several days."

As Kovalchuk left to prepare the team, Tarasenko turned back to the window. Rain had begun to fall, pattering against the glass in an irregular rhythm. In the distance, lightning illuminated the Mutapa skyline, casting momentary shadows across the warehouse floor. A storm was coming, in more ways than one.

CHAPTER 24

CIA OPERATIONS CENTER (BLACKBIRD), ARUSHA, TANZANIA

"Where's your partner?" asked Harley when Alex entered the room.

"He'll be here in a minute," she replied. "He's just . . . decompressing."

Harley gave her a questioning look but didn't pursue it. Her office wasn't fancy. It looked more like a temporary workspace in a mobile construction trailer than a long-term commitment to corporate accommodations.

"That you, Shooter?" came a voice from Harley's computer.

Mustang? Alex hadn't expected Harley to still be on a call with Deputy Director Thomas.

"Yes, ma'am. I'm here," Alex replied, circling to the other side of Harley's desk.

"I see no matter where you are on this Earth, Alex, you just can't stay out of trouble." Alex straightened up. Thomas waved dismissively at her own remark hanging in the air. "I'm sorry about your dad. He's a good man, and he's highly trained. He's a survivor."

To Alex's ears, *He's a good man* had all the ring of *He was a good man*. She didn't like the implication of the DD's words. They sounded like something one might say about the dead.

Thomas sat in what appeared to be her home office. Beyond the covered windows behind her, streetlights cast shadows of branches gently swaying in the breeze outside. Her office was bathed in the soft yellow glow of an incandescent bulb while the blue light from her computer monitor cast her dark skin in a spectral glow.

"Yes, ma'am," she said as Caleb and Trevor entered the room. "But I hope we're not relying on that alone, ma'am."

"Meaning?"

"Meaning that I would like to plan a rescue mission."

"You're not a singleton, Alex. We actually have teams for this, including the one you're supposed to be part of."

"I'm aware, ma'am. I wasn't implying—"

"You were implying that no one else is doing anything. You were implying that therefore you should do this on your own."

The deputy director normally spoke with a subdued Alabama accent. She was a code-switcher, meaning she could tone down her dialect when it suited her and when she needed to blend in with the Washington suits, or ratchet it up when she was feeling down-home. But she saved her most melodic and rich Southern tones for when she was unamused or being sarcastic. Like now.

"We've grown accustomed to you," she intoned. "So I'll ignore the insinuation that everyone else has been sitting around, lallygagging like a bump on a pickle. I've been having that very conversation about a rescue op with both Harley and JSOC. The latter will have a plan on my desk by morning, since it's their show and the general is one of theirs."

Alex glanced down at her Rolex Submariner, a gift she had given herself after earning her assignment as a Ranger medic—a combat medic with the 75th Ranger Regiment. The watch was dependable, attractive without pretense, and a trusted and trustworthy partner in the field. It was just after 2 PM in Arusha.

"Ma'am, if I may speak freely?"

"I've learned I couldn't stop you if I tried."

Caleb circled in behind.

"It's twenty-two hundred hours at Fort Bragg—"

"Here, too, Alex. And it's Fort Liberty now. What's your point?"

"JSOC will be so busy ignoring Tier One advisors and seeking consensus from their Pentagon masters, they won't have a workable plan tomorrow, if ever."

Harley looked like she was going to fall out of her chair.

"Why don't you tell us what you really think, Shooter?" Thomas said.

"So my point, ma'am, is that we have the resources right here—Caleb, myself, Harley, and her team. I'm sure you've been given the full situation report, so you know the location we identified as the place the general is most likely being held. Plus, Harley's team already has ISR stationed over the camp—"

"Oh, sugar honey iced tea, Alex. I know where you're going with this."

"It would take no time at all."

"Alex, when I said JSOC was working on it, I had hoped you would have understood the subtext that Joint Special Operations Command is talking to State who's talking to our embassy in Dar es Salaam who's talking to the Ministry of Foreign Affairs and East African Cooperation who no doubt is speaking with their law enforcement and military communities within this, their own sovereign country. And despite recent evidence to the contrary, the United States still respects the sovereignty of other nations. So it is not up to CIA through Harley and me—or you, for that matter—to unilaterally come up with and execute a plan to rescue your father. Quite the contrary, Shooter; despite your talents and experience in ground ops, you need to wait for this to play out."

"Yes, ma'am, but—"

"Any sentence that starts with a *yes, ma'am, but* is not a sentence you want to finish right now. It ends with *yes, ma'am, period.*"

"Yes, ma'am."

Alex literally and figuratively bit her tongue to keep from saying any more. In fact, she thought she tasted blood. What could she do to convince Mustang? She was about to speak up again when she felt a tug on her shirt from behind. Turning, she found Caleb gently, almost imperceptibly, shaking his head at her.

Kadeisha Thomas continued. "We have not received any demands from his abductors. There have been no communications directly or indirectly. No one has contacted the corporate entity that employs the general, our embassy, the State Department, CIA, or any other entity. But..."

But? A sliver of hope lifted her. Alex looked expectantly at Mustang on the screen in front of her.

"For what it's worth," Deputy Director Thomas continued, "we've heard chatter through a signals intelligence listening station in Nairobi, Kenya."

"And?"

"It picked up cellular communications between two parties that would indicate the general is alive. Now, you're not to construe that information as anything but what it is, Alex. Which is that, for the time being, I am able to give you some good news about your father. Call it *proof of life*."

"Then time is critical, ma'am."

Thomas's image loomed larger as she leaned close to her computer.

"Alex, I've been authorized to read you into something."

"Ma'am?"

"The president himself asked that you be made aware."

Alex straightened up and stayed silent.

"Your father was not acting merely as a government contractor on a tech initiative. He has been working in concert with us on Project Aegis."

"What's Project Aegis? And *us* who?"

"It's a next-generation drone system with advanced AI capabilities. The project is run under a joint Central Intelligence Agency and DARPA program."

She had to work a bit to recall that DARPA—the Defense Advanced Research Projects Agency—was a US government agency that developed new technologies for the military.

"What's so special about this program?"

"A whole shit ton, including that the drones can analyze battlefield conditions in real time and make independent tactical decisions without requiring direct human input. They act in coordinated swarms and can communicate with each other. They use adaptive AI that can learn on the fly, so to speak. They're resilient and can evade hacking attempts. And they're equipped with cutting-edge stealth technology." She looked up from her notes. "I'm not the expert. Trevor, you fill in the blanks I've missed."

Trevor continued. "Yes, ma'am. These drones are nearly undetectable by radar or infrared systems, making them ideal for covert operations. And most important, they are able to evade and defeat the process the Chinese discovered that allowed them to exploit a vulnerability in satellite constellation systems to track our F-35 and F-22 stealth aircraft."

"What's that got to do with the general?"

Thomas replied, "He was the project lead."

My father? The man who couldn't change the time on a blinking VCR clock back in the day? She was sure her jaw has hanging open, so she closed her mouth.

Trevor continued. "Not long ago, some intrepid Chinese researchers discovered a method called forward scatter detection, which uses disturbances in satellite signals to identify stealth aircraft. It's a passive approach that analyzes electromagnetic wave interference caused by stealth planes passing between satellites like SpaceX's Starlink or China's own BeiDou systems and ground-based receivers. By measuring subtle changes in these signals, the system can detect even low-observable aircraft like the F-22 and F-35 without emitting its own radar waves—making it harder for stealth countermeasures to evade detection—even high-tech systems can't know what they don't know. The technique works by leveraging existing satellite constellations to create a global detection network, challenging traditional stealth capabilities designed to absorb or deflect active radar emissions. Project Aegis will give us back the upper hand in stealth capabilities."

"Again," Alex said. "How exactly was my father involved?"

"As I said, Shooter, he was in charge of this project. Although he wasn't the subject matter expert, your father was—*is*—a highly skilled project manager who has previously worked on classified ventures for us and could keep the whole thing on track. The general played a crucial role in overseeing the integration of Project Aegis into US military operations. His expertise in logistics and his reputation as a strategist make him an essential asset in the project's development.

"This program is vital, Alex, not just for the drone initiative and the technology that will restore stealth capabilities to a costly aircraft program, but also as a necessary effort to counter China's expanding military presence in Africa and its use of similar drone technologies in proxy conflicts. It's critical that this program succeeds. Obviously, if the technology—or even knowledge of it—were to fall into the wrong hands, it could tip the geopolitical balance against us. Moreover, increasingly, intelligence chatter indicates that the Chinese may be involved in the general's abduction."

"The sooner we act—" she said.

"Alex, did you catch the whole bit about the strategic importance and the need to act with a strong plan to ensure mission success?"

"Yes, ma'am. But—" The tugging at her shirttail became more emphatic. She wanted to bat Caleb's hand away, but instead, she gritted her teeth, feeling a flush of anger race across her cheeks.

"No, Alex. There is not to be any cowboy shit done by you and your crew. You will wait until I give Harley an order for you to act on. There are layers and layers of personnel and departments working this out right now. Is that clear? Now, if you don't mind, I need to speak with Harley without y'all in the room."

More like layers and layers of bureaucracy, thought Alex. *What had Shakespeare said? "Full of sound and fury, signifying nothing."*

She respected JSOC. Or rather, she respected and appreciated the Special Mission Units and operators under its command. Their philosophy was simple: every member of JSOC was empowered to identify and solve problems. She had been part of that elite community only a few short years ago. Before CIA snatched her up, before the FBI, before Interpol, she had been a member of Intelligence Support Activity, the most secretive of the organizations within the US intelligence community. Alex had been part of the Activity's direct action element, the most covert feature of the most secret team in the US arsenal.

In her mind, though, high-ranking officers at JSOC were out of touch with the rank and file and the tactical needs of the mission. And though they understood operations and diplomacy—armed conflict being diplomacy by other means—they didn't have their priorities aligned with the men and women who served and sacrificed, as her father had. His recovery should be paramount for both tactical and humane reasons. But would it be? She had reason to doubt.

There was always reason to doubt.

So, thought Alex, *if every member of JSOC was empowered to identify and solve problems, then even as an alumnus, it's incumbent on me to do just that.*

And so she would find a way.

When they were out of Harley's office, she felt Caleb's hand gently grasp her by the elbow. He guided her down a hallway and out a back door. Outside, the air was muggy and she found herself standing in the op center's staging area—a compound one hundred by two hundred feet in size filled with SUVs, Humvees, and large green crates that Alex presumed had held the computers and other tech as well as water filtration systems and other supplies.

"Why'd you bring me out here?" she asked.

"I thought you could use some fresh air."

"What I could use is some action."

His eyes lit up.

"You dork. That's not what I meant." Despite herself, she smiled.

"Now *that's* why I brought you out here, Shooter," he said, pointing at her smile. "You need to defuse, Alex." Before she could lash out at him, he raised his hands in mock surrender. "And I know what you're going to say. So before you say, *What I need, boss, is a little support from you*"—his tone was mocking yet playful—"remember that I *am* your boss . . . and your friend. Your dad is also my friend. What you want is what I want. But tactically speaking, we can't go rogue on some renegade op to recover David. We have to trust that others know more about what's going on than we do. And maybe even I know a little more about what's happening than you."

"Meaning, trust you."

"Trust *us*, Shooter. Let others assume some of the burden for a change." He dropped his hands and tucked them into his pockets, strolled toward one of the OD green crates.

She caught up to him. "You know that's outside my comfort zone, right, Viking?" she asked, calling him by his Agency code name.

"I know it."

He stopped in front of one of the crates, while Alex wondered what was stored inside.

"Wait," she said. Recognition had dawned within. "I know what these are."

One by one, Caleb released the latches and pulled open the door.

"Holy shit," she said. "It's like Christmas came early!"

CHAPTER 25

PFA COMPOUND, BUTEMBA, TANZANIA

An afternoon mist and rain had settled over the village, bringing a heaviness to the air that lingered overhead and seeped into the confines of the run-down shack that served as David Martel's jail cell. His captors had provided him with food and water, treating him reasonably humanely so far. That is, if he didn't consider the rough handling he had endured upon his arrival and shortly thereafter. But there were no guarantees that such hospitality would last. In fact, the longer he remained in custody, the more likely it was to diminish.

The rain drummed steadily on the corrugated metal roof, creating a persistent hollow rhythm that marked the passing hours. Here and there, water seeped in. Occasional droplets found their way through rusted holes, forming small puddles on the floor. These puddles didn't last long, the water flowing in rivulets, finding holes in the floor to drain through.

Someone had removed the sheet of metal covering the window on the outside. Through the small opening—little more than a hole cut in the wall—he saw figures moving through the compound, their forms blurred by the rain. Armed men patrolled in pairs, AK-47s slung across their chests, conversing in a mixture of Swahili and another dialect he couldn't place. Occasionally, they would glance toward his prison, their expressions unreadable at this distance.

Martel sat on the floor, his back against the wall, wondering about the reason for his captivity. Express kidnappings were exactly that—brief incidents that usually targeted tourists and often lasted only until the victims could be taken to the nearest ATM to withdraw enough money to satisfy their abductors. A step beyond these were cases that targeted employees of medium-sized businesses, employing a more high-volume, rapid-settlement strategy. The approach involved abducting an individual, contacting their employer or a family member, requesting just enough money in ransom to make the act worthwhile, and then repeating the process.

Larger multinational corporations, on the other hand, often became targets of a different kidnapping and ransom strategy. In areas controlled by insurgent groups or politically motivated kidnappers—especially where terrorist organizations were active—captives were frequently held for long periods. Depending on the complexity of negotiations and the group's goals, these situations could last for several months or even years. High-profile cases involving foreigners or politically significant individuals also tended to be drawn out due to higher ransom demands or behind-the-scenes political negotiations.

Martel reflected on the fate of William Buckley, the CIA chief of station in Beirut, Lebanon. On a sunny morning in March 1984, Buckley was kidnapped by the Hezbollah-linked group known as Islamic Jihad. Investigators struggled to determine his whereabouts as his captors frequently moved him during his captivity, hindering any hope of rescue. He endured brutal torture for 444 days before dying in captivity. His death exposed Hezbollah's brutality and had devastating repercussions for US intelligence operations in the Middle East and around the world. Buckley's ordeal became a symbol of courage and sacrifice in the field of intelligence and would always remain so for Martel and generations of intelligence community officers to come.

David Martel was a junior military officer when Bill Buckley was abducted in Beirut. He distinctly remembered the somber mood of his friends and colleagues during Buckley's captivity. Martel had met Buckley once early in his career. His kidnapping and the subsequent investigation were exhaustively dissected and chronicled in the seminal work *Beirut Rules* by Fred Burton and Samuel M. Katz.

The book was required reading in several courses Martel completed on his path to the rank of general.

What very few people knew, not even his own daughter, was that for years Martel had been working as a CIA NOC—a nonofficial cover operative. It was one of the most sensitive and high-risk positions within CIA's intelligence-gathering operations. NOCs operated without any official connection to the US government, adopting covert identities within various organizations. In Martel's case, his latest role was as an undercover assignment working out in the open under his own name as a retired military commander in a senior-level executive position with a defense industry contractor. It was a story as clichéd in Washington as they came, and so it made for the best cover legend of all.

Would the past be prologue? he wondered. *I mean, I'm not Bill Buckley, but might the same fate await me, especially if I'm exposed?*

A shiver ran up his spine. The longer he remained in captivity, the greater the risk of being handed over to a group affiliated with Hezbollah, the Islamic State, or one of their fringe factions or other Iranian proxies. They would take great pleasure in torturing him to extract as much intel from him for as long as they could before killing him, or before he, like Buckley, perished from the cumulative effects of the physical and mental wounds suffered during his ordeal.

Do NOCs get a star on the Memorial Wall at Langley if they're killed? He couldn't remember but thought they did. *Shit! What am I doing conjuring up thoughts like that?* He knew it was the exhaustion and the effects of the long ride and carbon monoxide still in his system talking. And the sheer boredom of being sequestered away without anything to occupy his time—or his mind. The mind could be the worst prison of all.

Of course they do, he decided after remembering a memorial he had attended in the lobby of the Old Headquarters Building of the CIA a few years ago. He took a deep breath to clear his head and chastised himself for thinking such things. He knew he should focus on coming up with an escape plan, not on dwelling on the various negative outcomes that could befall him.

SERE training could and would take a soldier so far, but no one could withstand torture indefinitely. There came a point when even the most highly trained and noble warrior succumbed to *enhanced interrogation* and talked. The best the Seventh Floor at CIA could hope for from him was that he could buy them enough time to change program code words and crypts—the ciphers that hid the real identities and locations of valuable sources; change the code names of Directorate of Operations and Special Activities Center members; and retrieve operatives and vital agents from the field before they could be picked up, tortured, and killed themselves. It was a cynical and frightful hope, but sometimes that was all one had to cling to.

The intelligence community had learned a great deal from the mistakes that plagued the Buckley affair. While bureaucratic processes still sometimes took precedence over effective field operations, this had become more of an exception than the rule. There were now fewer institutional constraints than there had been before. Based on all the lessons of the past, he hoped that a rescue mission was being planned even now. However, it was essential for him to act as if there wouldn't be one. He needed to plan and execute his own escape, his own rescue. He couldn't sit back and wait for the cavalry to arrive.

Still, if there was one thing he knew as sure as he knew anything, it was that Alex would never leave him behind.

Blood of my blood, until my last breath.

CHAPTER 26

CIA OPERATIONS CENTER (BLACKBIRD), ARUSHA, TANZANIA

Caleb flung open the doors of the mini sea can, a weapons systems storage container measuring six by eight by eight feet tall. "It's part of the logistics reserve to support special operations down south. It's in addition to the cache stored inside the building."

"Don't the other teams have their own storage and backup systems?"

"Two is one and one is none," he said, reciting the mantra of logistics and supply personnel everywhere in the special operations community. The saying emphasized the critical importance of redundancy in military operations, where equipment failure could jeopardize mission success or survival. "It's part of the overall JSOC and Special Activities cache."

"So we should be able to use what we need if we get the green light, right?"

He shrugged.

Alex pushed into the green can used for transporting small arms and light weapons. This particular one held pistols, rifles, carbines, squad automatic weapons, night vision goggles, crew-served weapons, and more. Beneath the open weapons racks were drawers and cabinets packed with uniforms, gear, and ammo.

"And is there any chance we'll get a green light?" she asked. He shrugged again. "But if we do," she continued, "are you on board with us launching a rescue?"

She ran her fingers along the handguards on a row of M4 rifles standing in racks, the way a musician checks the strings of her treasured instrument.

He looked at her as if she were out of her mind to think otherwise. "The second we're a go, I'll take point, Alex."

She smiled. His rugged face stared back at her, his eyes boring into hers. He was the quiet kind of fighter that she was sure many had underestimated in a schoolyard or a barroom brawl. He was built sturdy and strong, but his mannerisms were self-effacing. He was a leader who led quietly, with no drama.

"I'm glad to hear you say that. It feels like no one wants to do anything," she said.

"I think there's more happening than you could know. Between JSOC and whatever Mustang is cooking up, I'm sure things are starting to fall into place. You saw it yourself—they already had an ISR drone stationed over the camp when we arrived. I'm pretty sure it wasn't just passing by on its merry way back to its home base. Someone had to retask it from somewhere else. No one deploys a hundred-million-dollar piece of hardware and tech without someone much higher up the food chain authorizing it."

He was right. Whatever drone was flying over the People's Freedom Army of Tanzania compound, deploying an Intelligence, Surveillance, and Reconnaissance (ISR) platform into the sky required approval from US Africa Command, or AFRICOM, the Department of Defense—likely the SECDEF herself—and maybe even presidential approval, not to mention the necessary approvals, or at the very least notifications, to the host country. Those processes typically didn't happen quickly outside planned operations, but in this case, approvals seemed to have materialized within hours.

She sighed and stepped closer to him. "Maybe they *are* taking it seriously," she conceded.

"You think?"

"Look, you know me. I don't do *slow and easy*."

"No. You don't."

Her gaze drifted to his lips, the memory of their storage room kiss still burning in her mind. Looking at him now, she felt a hunger she hadn't experienced in years—not since Kyle. The other men in her life had merely been shadows, poor substitutes for what stood before her now. For *who* stood before her now. A restlessness stirred inside her that she could barely contain. She had been with other men recently—okay, one other man—but she knew that even he had been a proxy for what she really wanted. *Who* she really wanted.

She closed the distance between them, drawn by an irresistible pull.

"Alex," he whispered.

She saw the recognition in his eyes—he understood exactly what was happening. She placed a hand on his chest, over his heart. He was well-muscled. She remembered seeing him shirtless not long after they met, when an assignment had taken them to Turkey together and he had been injured. She had watched as the paramedics assessed him, then released him against medical advice into his own care. His swimmer's physique had captivated her even then. Now, beneath her fingertips, his heart thundered a primal rhythm that matched her own. Rising on her toes, eyes fluttering closed, she sought his mouth with hers, drawn to the intense heat radiating between them—a force as powerful and dangerous as a nuclear reaction.

"Sir? Ma'am?"

The voice had come from behind them. Alex opened her eyes and planted her feet back on terra firma, pushing an arm's length away from Caleb. It was Trevor again, the same analyst who had found them together in the storeroom.

Jesus, she thought. *Could his timing be any worse?*

"I don't mean to interrupt. Again." He smirked.

"Spit it out, kid," Caleb said, positioning himself to block Trevor's view of Alex.

"You're needed inside. Harley wants you back in the op center."

Saved by the bell, thought Alex.

Trevor turned and went back in, leaving the two of them in the weapons crate.

"Look—" began Caleb.

"Don't say it. I know."

"I know we talked about this back at the lodge last night, and we were going to—"

"Caleb, you don't have to say anything. I'm on edge; I'm upset. My gyroscope has flipped upside down. This isn't just a craving for a random hookup. There's something here that . . . ," she trailed off, knowing that whatever she had said and was about to say wouldn't make much sense. Emotions were running high, and she needed to acknowledge that she wasn't exactly herself. She was frustrated by her lack of activity and felt like she was on tenterhooks. Apparently, that was now manifesting itself in her lust for Caleb.

Talk about bad timing.

"No, I want to," he said. "Let me speak. I thought about what you said last night. What *we* said. I agree I need to be more open with you. To open up more *to* you. But this isn't the right time or place. We need to have only one focus, and that's your dad. Getting the general back is our only priority. Everything else is a distraction that can only muddle that objective. And muddle whatever this is or will be."

She felt a combination of rejection and relief wash over her. She wasn't highly experienced in the world of . . . of whatever *this* was. But it was getting messy, and he was right—*messy* would only interfere in their work. Her only goal right now should be to get her father back safely, and anything that could stand in the way of that was something she needed to reject. As someone smarter than her had said, if it's meant to be, it would survive whatever came and would wait for them.

But would it?

Caleb buttoned up the weapons storage crate and the two headed back into the building. They walked up the hallway in silence until they reached the command-and-control room and the banks of computers and monitors bringing images of Africa into the room.

Caleb addressed Trevor. "Any new developments?"

"Not on this front," he replied.

Harley breezed in behind them. "Oh, good, you're here. Come on, you need to say hi to someone."

* * *

CONFERENCE ROOM, CIA OPERATIONS CENTER (BLACKBIRD), ARUSHA, TANZANIA

Harley swung the door open into a conference room as Alex and Caleb trailed behind.

As she entered the room, a voice deeper than a Louisiana swamp echoed across the meeting room.

"Ain't you a sight for sore eyes!"

"Moose!" shouted Alex, rushing past Caleb and Harley to embrace the newcomer.

At six-four and weighing in at two-sixty, the man seemed every bit the size of his namesake.

"Alex!"

"Well, look who it is," Caleb said.

"Hey, boss!"

"What am I, chopped liver?" came a voice from somewhere beyond.

Alex peered around Moose to see Rocky standing there. Rocky was a former boxer best described as compact and densely muscled. But his ever-present smile betrayed his obvious joy at seeing Alex again.

"Sorry about your dad, kid," he said, wrapping his arms around her in an embrace that almost crushed her. "But we're going to get him back, don't you worry."

"What is this?" she asked, turning to Caleb and Harley. "What's going on?"

Without fanfare, Harley announced, "Mustang's authorized a close-target recon on the rebel camp. So once this little lovefest is over, we'll brief and then head out to the vehicle bays to gear up."

"We're here not five minutes," said Moose, "and we're already going on a recce!" He was positively gleeful.

It was good to have the band back together again.

The door to the conference room swung open and in strolled the two men who had acted as Harley's close-protection detail when she came to pluck them off the savannah.

"Good, you're here," she said as they filed in. "Team, I want you to meet Kurtz and Santiago. They'll be joining you on your little reconnaissance mission."

The men waved and walked silently to the side of the room and propped themselves on a desk along a wall.

"Don't worry about them," said Harley, picking up on the vibe in the room. "They're some of the most experienced members in Special Activities."

"Then why haven't we seen them before?" asked Moose, eyeing them suspiciously.

"Because while you were hanging out in the Starbucks at Langley," said the one Harley identified as Santiago, "we were out actually kicking ass."

Cute and cheeky, thought Alex.

"Alright, alright," said Harley. "We don't have enough measuring tape to go around, so put 'em back in your pants, boys. And if you all don't mind, I'll get to the briefing. That okay with you, Santiago?"

"Yes, ma'am."

"Moose?"

"All good here, ma'am."

"Good. Here it is."

The analyst seated at a workstation brought the screen on the wall to life.

"The weather is . . . changeable," Harley began. "We have ISR on the rebel compound—for now. But given how long our UAV was loitering on the other op down south, it'll be past its endurance window and need to return to its base soon. We'll bring in another Reaper as soon as we can, but as Moose said, you might be doing an old-school reconnoiter on the PFA camp, which means mostly without eyes in the sky."

Aerial images of the People's Freedom Army compound and the surrounding landscape flashed onto the screen. The camp was encircled by bush and perimeter fencing, with a single road leading in and out. It was nestled in an area on the outskirts of Butemba, sharing the space with other homes and a church.

"We'll load up in a Black Hawk and set down here"—she pointed a red laser dot onto the image—"in a field on the opposite side of a hill east of our target . . ." She circled the compound with the red laser dot. "Over here."

"What's the terrain?" asked Moose.

"The nearby city of Mwanza is nicknamed Rock City, and the entire region, including our target village, Butemba, five klicks north of the airport, is strewn with large boulders. That hill next to our target is two hundred meters tall, give or take. The distance from the landing zone to the compound is one-point-five klicks, so you'll have to hump it over the hill to get there. You'll set up reconnaissance points on the west side of the hill and call in coordinates. We'll pass your intel to the Delta team coming in after you to effect the rescue."

"What's the catch?" asked Caleb.

Harley made eye contact with Alex.

"The catch is we need to get a positive ID on the general, or the mission gets scrubbed."

Alex wanted to protest, but Harley was right. They couldn't risk putting operators on the ground on a *maybe*. It wasn't just the lives of the Delta Force members that would be in jeopardy; it would be all the noncombatants—the women and children mostly—inside the camp who would be put in danger if shooting broke out, which it surely would, given the nature of the mission.

"And, not unironically, your team's call sign for the op is Ronin."

"Ah, *Kon'nichiwa!*" Moose said.

"We good, Shooter?" Harley asked.

"Good," Alex said. "You're not coming?"

"Much as I'd like to, I'll coordinate the op from here."

"Where's Delta coming from?"

"They'll be flying in from the south. They're currently on Tanzania's border with Mozambique. But again, they can't put boots on the ground until we have a definite ID and location of the general. Understood, Shooter?"

"Hooah!" she replied.

"Our job is to put eyes on the compound, find out where the general is being held, specifically, and point the way. We are not to engage except in support of the Unit."

"It would be nice to snatch him back ourselves," said Rocky.

"Suck it up. We're to provide intel only until otherwise requested. Near as we've established, there are fifty or sixty fighters in that camp and too many women and children. We're looking for a precision op by an official special mission unit. CIA Ground Branch paramilitaries like you dumb clucks don't fit that bill."

"A sniper rifle, not a scattergun," Alex said. "We get it."

CHAPTER 27

CIA OPERATIONS CENTER (BLACKBIRD), ARUSHA, TANZANIA

Catherine Harris—call sign Harley—sat alone in the sensitive compartmented information facility, a SCIF, essentially a bunker within a bunker, its twelve plasma screens painting the space with the colors from the drone feed across the room. She focused on the image flickering on screen 12. The storm over Lake Victoria had rendered the Reaper MQ-9's thermal imaging into pixelated ghosts. What might have been General Martel's heat signature pulsed weakly in hut 4—alive, for now. She didn't need the biometric overlay to know his heart rate would be steady. The man had survived Fallujah. He would survive this.

The secure line chirped. Deputy Director Kadeisha Thomas appeared on a center screen, her DC office blurred behind her. To her left, CIA director William "Iron Mike" McAllister—Army Intel, two tours in Iraq with General Martel before trading BDUs for a Langley corner office.

"Status," McAllister barked.

"Hunter's wheels-up in ninety," Harley said, referring to the team of Delta Force operators flying in from the border with Mozambique. "They have a long flight. Ronin's prepping for insertion at dawn. Lemarti's dug in deep."

Thomas's gaze sharpened. "Extraction probability?"

"Forty percent. Maybe less if PLA assets interdict."

McAllister grunted. "Martel knew this could happen. He's the only one who can reinitialize Aegis's countermeasures if the Chinese crack the algorithms."

"That was the project's fail-safe," Thomas said. "Everyone signed off on it."

Harley's fingers hovered over the strike authorization. "And if they do crack the algorithm?"

"Then every Aegis drone from Niger to Somalia becomes target practice." McAllister's voice hardened. "Beijing's BeiDou satellites already track our F-35s. Martel's the reason they can't see Aegis. And with the next phase, our adversaries will be blind to all our stealth equipment again. You know what he embedded in those drones?"

"Spoofing protocols," Harley said. "Randomizes their radar cross-section to mimic civilian aircraft or blots them out entirely."

"Chinese scientists developed a method for detecting stealth aircraft by analyzing the disruptions these aircraft cause to electromagnetic signals emitted by specific satellites," McAllister noted. "But DARPA and the Project Aegis engineers eliminated that capability by developing an algorithm that keeps them and our newest generation of autonomous drone swarms hidden. Except—" He hesitated before finishing.

Thomas picked it up. "Except that if the PLA gets the seed codes for that randomization, they'll tweak their satellites, and suddenly our trillion-dollar stealth fleet and next-gen drones light up like Christmas trees. AFRICOM—hell, *America*—loses air dominance and a vital strategic and tactical edge overnight."

A flash of lightning lit the monitors. The storm was grounding the Reaper in eighteen minutes.

McAllister leaned closer. "You briefed Hunter on the abort protocol?"

She tapped her keyboard. The Reaper's feed populated screen 12: crosshairs locked on hut 4. "Operation Ironclad. Yes, sir. Laser-guided AGM-176 Griffin air-to-ground missiles—right-sized for minimal splash. Plausible deniability. Command of the missile strike will be initiated by Hunter at their discretion in the event they can't recover the general. Blackbird is the fallback for Hunter in the event they can't initiate Ironclad."

Thomas frowned. "So Ironclad is good to go, Harley?"

"Ironclad is good to go, ma'am."

"No issues?"

Harley swallowed hard. To initiate Ironclad and kill General Martel in the event of imminent capture by Chinese Ministry of State Security operatives was a fundamental necessity. It had to be done if they wanted to keep the program's intel secure, saving lives and billions—possibly trillions—of dollars. America's strategic advantage for the next decade depended on Aegis remaining secure.

"No issues, ma'am."

"Good. And our girl?"

"Shooter? Unaware."

A beat of static. McAllister's eyes narrowed. "I served with Martel in '03. Man could sweet-talk a Bedouin into selling his camels *and* his mother. You think that charm'll hold against sodium pentothal? Or *ling chi*? The Chinese can be very creative. *Ling chi* was also known as *slow slicing* or *death by a thousand cuts*. It was a method of torturous execution practiced in China where the condemned was tied to a post and bits of skin and limbs were gradually filleted and removed one by one, usually culminating in a final cut to the heart or decapitation. The practice was used as early as the tenth century, and continued for nearly a thousand years, but I'm sure they've developed other methods that are equally unpalatable and just as effective."

Thomas's expression mirrored her own revulsion. Harley's fingers hovered over the strike authorization. "If they move him, we'll have a ten-second window from the docks."

"Make it five."

Thomas lingered. "You understand what this costs her—*us*?"

"He'd want it this way," McAllister said quietly. "Believe me, he knows the alternative."

"With respect, sir, *want* doesn't factor. You're asking me to green-light a strike on an American flag officer."

"I'm asking you to prevent a global paradigm shift." McAllister's knuckles whitened. "That AI isn't just code—it's the only reason China hasn't shot down our drones over the Mozambique Channel and the South China Sea. You let Martel spill those secrets, and every Aegis bird and stealth aircraft becomes a liability. We'll have to scrap the entire fleet. Look, Harley, you'll be acting under Title 50 authority. And since Hunter is working a joint operation with CIA here, they're covered by Title 50 as well."

Thomas cut in. "There's another angle. If the Chinese take him, they might not kill him. They'll own him. Imagine Martel on state TV *advising* their drone program. The psychological blow alone..."

"And the daughter?"

Harley's gaze drifted to screen 4. Alex's dossier glared back: Martel, A. L.—Code name: Shooter. Call sign: RONIN-6. No red flags. No psych waivers. Just a service record littered with confirmed kills.

"Liable to do something stupid," McAllister said. "Which is why you're not telling her about this."

"She'll be in the air with Ronin soon."

"You better pray Hunter and Ronin work nice together and get the general back. If they don't and if the Chinese *do* get their hands on him, we'll pay a heavy price."

"We'll all pay a heavy price regardless, sir," Harley said.

The screens flickered.

Somewhere over Lake Victoria, the Reaper circled.

The feed died.

* * *

PFA COMPOUND, BUTEMBA, TANZANIA

Lemarti rolled off the woman and sat on the edge of the bed, glancing back over his shoulder at her. She was a masterpiece sculpted in ebony, a midnight-black statue of gentle curves and valleys of dark, shimmering skin that captured the meager light filtering through the grimy window. Rivulets of sweat trickled down her neck, pooling between her breasts. She didn't look at him. In fact, she had been staring out the window the entire time he was inside her. Even now, her eyes remained fixed on some distant point beyond the glass as if her spirit had fled there, leaving behind only the vessel of her body.

Sitting there, he felt the familiar ache of rejection stirring in his chest, echoing through the years to another woman, another bed. His third bride had worn that same vacant stare back in the village when his family's meager cattle offering had sealed their fates. He had learned then how shame could hollow a person from the inside out. But villages had their own laws and rhythms—given enough seasons, even the most reluctant seed might take root and blossom. Here, in this sterile room with its feeble light, he felt those old certainties slipping through his fingers like sand.

After her husband was killed, Lemarti claimed her for himself. It wasn't a Maasai wedding—there had been no ceremony. The first time they lay together, he saw she hadn't undergone the same rite that every Maasai girl goes through to become a woman. In his village, such women didn't exist, and it was forbidden for a man to be with such a woman. But Adiya was useful, so he kept and protected her as his own. She was his now, and over time, she would come to appreciate what he provided, perhaps even look into his eyes when they had relations as man and wife.

He retrieved his pants from the floor and pulled them on. Then, without a word, he left Adiya to stare out the window at the rain. He walked under the camouflaged canopy from his hut to the main building. The canopy was made to filter light and hide what moved beneath, not to block the rain, so his skin and clothing got wet in the gentle downpour. Around him, the village was cast in the shadow of heavy clouds rolling in off Lake Victoria. Usually, storms grew less frequent this time of year, but that hadn't been the case for the past few years. The shoulder seasons had grown less predictable, and storms that brewed over the lake were more common and lasted longer than they had before. He had seen this with his own eyes, and local villagers had told him so.

Inside the Nissen hut, Desmond waited for him.

"Boss," acknowledged Desmond in Swahili as Lemarti approached.

Lemarti sat in his thinking chair and contemplated his next move. Such an important American being held hostage would stir the emotions of many, not least of which were the general's countrymen. The US government, for all its bluster, had behind it the lethal might of its armed forces. And Lemarti knew better than to question their capabilities—their command and control, he had heard, but not the skill and determination of frontline soldiers.

"Should we move the general now?" asked Desmond. "Or wait until morning?"

"Morning," he answered. "The Americans will be planning to rescue him, and it won't take them long to learn it was us who took him. But they won't come until the new day is here."

"It would be hard for them to get past all of us, would it not?"

Desmond was a loyal and trusted aide, but he was arrogant and prideful. Not the best combination in a soldier.

"Maybe, but we do not wish to fight with American soldiers, especially here. Increase patrols along the perimeter of our village, in case somebody makes a hasty move against us."

"Let the *wazungu* come for the general. They will wish they had stayed home in their featherbeds." *Wazungu* wasn't always a pejorative for whites or Westerners, but that's how he meant it here.

Lemarti laughed at his friend. "Good thing I am in charge and not you, my friend. You are forgetting that we have also enraged our Russian friends by our actions. They may try to come for him, too."

Indeed, Leopard Group PMC wasn't happy that he had unilaterally changed the terms of their agreement. Tarasenko had wanted General Martel dead. But Lemarti estimated that the profitability of that was low, and a buyer who was ready to pay more—by a factor of ten—had already surfaced to take possession of the general in a couple of days. As low a probability as it was, the Russians might attempt to recoup their investment and kill the general themselves—and anyone associated with the double cross or who stood in the way of that outcome. The ruthlessness of Tarasenko and his men wasn't to be underestimated. Africa was dotted with the headless corpses of those who had made such miscalculations.

"We have not made many friends these last few days," Lemarti reflected.

"Perhaps not."

Kijana entered the building and approached.

Desmond nodded toward him. "The boy almost shot the general when he thought he would attack me." He didn't think it was important to mention that what had provoked the general was when he had raised his hand to Adiya, Lemarti's woman.

Lemarti placed a hand on top of the boy's head.

"Soon, you'll be killing men alongside the rest of us, Kijana." He felt a swell of pride in his chest at the thought of the boy becoming a real soldier, a warrior of his ad hoc tribe. "You will come with me," he said to the boy. "Arrangements have been made. At first light, we will move General Martel to a safer place not far away."

CHAPTER 28

PFA COMPOUND, BUTEMBA, TANZANIA

The memories haunted Adiya like ghosts, fragments of a life stolen from her three years ago. She lay motionless on the thin mattress, her gaze fixed on the rain-streaked window as Lemarti's weight lifted from the bed. She didn't flinch when he glanced back at her, didn't acknowledge the sweat cooling on her skin or the hollow ache spreading through her chest. Her mind had already escaped to that sacred place beyond the glass where Lemarti couldn't follow.

Three years ago, she had been Adiya Okello, a respected teacher in a lakeside village, wife to Jabari. They had built their life brick by brick—she with chalk dust on her fingers from the schoolhouse, he with the easy confidence of a man who guided foreign researchers through the mysteries of Lake Victoria. Their small home had been filled with books and laughter and whispered plans for children who would never come.

The PFA militants had descended on their village like locusts at dawn, the rumble of trucks her first warning that the world was about to collapse. Lemarti hadn't been just another armed man that day. He was the one who had stepped forward when Jabari dared to defend an elderly villager, the one whose finger had squeezed the trigger without hesitation. The gunshot still echoed in her nightmares, a sound that had cleaved her life into *before* and *after*.

"You are educated," he had told her later that night, examining her ID card while the village burned behind them. "You will be useful."

Useful. Not human, not woman, not widow. Just useful.

The compound at Butemba became her prison, a place where she translated documents and communications for the PFA while Lemarti claimed ownership of her body. She learned to read the shifting alliances between the militants and their Russian partners, to understand the value of hostages like the American general currently held in the adjacent building. Knowledge became her weapon, her only defense in a world where she had been reduced to property.

Adiya watched Lemarti pull on his pants, his movements mechanical, practiced. He didn't speak before leaving—he never did. Words would have required acknowledgment of what transpired between them, would have made it real in ways neither could bear. The door clicked shut behind him, and only then did she allow herself to breathe fully, to reclaim the vessel of her body inch by inch.

Rain pattered against the corrugated metal roof, a gentle percussion that masked the sound of her shifting on the bed. She sat up slowly, wrapping the thin sheet around her nakedness, a futile shield against memories of Lemarti's hands. The compound would be busy tonight with the American general's presence.

Tomorrow they would move the general. Lemarti had mentioned it while believing she was asleep. One day, she hoped to run away. Maybe that day would come after they moved the general and there were fewer soldiers in the camp. Kijana might help her. The boy soldier had shown her small kindnesses when others weren't watching. She had been secretly teaching him, feeding his eager mind with knowledge that Lemarti would never approve of. There was still something human in the boy, something not yet corrupted by Lemarti's influence.

Outside, the rain intensified, drumming against the roof like impatient fingers. Adiya's gaze returned to the window, to the darkness beyond. Somewhere out there was freedom, a life reclaimed. Lemarti believed that eventually she would break, would look into his eyes and accept her fate as his woman. He didn't understand that her spirit had never been captured, that what remained in this room was merely a shell, waiting for the perfect moment to shatter its chains.

Tomorrow, she thought, *tomorrow everything changes.*

CHAPTER 29

BUTEMBA, ON THE SHORES OF LAKE VICTORIA

It was zero dark when Alex and the team executed a low-hover exit from the Black Hawk. As each member emerged, they fanned out in a defensive perimeter next to the helicopter. Taking a knee, each of the six operators remained at the ready with their rifles extended, scanning the landing zone and beyond for threats.

They were kitted out in a mix of civilian clothing and tactical gear—a favorite ensemble among Special Activities Center paras. They wore Kevlar vests and ballistic helmets fitted with ground panoramic night vision goggles, or NVGs for short. These odd-looking devices featured four tubes that combined to offer high-definition vision.

By the time the Black Hawk deposited them in the designated landing zone, the temperature had fallen to sixty-four degrees. The rotor downwash intensified the chill in the air, and was strong enough to make it difficult to hold their position for long. Alex was thankful for the thick fleece she wore over her shirt. She carried yet another layer inside her Arc'teryx backpack. One thing her dad had taught her when they lived in the mountains was that layering saved lives. She made it a point to wear a good technical base layer under her clothes and, whenever possible, to ensure she had a windproof and waterproof layer nearby.

Fuck, I'm getting soft, she thought.

Her NVGs gave her a high-definition view, near and far. The field they occupied was flat and maybe a couple hundred meters across, bordered on three sides by small homes. A few were lit sparingly while the rest remained pitch black, which, given the hour, wasn't surprising. To the west of their position, a hill rose into the sky seven hundred meters ahead. Assuming they encountered no obstacles or tactical challenges, she figured it would take them less than ten minutes to reach the hill.

Caleb's voice sounded in her earpiece. "Blackbird Zero, this is Ronin Actual. Radio check, over." Blackbird Zero was the call sign for the CIA operations center in Arusha. Ronin was their team's call sign, and as team leader, Caleb was Ronin Actual.

A voice came back that Alex recognized as Trevor, the analyst. "Ronin Actual, this is Blackbird Zero. You're roger, over."

"We're at LZ Crow. Moving to OP Sunray."

"Copy. Notify when you're in position."

"Roger. Ronin out."

Caleb spent nearly a full minute scanning the hillside ahead with binoculars before giving the team the signal to move out. Rocky took point and led the advance while Alex, assigned as the designated marksman and security for the section, brought up the rear of the formation. Every team member, except for Alex, carried a rifle equipped with a holographic sight and a separate 3x magnifier. Alex, however, carried the designated marksman rifle variant of their HK416 rifle—the M38 DMR. This customization included a SIG Sauer TANGO-DMR 5–30x56mm scope that she had previously used in combat. While she loved its 30x zoom magnification, she wasn't thrilled about the sixteen-and-a-half-inch barrel, especially since the rest of the team's rifles had fourteen-and-a-half-inch barrels. She knew that the extra two inches could hinder her maneuverability if they found themselves in a close-quarters battle within the village or the People's Freedom Army compound.

On a mission like theirs, though, versatility was the key. This choice of weapon was tactically sound for long-range shooting out to eight hundred meters while maintaining some utility for close-quarter battle situations.

Rocky led them toward the hill ahead, the team keeping appropriate distance between squad members. As they walked, they encountered large boulders scattered throughout the field in front of them. Their presence necessitated that they weave as they walked. The obstacles were easy enough to navigate around or between, but it would slow them down, and Alex was eager to get into position.

The rocks looked like they might be composed of granite, similar to those surrounding the family's homestead in the Wind River Range. There, the land was known for its dramatic mountain landscape of soaring peaks that reached into the sky. Large boulders behind her cabin and around Shoshone Lake were more jagged and less rounded than these. She thought this difference might be because those boulders had not undergone the gradual effects of weathering and erosion over the eons like these appeared to have, but instead had fallen off the high peaks in more recent history, split off by the activity of wind and rain and ice over the ages.

Rocky's voice came through her earpiece.

"We expecting trouble, boss?" he asked.

"Never say never," came Caleb's reply.

Moose chimed in. "Never mind bogeys, Rocky. Watch out for snakes, hyenas, and lions."

Not likely, thought Alex. *But hey, the odds are low, but not zero.*

"Lions?" said Santiago. "Never had trouble with no lions. Cougars on the other hand . . ." His smooth Colombian accent was as rich and expressive as the coffee from his homeland. "*León de montaña!*"

Alex groaned into her mike.

"Knock it off," Caleb said. "Let's maintain noise discipline, yeah? Stay frosty."

In other words, *Shut up and stay alert.*

It wasn't likely the PFA had sentries up on the hill. And the approach of their Black Hawk had been well below the top of the hill in order to block most of the rumble before it could reach the rebel camp on the other side so as not to raise the alarm. But that, too, wasn't guaranteed. Nothing in combat was. So, as Caleb had said, they needed to stay frosty, just in case.

They reached the slope and began the ascent up the hillside, where still more rocks and boulders obstructed their path. As they navigated through them, she wondered what geological processes had formed them or deposited them there eons ago. But she didn't dwell on it for long, preferring to focus on where she placed her feet to avoid twisting her ankle in the dark—or stepping on a cobra.

Rocky's arm shot into the air, his fist balled. The formation froze.

"Hold," he whispered into his mike.

The squad took a knee and watched as he brought his rifle up, advancing slowly, stepping deliberately through the low shrubs and grass. It was clear to Alex that he had seen or heard something, but she couldn't see what he saw. She turned 180 degrees to scan their six, panning her rifle from left to right and back again to be sure no one—not man nor beast—was riding up on them from the rear.

She turned to face the front again as movement ten meters in front of Rocky caught her eye. Rocky squared to the threat. Others who'd had their rifles guarding their sides and flanks now turned to the threat, too.

A tiny antelope, no bigger than a foot tall, burst from cover and bolted, joining its mate halfway down the hill.

"Jesus!" he cursed.

"We good?" asked Caleb.

"Yes, boss. It was only a little dik-dik," he reported.

"Is that what she told you last night?" asked Santiago.

"Funny guy. Why don't you come up here and find out?"

"Hey, numpties," Alex said into her radio. "Knock it off. Can we try to remember why we're here?"

Caleb remained silent, letting the squad work it out.

"Sorry, Alex," said Rocky, giving her a wave.

Awash in the green light of her NVGs, Santiago acknowledged her with a dip of his shoulders and a smug smile.

"Move out," Caleb said.

Rocky signaled and their trek resumed up the hill.

Ten minutes later, they reached the summit, a rounded crest of hilltop high above the landscape to the west. Like the ground around them, it was dotted with boulders three, four, and six feet tall and wide. Cover and concealment weren't going to be an issue as the team spread out, silently getting to work establishing observation points.

Caleb spoke to Rocky. "Call it in."

Rocky got on the radio to advise the ops center that they had reached their first observation post.

"Blackbird Zero, Ronin Two, over."

"Ronin, go for Blackbird."

"We're at OP Sunray. We'll advise when we're moving to OP Seagull."

"Roger, Ronin Two. Blackbird out."

Through the monochrome green of her NVGs, she had a clear view of the surrounding countryside. Little blooms of light dotted her field of view. Like the houses to the east where they had started their climb, the ones laid out below her were mostly dark. But here and there in the distance, a streetlight shone. A porch light. A light through a window. A few hundred meters farther away, just beyond the collection of irregularly placed homes built around the patchwork of rocks, was a denser settlement.

She flipped up her NVGs. A crescent moon hung low over Lake Victoria, bathing the town in pale blue light and painting long, wispy clouds a faint pink. Soon they would catch fire as night turned to twilight and twilight to dawn, marking the inescapable rising of the sun. The beauty of it lifted her heart, and for that, she was grateful. But she knew why she was here. Knew that the mission had hardly begun. While outwardly displaying the courage of a warrior—a bravado born from her confidence in her skills and those of the team around her—inside, she trembled like a little girl, unsure of herself and wondering if she could complete the dangerous task ahead of bringing her dad safely home.

She removed her pack and leaned it and her rifle against a five-foot-tall boulder. She opened it and loosened the top compression strap, then took out a pair of laser range-finding binoculars with their own night-vision capability. While her teammates spread out and claimed their spots across the hill from which to observe and provide overwatch for the Delta Force rescue team, she rested her elbows on top of the rock, peering down at what she knew was the People's Freedom Army of Tanzania compound.

It had been given the code name Forge. The buildings were smaller and more square-shaped than the homes immediately below her, and they were aligned in a grid pattern along narrow roads and pathways. A chill ran up her spine as she noticed the netting strung along paths connecting many of the buildings. It was the camouflage netting she had seen on the feed from the overhead drone. Somewhere below her in that compound was her father.

She could feel it.

Memories of a promise she had made long ago washed over her.

I would look for you, too, Dad. I would search everywhere for you and I'd bring you home.

It wasn't just a promise but a vow consecrated in blood.

Blood of my blood, until my last breath.

A blood oath.

She continued to scan the compound, seeing him in every doorway, every shadow.

Where are you, Dad? Give me a sign.

But no such sign came. Nothing seemed to be stirring in the camp at this hour, only emptiness. Enough emptiness to block out hope.

She removed the hydration pack from its sleeve in her Arc'teryx backpack and took a long draw on the drinking tube. The tepid water nevertheless quenched her thirst, and she took another long sip. The thing about special operations recces was you could never be quite sure whether you were going to be sitting in place for hours or if the assignment would go kinetic. So, best to stay fed and hydrated. Reaching back into her pack, she pulled out a chocolate Soldier Fuel bar and peeled back the wrapper, biting off a chunk of the slightly slimy, malleable bar. It was just as she remembered with that familiar chocolate energy bar taste and crunch imparted by those crispy flake things dispersed throughout that made it all the more interesting, whatever they were. It was nostalgic and sweet, but not overpowering of either.

She looked down the line at her teammates. Kurtz had the watch along with Santiago. The two had been silent sentinels when they flanked Harley to pluck her and Caleb off the savannah. In hindsight, it was understandable—what could they have said? They were already aware that her father had been taken, a fact she would only learn soon after getting airborne in the Black Hawk.

But they were okay. Kurtz was over six feet tall with plenty of lean muscle. He wore his dirty-blond hair longish on top but with the sides buzzed. He reminded Alex of a young and rakish Dolph Lundgren. The strong, silent type. Santiago, on the other hand, was going to be trouble. He was already making eyes at her. Worse, he knew he was good-looking. Of medium height, he had broad shoulders, dark wavy hair, and smoky eyes. Beneath his long sleeves, his thick arms were well defined, like the rest of him. Plus, he had dimples.

Beyond them was Caleb—well beyond them, in fact. He was simply out of their league entirely. While Kurtz and Santiago seemed like squared-away soldiers and must have had the background to earn a spot on a CIA Special Activities team, Caleb was a branch chief who led his own team with a global mandate for covert action. Having worked with him on previous assignments, she understood how his mind operated. He could distill information seemingly from nothing and acted with courage and conviction when executing a mission. He reminded her of her late husband, Kyle, and perhaps that was the issue. Could anyone expect to be struck by lightning twice in their lifetime? Did she have the right to hope for a love like that ever again? Was she even deserving of it? And could she expose herself to the risk of such pain once more? The grief was only now beginning to ebb.

As if hearing her thoughts, Caleb walked toward her. He stopped first to speak to Kurtz and Santiago before strolling over, one hand on his rifle, the other wrapped around his own Soldier Fuel bar. She took another bite of hers as he sat down on the ground next to her, his back propped against the rock.

"Great minds," he said, eyeing her bar. She nodded. "You good?" he asked. She gave him a thumbs-up as she took another bite out of her energy bar, chasing it with a gulp of water from her pack.

"I've always liked these." His words came out mumbled through a mouthful of Soldier Fuel bar. "And they don't raunch my gut out."

"It's the soy protein," she said after swallowing a chunk. "It's better for you old guys than milk protein."

"And you know this how?"

"I watched how slow you were climbing the hill."

"Funny."

"Seriously."

She was having fun at his expense. Truth was, he was as fit and agile, if not more so, as anyone on this squad. He was likely ten years older than the youngest member and probably the only one who'd had a bullet lodged in his heart, a souvenir from a skirmish with a group of insurgents intent on obliterating the outpost he occupied along the Arghandab River as it flowed southwest past Kandahar. To this day, he kept that bullet as a memento chained to his ever-present Kubotan.

"This will all be over soon, Alex."

She thought about that. And she thought about the unintended double meaning in his words.

"The Unit will be here before sunup," he said, referring to the troop of 1st Special Forces Operational Detachment–Delta, or Delta Force, commandoes flying up from somewhere south of them. "And, God willing, all will go according to Hoyle. They'll put down on that beach"—he pointed with his energy bar to a faint line of light where the land met the lake about one and a half klicks away—"and advance to the rebel compound. In about five minutes, we're going to walk along this ridge to that point over there"—he pointed to a shadowy outline in the distance—"from where we'll observe and cover their advance. That will put us within a hundred meters of the camp."

He tapped her leg, stood up, and moved back to a position in the middle of the group, checking in with each member of the team as he went. A leader.

A minute later, "Ronin Actual, this is Blackbird Actual," came over Alex's earpiece. It was Harley's voice, Blackbird Actual.

He looked at her and pointed to his radio, as if to say, *See?*

"Go ahead," he replied.

"Hunter is delayed."

All heads turned to Caleb, and then to Alex. Hunter was the call sign for Delta Force's A Squadron that had been attached to the hostage-rescue mission.

Caleb looked off toward the lake as if gathering his thoughts. Then he turned and looked back at Alex, too.

"Ronin, how copy?"

"Good copy," he said, letting go of the transmit button. Then, keying it again, "How long?"

The air was silent for a full twenty seconds, then, "Forty-five minutes."

The team let out an audible groan. Caleb waved a hand to silence them.

"We're going to proceed to Seagull," he said.

"Negative, Ronin. You're not authorized to move to that position until Hunter's arrival is imminent."

Caleb didn't respond right away. Instead, his eyes bored into Alex's as if he could read her anxieties and worry over the delay.

"Due respect, Blackbird, but Ronin is on the move now. Ronin out."

He summoned his squad to form up. The team scooped up their kit and gathered around their leader.

"Okay, HRT is delayed," he said. "We can sit our asses down at this observation point until Hunter lands on that beach over there, or we can proceed to our next objective and establish an overwatch position at OP Seagull. By the time Hunter gets their asses on the ground, it'll be almost daylight. Their approach will be visible. Our movement along the ridge will be visible. Best to do it now while we still have the cover of darkness. Agreed?" He searched his team's eyes for dissent. None. "Once there, we'll provide cover and give them the most recent SitStat. And if shit goes down before they're on the ground, we'll be in a better position to react and respond. We're not doing anyone any good sitting behind these pretty rocks. Yeah?"

Alex scanned her teammates' faces. Their silent consensus hung in the air, heavy as a promise written in blood.

CHAPTER 30

PFA COMPOUND, BUTEMBA, TANZANIA

David Martel lay on the thin mattress, its straw stuffing long since collapsed into uneven mounds that pressed against his spine. Decades ago, during a rare family trip to Kyoto, Alex had sprawled on a futon just like this, giggling as she plucked edamame from their pods. Now, the memory felt as distant as the stars winking through the tin roof's jagged cracks.

The predawn air clung to his skin, thick with the musk of damp soil and woodsmoke. Somewhere beyond the compound's walls, a hyena's laugh sliced through the silence—a sound he'd once found hauntingly beautiful during safari nights with Alex. Now, it felt like a taunt.

He counted the rhythm of sentry boots outside: eight paces east, twelve west, repeat. Lemarti's men had grown lax, their footsteps uneven, but their numbers hadn't dwindled. Two guards were stationed outside his hut, even throughout the night. Especially throughout the night.

Martel's fingers traced the scar on his palm, the one that mirrored Alex's.

Blood of my blood.

The oath had been a child's promise; now, it was an operational mandate.

The door creaked. Adiya slipped inside, her silhouette sharp against the gray light. She carried a clay jug, her eyes downcast.

Water sloshed as she filled a chipped mug, her hands trembling—not from the weight, Martel realized, but fear.

"*Asante,*" Martel murmured, his Swahili deliberate, probing, passable for the most basic needs. He didn't stand or reach for the water. Not yet.

Adiya's gaze flickered to the door, then to the faded kanga cloth wrapped tight around her shoulders. A vibrant red-and-yellow pattern. When she spoke, her voice was a blade sheathed in silk. "They come at first light."

Martel kept his face neutral, but his pulse spiked.

They're going to move me. But move me where? Or to whom?

Project Aegis's schematics burned in his mind like a lit fuse. DARPA's AI-driven drones and access codes—the stealth tech that could outmaneuver China's satellite trackers—all of it compartmentalized behind mental firewalls. SERE training had taught him to fracture intel, to bury truths under layers of half-truths. But how long could he play that game under a blowtorch, drill, or a hole saw?

The night before, he'd overheard Lemarti on a satellite phone, his voice low but unmistakable. *The amount is nonnegotiable.* A pause. *No, not damaged goods. He is very much intact—for now.*

Kijana appeared in the doorway, his AK-47 slung haphazardly. The boy's cheeks still held the roundness of youth, though his eyes were older—too old. Martel tracked the rifle's safety selector. Still on safe.

"You stare like a leopard," Kijana said, chin jutting. His finger hovered near the trigger guard, a hair's breadth from breaking protocol.

Martel shrugged, the chains around his ankles clinking. "Leopards are survivors. You learn that when the hyenas come."

The boy stiffened. Hyenas had taken his brother last year—Martel had overheard the guards whispering. A cheap psychological play, but war was chess with bloodstained pieces.

Martel had been watching Kijana, studying him like he studied Lemarti and Adiya. He was cocky and liked his rifle a little too much. Yet something in his eyes spoke of doubt. Of questions that Lemarti's ideology couldn't answer. The boy had smuggled extra water to Martel twice now, had loosened the chains once when no one was looking. Small mercies that spoke volumes.

Adiya hissed something in Maa, the Maasai dialect sharp as a scalpel. Kijana's jaw twitched, but he stepped back, the rifle's muzzle dipping toward the dirt. Martel filed the exchange away: *Divide them. Leverage the woman.*

He'd seen the bruises on her wrists, the way she flinched when Lemarti entered a room. She wasn't identifying with her captor. She was surviving him. Martel recognized the fear and calculation behind her eyes; it mirrored his own. They were both playing the long game.

Footsteps pounded outside—heavy, impatient. Desmond filled the doorway, his rifle slung like a scepter.

"Up, *mzee*." He spat the Swahili word for *old man* like a curse.

Martel rose slowly, newly added chains rattling at his ankles. Desmond secured the general's wrists with zip ties. Martel flexed his fingers, testing the circulation. The bindings they'd used had left angry welts around his wrists. Amateur work. The real professionals—the ones who'd trained at the same black sites he had—would have known better. Would have used techniques that left no marks but broke men from the inside out.

Desmond—former child soldier, now Lemarti's enforcer. A scar bisected his left eyebrow. If the rumors were true, he'd killed a dozen UN peacekeepers before defecting to the PFA. His hands were steady, his eyes clear. No drug addiction, unlike most of Lemarti's inner circle. Dangerous.

"Where's Lemarti? Doesn't he want his prize?"

Desmond backhanded him. Martel's head snapped back, copper flooding his tongue. Classic interrogation opener: disorientation before the dance. He'd taught this at the Farm.

The blow was calculated—enough force to show dominance, not enough to cause real damage. Desmond was under orders to deliver the package intact. Martel filed that away: whoever wanted him needed him functional. That narrowed the list of potential buyers.

"You think you're worth more alive?" Desmond grabbed Martel's shirt, hauling him close. "Lemarti has already tricked the Russians. And now the Chinese will pay well for the scraps."

So, in the end, it's the Chinese. Martel almost smiled. Beijing's spies would peel him layer by layer, hunting for Aegis. He let his voice fray, the perfect portrait of a broken man. "They'll kill you after. You know that, right?"

For a heartbeat, Desmond hesitated. Martel pressed. "Lemarti trades you next. Or the boy. That's how hyenas eat."

The metaphor wasn't subtle, but subtlety was a luxury he couldn't afford. Not with the clock ticking down on whatever extraction plan Alex might have set in motion.

Two PFA fighters shoved into the hut. They barked orders, their Swahili slurred by *pombe* liquor. Zip ties bit into Martel's wrists again as they dragged him out. He caught Adiya's eye. Silent, she dipped her chin—a nod so slight it could've been a tremor. A crack in the wall.

Kijana trailed behind, the rifle's safety still on. Martel's training screamed: *Disarm him. Run!* But the boy's eyes glistened—not with malice, but fear. Martel's ankle chains clanked as he stumbled, his hand brushing Kijana's. The boy recoiled.

"*Rafiki*," Martel whispered.

A half smile flickered.

The Swahili word for *friend* hung between them, fragile as spider silk. Martel had spent twenty years building networks of assets across five continents. He knew the power of that word—knew how it could turn enemies into allies, how it could create breathing room in the suffocating confines of captivity.

Desmond kicked the back of Martel's knee, causing him to stumble again. But Kijana caught his arm, steadying him.

"*Asante*, Kijana."

Outside, the compound stirred. Lemarti stood by a rusted Hilux, his silhouette sharp against a row of torches and the harsh glow of floodlights. Next to him, the woman, Adiya.

"You'll fetch a fine price, General," he said, tapping a tablet, its screen flickering with Chinese characters.

Martel scanned the compound perimeter. Three guards on the eastern fence line. One technical vehicle by the main gate, a .50-caliber machine gun mounted on its bed. A communications array had been mounted on the central building—new equipment, satellite uplink. Someone had upgraded Lemarti's operation recently. Someone with deep pockets and deeper motives.

Martel's laugh was a dry rasp. "You're dead already. Tarasenko doesn't forgive betrayal."

The warlord's smile faltered. The Leopard Group's reputation wasn't just for efficiency—it was for creativity.

Lemarti recovered quickly, but not before Martel caught the flash of genuine fear. So it was true—Tarasenko had been bankrolling the PFA, using them as proxies in whatever game he was playing. And now Lemarti was selling out to the Chinese, double-crossing the most dangerous man in the private military sector.

As they shoved Martel into the back of Lemarti's truck, he exchanged looks with Adiya. She stared back with soft eyes. Her fingers lightly brushed the kanga cloth. A sign of empathy? He hoped she'd find the courage to help him. Somehow.

The engine roared. Dust swirled, stinging Martel's eyes. Somewhere out there, Alex would be watching. He felt it.

He clenched his scarred palm.

Blood of my blood.

He'd hold on.

Until his last breath.

CHAPTER 31

OP SEAGULL, BUTEMBA, TANZANIA

The trek across the ridgeline from OP Sunray to their new observation point hadn't taken more than twenty minutes. The team established their watch positions, with Alex locating a patch of granite to set up on behind her M38 designated marksman rifle.

Santiago strolled up and settled beside her, where she lay on her belly, ranging targets through her riflescope. Without encouragement, he sat on the ground next to her, wrapping his arms around his knees like he was at summer camp, listening to the camp director read the morning announcements.

"You good, Shooter?"

It was awkward hearing someone other than Caleb or Deputy Director Thomas call her that. Yes, it was her call sign—not exactly a secret code name—but it still sounded odd coming from this operator's lips.

"I never have sex on the first date," she said.

"What?" he stammered.

"Just clearing the air. Don't want to lead you on."

"But you'd go out with me on a . . . date?"

"Nope."

"But you just said—"

"No, I didn't. You heard what you wanted to hear. Look, I know when guys are sniffing around for a quick piece."

"Alex, you got me all wrong."

She looked over and laughed at him. "You should see the panic in your face, Santiago. What, none of your Puerto Rican girlfriends ever yank your chain this way?"

"Colombian."

"Got something against Puerto Ricans? They're American, you know."

"No, I know." He stammered again, clearly frustrated. "*Me estás mamando gallo?*"

Alex laughed again. She *was* messing with him. It felt good to see him squirm, a delight she relished after years of perfecting the art of redirecting men's attention and endless come-ons. It didn't happen as often as it used to, but it still happened here more than in the civilian world. She thought it must be the same for cops. And for women who had close and regular contact with men in what could be called more *casual* work environments.

"Relax," she said. She scanned the rebel compound—Objective Forge—through her riflescope. "I just need you to know where the bullshit stops." She had ranged a number of points within the camp—and a few on its perimeter, too—and transferred the data into a small notebook that lay next to her rifle while he watched.

"DOPE card, huh," he said. "Kind of a sniper's bible?"

"It'll have to do," she replied. This was the first time she'd be using this rifle, so she didn't have a history of previous engagements implied by calling it a DOPE card, but it was close enough. "The only bible I keep faith in."

"That can't be true," he said. He reached down and flicked the medallion that dangled from a box chain around her neck. "St. Christopher?"

"St. Michael," she corrected, tucking it into her shirt.

"I know. Now I'm messing with you." He reached over and faux punched her in the shoulder.

"Got me," she said. "Funny guy."

She continued ranging and writing in her notebook. The average distance to targets in and around the People's Freedom Army compound hovered around three hundred and fifty meters, well within the capabilities of her rifle and match-grade ammo.

Underneath her, the ridge's jagged granite bit into her knees as she adjusted her position. The black of night had given way to inky twilight. Under the pale glow of generator-powered floodlights, Forge began to stir like a mall full of Black Friday shoppers. Figures darted between huts and tents, their shadows stretching out around them. She dialed her SIG Sauer scope's magnification to 8x, the crosshairs trembling slightly as she panned across the central clearing, hunting for potential targets.

Searching for her father. Thermal had previously pegged him in hut 4 but she'd had no visual confirmation of that, and ISR wasn't currently loitering on station above.

Behind her, Kurtz's voice: "Boss, you might want to see this," he said.

Alex raised her binoculars in the direction Kurtz was pointing. In the distance, the unmistakable blinking navigation lights of a large aircraft were visible as a plane banked on final approach to Mwanza Airport.

"You clocking this?" she asked.

"I am," Caleb replied. "Moose?"

"Yeah, boss," he said, already stirring from where he'd settled in. "I see it."

"One of ours?" she asked, wondering if reinforcements to aid with the rescue mission might be arriving, though they'd had no such report.

"Not likely," Caleb said. "And Blackbird would have shared that with us."

Moose peered through his binoculars. "It's too far to get a good view of the bird, but it's maybe a Herc or a Globemaster," he said, referring to the Hercules C-130 and the C-17 cargo and transport aircraft.

"Can't be a Hercules," said Kurtz, staring through his binoculars.

"Why not?"

"The Herc is a prop plane; that's a jet. Looks like four engines. From the shape of it, I'd guess it's an Antonov."

"He's right," Alex said. "Four-engine strategic airlift."

"My bad," said Moose, still following the aircraft along its descent path.

Alex pivoted on the ground, swinging her rifle toward the Mwanza Airport five kilometers away. Her rifle scope was more powerful than any of their binoculars. The runway was aglow in her reticle, lit by floodlights that reflected off the aluminum skin of the white-painted aircraft.

"It's an Antonov, alright," she confirmed.

Mwanza Airport's runway lights blinked as the Antonov AN-124 descended through broken cloud cover, its four Progress D-18T engines screaming against the night. Cranking her scope to 30x, the aircraft's tail number resolved into focus: RA-82049.

Leopard Group's logo—a snarling leopard head—was painted beneath the cockpit. Her finger hovered uselessly over the trigger. Five kilometers. Even her father's custom .338 Lapua back in Wyoming couldn't bridge that distance.

"Tarasenko's PMC," she spat.

The massive cargo plane touched down, coasted to the end of the runway, and taxied toward a distant hangar. Armed figures, about two dozen or more, spilled from its yawning rear ramp—European builds in matching tactical gear, dragging crates.

She summarized her observations for Caleb and the team.

Caleb called on the radio. "Blackbird Zero, Ronin Actual."

"This is Blackbird, go ahead, Ronin."

"We're at OP Seagull and need a sitrep for Hunter. A Russian transport aircraft just landed."

"You're sure?"

"Tarasenko's PMC. We got tail numbers and everything. Sending you intel and photos now."

He nodded to Rocky, who was pecking away on an encrypted mobile device.

"Stand by, Ronin."

A full thirty seconds passed before Trevor came back over their talk net.

"Hunter will be arriving aboard a Black Hawk. ETA is six minutes."

"You better advise Hunter. Not sure if this'll change their plans."

"Ten-four, Ronin Actual, will advise Hunter of the new SitStat. Mwanza Airport isn't answering their phones. I'd say stay alert—you may have company soon."

"Boss?" It was Santiago. "Activity at twelve o'clock."

Caleb spied through his binoculars.

Santiago muttered through the squad's encrypted comms. "Technical with mounted Dushka."

Alex swung her rifle around and dialed her scope's magnification back down to 8x. The aging Soviet DShK heavy machine gun sat unmanned on its truck bed, its barrel angled skyward, parked in front of a Nissen hut. "No crew. Looks like they're mobilizing for—"

Six Toyota Hilux pickup trucks roared into formation beside the technical. Alex's breath hitched as her scope settled on a figure being marched out to the lead vehicle. The figure yanked at his restraints—General David Martel, his left eye swollen but posture rigid. Someone shoved him into the back seat of the lead pickup.

"Blackbird Zero, Ronin Actual," Caleb barked into his mic. "Confirm Hunter's ETA. Advise them package is being loaded into a pickup truck. I say again, we have eyes on Condor. They're mounting vehicles."

Static hissed before Harley's voice sliced through, cool and firm: "Ronin Actual, this is Blackbird Actual. Hunter landing in three mikes. Maintain observation. Do not engage."

The Night Stalkers were famous for their pinpoint-accurate ETAs. If they said three minutes, it wouldn't be a minute later, but likely not sooner, either. That might be too late.

A man Alex recognized as the PFA's leader, Lemarti, followed the general to the vehicle. A woman wearing a lime-green skirt walked beside him.

Moose's growl vibrated through the comms. "Boss, they're going to roll out before Hunter can get there. If they hit the shoreline road and reach those fishing villages up the coast . . ."

"Understood. We'll lose 'em." Caleb's jaw muscle twitched. "Shooter—range to lead vehicle."

Alex checked her laser range finder. "Four hundred twenty meters and counting. Wind three-quarter value left."

"Can you disable?"

She glanced at the M38 DMR's sixteen-and-a-half-inch heavy barrel. "Tires? Maybe. Engine block? Not a chance with this five-five-six," she said, citing the rifle caliber. What she wouldn't have given at that moment to have her trusty .300 Norma Mag with her, the one she used from the side of Mount Hoverla in the Eastern Carpathian mountains of Ukraine nine months ago.

"Then we watch."

The rebuke stung. Alex ground her molars, watching the convoy in her scope as it idled in front of the Nissen hut. Soon, Lemarti and his crew would go mobile and drive out through the gates of the compound while they sat here watching and waiting for something to happen. Waiting for a helicopter full of Tier 1 operators to do what she should be doing—rescuing her dad. She felt helpless.

She knew it was the PFA's leader, Lemarti, from the surveillance and intel package they'd seen in the ops center in Arusha. In front of her eyes, Lemarti's frame filled the passenger seat of the lead Toyota pickup, his trademark red *shuka* wrapped around his shoulders like battle flags. Behind him, sitting next to her father, a shock of curly hair bobbed—a boy in his early teens, clutching a rifle with nervous reverence.

Caleb keyed his radio: "Blackbird, situation as follows: hostile PMC insertion at Mwanza Airport. Two or three dozen armed mercenaries deplaning with vehicles and equipment from an Antonov. By road they're twenty minutes to Forge, the PFA camp. Condor is about to be moved in a convoy guarded by a technical. We're useless here, and soon we'll be blind, too. Request ISR overwatch."

Harley's response crackled with rare uncertainty: "Satellite's blind for another twelve minutes. A Reaper UAV will be on station soon, but without airbases in Tanzania, it's coming from up the continent. I copy your sitrep, Ronin, but hold your position. Do not move in. Do not engage. Hold your position."

In front of them, four hundred meters away, Lemarti's convoy loaded up. Soon they would drive toward the road that hugged the shoreline and disappear into villages five or six kilometers up the coast. Alex's fingernails bit into her palm. Every meter her father traveled northeast took him farther away from the Delta team's planned LZ. And from her. She willed his convoy to sit tight, blow an engine, anything that would delay its departure.

A new voice cut through her comms—gravelly, urgent but composed. "Hunter Actual to Ronin. Blackbird has given us the sitrep. We're approaching the LZ from the southwest. Two mikes out."

Alex glanced up, alerted by a new sound. Against the twilight sky, the faint *thwap-thwap* of rotor blades grew audible.

CHAPTER 32

MWANZA AIRPORT, MWANZA, TANZANIA

Airport operations in Mwanza typically adhered to a strict daytime schedule, but exceptions could always be made for those willing to pay the right price. In this instance, a dedicated ground crew had been hastily assembled to fulfill the urgent demands of Leopard Group and their imposing Antonov AN-124. With the right financial incentive, men could always be encouraged to disrupt their routines. And so it was tonight, under the dim glow of the tarmac lights, that a scene driven by urgency and opportunity unfolded, where the night air buzzed with the promise of adventure and the thrill of last-minute logistical challenges.

Tarasenko stood at the top of the ramp at the back of the aircraft. He appreciated that this plane could kneel forward and the front cone could be raised on a hinge so vehicles and equipment could be driven or otherwise loaded aboard. Once at its destination, everything could be driven straight off the ramp at the back. Only Russians could be so ingenious.

He inhaled deeply. The night felt different here. Tanzania had a scent unlike any other place he had visited—more vibrant. The land, air, and water seemed to breathe as if they were alive. Did they object to humanity's presence? At times, it felt like they must; otherwise, why would everything in nature here strive so hard to rid themselves of it? No, Tanzania—all of Africa—was a place for survivors. One had to be made of sturdy stuff not to be overwhelmed by the challenges the natural world here could present. But Artemi Tarasenko was a survivor.

The Russian squad unloaded their kit and drove their trucks down the ramp onto the tarmac. Tarasenko's advance crew of four was already at their destination near the rebel camp, keeping an eye on things. He would receive a situation report from them soon. As Tarasenko waited, a Tanzanian Air Force officer approached. On his epaulets, he wore the rank insignia of a general.

"It's a clear night, Colonel," he said, addressing Tarasenko by his former military rank. Then, glancing up at the enormous airplane, he added, "Such a magnificent beast."

Tarasenko often used his military rank to communicate requests to government and other officials. It was more expedient to keep up such appearances as in this case.

"Yes, General. It made for a very smooth flight."

"I asked my men to check. The roads are clear to your destination. It's a ten-kilometer drive, which will take you twenty minutes."

"Excellent! I am most grateful."

"But this is Africa; you must always be aware of large animals and such that could wander onto the roads."

And such?

"Thank you for the warning, General. We will keep our eyes open."

* * *

OVER LAKE VICTORIA, BUTEMBA, TANZANIA

Sergeant First Class Mateo "Rook" Castillo flexed his gloved hand behind him against the Black Hawk's bulkhead, the vibration of the rotor blades thrumming through his bones like a second heartbeat. His PVS-31 night vision cast the world in spectral green—Lake Victoria's chop shimmered below, its waves fracturing moonlight into jagged shards. Across from him, Delta operators Viper, Ghost, and Doc sat motionless, their HK416 rifles angled toward closed cabin doors. His team's leader and two other operators filled the bench seats opposite.

The mission brief played in Rook's mind like a broken reel: *Insert at LZ Disciple. Locate and secure General Martel. Weapons tight unless compromised. If hostage rescue opportunity is lost, go to Abort Protocol: Operation Ironclad.*

The prospect of eliminating a friendly didn't sit well with him, but those were their lawful orders, and he would carry them out if it came to that.

"Hunter Actual, this is Blackbird. You're cleared for final approach. Winds light and variable, no hostile signals detected."

CIA Deputy Chief of Station Catherine "Harley" Harris's voice crackled through Rook's earpiece, all business, echoing from the operations center in Arusha. They had worked black ops together in the field before, prior to her becoming CIA's DCOS in Tanzania. She was a switched-on operator—cool as a cucumber. Now, there was no trace of the sardonic edge she had shown during the pre-mission conversation the team had with her a couple of hours earlier. She sounded tighter than a tripwire, detached and clinical.

Captain Elias "Striker" Voss raised three gloved fingers, then keyed his microphone.

"Copy, Blackbird. ETA three minutes." Striker's drawl betrayed none of the tension coiling in the cabin.

Rook knew they didn't have ISR overhead, so they'd have to stay alert despite her assurances that the landing zone appeared clear of hostiles. His gaze swept the shoreline. Scattered boulders hulked like sentinels in the shallows, their shadows stretching toward the beach code named Disciple. Mwanza's Rock City nickname lived up to its reputation.

Perfect kill zone, thought Rook. His thumb traced the safety selector on his rifle.

CHAPTER 33

OVER LAKE VICTORIA, BUTEMBA, TANZANIA

The MH-60M banked hard left, nose dipping as the Night Stalker pilot threaded between granite outcrops. Rook's NVGs flared—four light blooms near a collection of boulders two hundred meters inland.

"Striker, three o'clock. Movement in the rocks."

"Visual." The captain leaned into his harness. "Blackbird, confirm sweep on LZ."

Static hissed. Then Harley: "No visual right now, Hunter."

"Get ready," Striker told his men. "We might have company."

Viper muttered a Hail Mary in Spanish. Ghost tightened his grip on the fast-rope carabiner.

The rotors' whine dropped to a throaty growl as the Black Hawk flared over Lake Victoria's ink-black waters. Through his NVGs, LZ Disciple resolved into a jagged mosaic of granite boulders and wind-rippled sand. The four bodies they had seen off in the distance were no longer visible through the debris being kicked up by the rotors.

Striker flashed a gloved thumbs-up. Across the cabin, Viper tightened his sling while Ghost triple-checked his breaching charges. Standard pre-LZ rituals. Trust in the machine.

The lake rushed up to meet them. Rook's inner ear screamed as the pilot flared—standard combat insertion profile, rotor wash churning the shallows into a froth.

Rook dialed into the comms channel with Ronin. "Hunter Actual to Ronin. Blackbird has given us the sitrep. Be advised we're approaching the LZ from the southwest."

Thirty feet above the beach, the world erupted.

Twin fiery contrails lanced from the rocks—RPG-7s.

"INCOMING! RIGHT SIDE!"

Rook's training overrode instinct—his left hand locked on the bulkhead grip, his right pinning his rifle. The first rocket punched through the tail rotor with a ceramic scream. The second impacted the fuel cell behind the copilot's seat.

Fire engulfed the cabin.

"MAYDAY, MAYDAY—BIRD'S GOING IN!"

The Black Hawk yawed violently. Rook's harness snapped taut as the floor tilted. Something smacked him across his face and he tasted copper, felt wetness sheet his cheek. Outside the window, the lake inverted itself as they dropped out of the sky in a yawning arc. Sky became water, water became fire. Darkness. Cold. Pressure. He sensed he was underwater more than he knew it. Then his crash survival training kicked in.

Rook kicked toward fractured moonlight. Pieces of the sky fell in on him—but it wasn't the sky. It was metallic pieces of the helo's fractured airframe. He wrestled free of whatever held him and broke the surface beside burning wreckage. Gasping and sputtering, he fought to draw in big lungfuls of air.

Control your panic, Rook. Slow it down. Breathe.

He scanned his immediate vicinity, turning his body in the water. Ghost tread water nearby, Viper, mostly limp, hanging onto his shoulders.

"Striker?" Rook rasped, inquiring after the team leader.

Ghost shook his head. Doc's head broke the surface, gasping for air.

"You good? Doc . . . you good?"

Doc settled down and slowed his breathing. "Yup," he stammered between coughs.

Rook looked around again. Ghost, Doc, and Viper were alive,

but Viper was in rough shape. He didn't know where the rest of his team was—Striker, Hammer, and Hawkeye. He kept looking. The pilot and copilot were likely killed when the second RPG hit near the cockpit.

Three KIA. Probably the pilots, too. Four alive.

The beach loomed thirty meters through fuel-slicked waves.

"Let's go," he said, but his fellow survivors didn't need prompting.

Rook and Ghost each hooked an arm under Viper's plate carrier and began the swim, every stroke igniting fresh agony in Rook's ribs. He must have bounced off the wall or door as he was thrown around. Hell, they had crashed. He was lucky to be alive at all. As they made for the beach, the lake drank their curses.

They crawled ashore, weakened and wounded, armor dripping. Rook collapsed beside a guano-encrusted boulder. Most of their weapons were gone, including his M249 SAW, the squad automatic weapon he used to lay down a barrage of suppressive fire, but a few miraculously survived—three HK416 rifles and Viper's Glock pistol. Everything else—comms, med kits, NVG batteries—lay at the bottom of Lake Victoria.

"Comm check." Rook slapped his drowned radio, the only one that wasn't on the bottom of the lake. Tapped his earpiece. "Blackbird, Hunter Actual. We are down. Repeat, bird is down."

Nothing.

Ghost spat lake water. "Antenna's fried—or worse. We're dark."

Doc probed the shrapnel wound above Rook's eye, hands shaking as he applied pressure and a bandage. Viper's breathing rattled, one hand clutching his chest.

"Phoenix Protocol?" he asked.

Adapt. Improvise.

Rook nodded. The Phoenix Protocol was a plan of action employed by Delta Force operators after a catastrophic mission failure or malfunction. It involved salvaging materials from downed aircraft, equipment, or vehicles and creating a beacon of some sort—a visible or thermal signature that rescuers could target. He inventoried their status: four remaining operators, one badly injured, no comms, no spare ammo.

"Beacon requires—"

Ghost jabbed a finger at the burning wreckage as secondary explosions lit the shallows. "Requires swimming back to that?" Then he pointed farther up the beach. "You see the fucking patrol?"

Two hundred meters away, four figures walked toward them as if enjoying a leisurely stroll. The shooters spread out in a grove of trees and knee-high grass, advancing toward the shoreline. The last update they'd received from Ronin was that Leopard Group had arrived at the airport five klicks away. That's probably who made up their welcoming party. They suspected they might have company, but JSOC and the Op Center in Arusha hadn't picked up on it. Unusually, they had to forgo ISR in favor of rapid deployment. ISR would come later.

As well, reports were that the general was about to be moved, and they couldn't afford to lose him. They'd seen that movie too many times before—hostages moved multiple times, teams always chasing ghosts and never catching them. The specter of success looming, but never attained.

And Ironclad—the plan to kill General Martel if it seemed he would fall into the hands of other hostile forces—loomed unappealing now as well. The decision to proceed this time had cost them, but they had been aware of the risks.

"I can rig a visual signal with the pilot's survival kit," said Rook. "I saw it behind his seat during insertion."

"That's twenty meters out in a firestorm! Then twenty back! I think the burning aircraft is a beacon unto itself, Rook."

"There's classified tech on board. We have to make sure the bird gets completely scuttled," Rook said, but he was already moving.

The lake numbed him to the marrow. He dove under the fuel slick, the Black Hawk's carcass glowing like a hellish chandelier. Bullets sparked off the fuselage—Leopard Group's beach patrol tightening the noose. Ghost returned fire from behind cover, keeping the hostiles occupied and off-target.

Breathe. Move. Ignore the dead.

The survival kit dangled from its melted bracket. Rook wrenched it free as a secondary explosion rocked the airframe.

Surface. Breathe. Swim.

Doc had Viper propped upright when he returned. Ghost kept watch, rifle steady in his hands, laying down suppressive fire periodically.

"How bad?" Rook asked.

"Collapsed lung, TBI," Doc answered.

Rook was the team's automatic rifleman, but he was also the team's second medic. Viper appeared lethargic, with his head slumped to the side, yet he remained responsive to voice commands and could still move with assistance if necessary. *Traumatic brain injury*, Doc had said.

"Hopefully just concussed."

Doc nodded.

Ghost kept watch with his rifle pointed off the beach, waiting for an opportunity and a target. It didn't take long, and he dropped a shooter at a hundred and twenty meters.

Rook tapped the watertight pouch he had retrieved. "Got C-4 in here." He unzipped it. "Timer. Wire."

"You're not serious."

"I didn't swim out there for nothing. Burn the bird. Smoke and light will signal Ronin in case they're blind and can't see this. Scuttle the Black Hawk."

"Or bring every shooter in Tanzania."

He met Ghost's stare. "Got a better idea? We're already on their dance card."

They worked fast. Ghost helped him rig a device, then provided cover for Rook as he swam back out to the semi-submerged airframe of the Black Hawk. He had to move Striker's body out of the way so he could wedge the plastic explosive in the fuel line of the second auxiliary tank. He set the timer for five minutes, then swam back.

Back behind the rock, Ghost gave him that look.

"What? No easy day, remember?" said Rook.

The detonation lit the night. Flames clawed at low-hanging fog, casting their shadows giant against the rocks.

"Now we wait," Ghost said, scanning the tree line.

"Now we fight," Rook snapped, grabbing a branch from a gnarled tree as he stood.

Another RPG team would come. They always did.

"Doc, stay here with Viper. Ghost, on me."

They hadn't moved twenty meters. "Contact right!" Ghost shouted.

The men advanced diagonally toward two fighters who had come within fifty meters. Bullets ricocheted off nearby rocks. Ghost fired first, followed by Rook. The two hostiles fell. They advanced, making sure they stayed down for good, and relieved them of their weapons and spare mags. The last of the four shooters popped out and Rook took shrapnel from a ricochet to his arm before silencing him with a volley that zipped up his torso, punching holes through the Russian's ballistic armor.

"You good?" asked Ghost.

"Good," Rook lied.

"Shit, let me see that." Ghost reached into his pocket, pulled out another damp combat dressing, and expertly applied it over the wound on Rook's forearm. "There, now you won't bleed out."

"Yeah, now I'll die a slow death from a parasitic infection from the lake."

"Probably."

"What do you notice?" Rook asked, looking down at the dead men.

"They're three ugly white dudes." Ghost, not unironically, was Black.

Rook nodded. "Eastern Euro, probably Russian."

"Leopard Group."

"We kind of knew it, but nice to have our biases confirmed. Come on. Let's go before their reinforcements arrive."

They regrouped with Doc and Viper down along the shoreline.

Rook indicated out to the water. "I'm going to bring them in."

Ghost's jaw muscles clenched, but he nodded. The alternative was untenable.

"I'll go with you."

"No way, Ghost. Cover me."

The lake had delivered most of the men closer to shore on the gentle waves. He'd only had to go all the way back to the downed helicopter to recover Striker, his team leader. Ten minutes later, the bodies of their three fallen teammates—Captain Elias "Striker" Voss, Hammer, their breaching specialist, and Hawkeye, the team sniper, as well as the two Night Stalker pilots—were ashore. He and Ghost laid the bodies beneath a copse of trees for recovery later. Although Viper was a master sergeant and the senior operations NCO serving as second-in-command, he was injured and effectively out of the fight. So Rook, sergeant first class, assumed command of the team.

Behind the orange glow of the burning Black Hawk, a faint line of pink light hovered over the horizon. Soon it would be dawn.

"Let's move," he said. "That burning helo should have caught the attention of our CIA friends. But it's going to draw a bunch of anxious Russians this way, too."

The four-man team moved northeast along a line fifty meters inland from the beach.

No easy day, he repeated to himself, a smile tracing across his lips.

CHAPTER 34

OBSERVATION POINT SEAGULL, BUTEMBA, TANZANIA

Caleb's voice sounded bleak in her earpiece: "Blackbird, Hunter is down!"

Alex had witnessed the events unfold in real time, but Caleb's sitrep still sent chills down her spine. She scanned the beach, initially spotting only two survivors. Those operators had engaged four fighters, then returned to the water's edge to set off explosive charges on the Black Hawk—in principle, a signaling beacon. The light bloom in her NVGs from the burning Black Hawk made it difficult to discern additional details. There might have been more survivors; perhaps there were not. But Hunter was radio silent, either by choice or due to a failure in their communications systems. In any case, the lack of communication compelled her and her teammates to take action.

Now, Ronin faced two competing priorities: rescuing what remained of the Hunter element and losing situational awareness on her father, or pursuing her father—still in the custody of Lemarti and his crew—and effectively abandoning any survivors of the Delta Force hostage rescue team to their own devices.

Who had attacked Hunter? She couldn't tell. She could see them through her optics, but their physical features were obscured. They might have been part of Lemarti's militia, but more likely, they were an advance team from Tarasenko's Leopard Group.

"They're not answering on comms," replied Harley.

"Copy that," Caleb said. "I count two survivors, but we don't have a good visual."

"We'll have to assume the rest of the team is down for good." Harley's voice crackled through the encrypted channel, sharp as shattered glass: "With most of Hunter down, you're the tip of the spear now, Ronin. Shift mission priority—intercept the PFA convoy. Recover Martel."

Caleb's eyes met hers. "Shouldn't we grab Hunter on the way?"

Maybe he thought Alex wouldn't approve of that course of action, but Harley made it so they didn't have to weigh their options.

"Negative. JSOC will send a QRF. Your tactical priority is to recover the general. We can't lose him." Then, emphatically: "Viking," she said, using Caleb's CIA call sign. "Do not lose Condor."

Hearing Harley's order, Alex could barely contain her excitement. That's what she had wanted from the very beginning—to go kinetic and bring her dad home. She'd had enough of waiting for others to do what she and her team should have been doing all along. Childish vow or not, he was her father, her responsibility, and a premium intelligence asset to the country.

Her gloved hand tightened around her M38's pistol grip, knuckles bleaching to the color of sun-bleached bone. Below OP Seagull, two armed men scoured the beach, looking to finish off Delta's survivors who had made their way inland and north. To the west, the Black Hawk's wreck smoldered in Lake Victoria's shallows, its dying heat signature flickering on her scope's display. Hunter's survivors—now numbering four—made their way away from the crash site. One appeared badly injured. They huddled behind a boulder bracketed by converging Russian fighters, four in total.

Her breath fogged the scope's ocular lens. For three heartbeats, she let herself be eleven again—the girl who'd carved a blood pact into her palm with a hunting knife, who'd believed oaths could armor loved ones against the world's chaos. Then the professional reasserted control, parsing the dilemma through doctrine. Her assessment: recovery of Hunter element was high-risk due to open terrain and proximity of enemy forces. Martel extraction equaled low probability of success at this moment—moving convoy, unknown defenses. Martel's capture, though, risked exposure of Aegis AI to Leopard Group's backers, most likely the Chinese.

"Shooter—" Caleb's verbal nudge cut deeper than the serrations of Alex's combat knife.

"Boss?" Her index finger hovered above the DMR's trigger. Through the SIG Sauer scope, a Delta operator cradled a bandaged arm. Blood seeped through his pressure dressing, black as crude oil and glistening under night vision. Another seemed to be slumped down, unable to bear his own weight.

Leave no man behind.

The creed wasn't just doctrine; it was DNA. She'd carved it into her palm at the age of eleven, a blood oath sealed with her father's Ka-Bar. Now the blade's ghost cut deeper than the Taliban shrapnel embedded in her spine. It was a promise that bound Tier 1 operators into a single organism. She'd lived it at Al-Tanf, watching teammates loop back and rush into ISIS mortar fire for a wounded comms specialist. To break that covenant was to unravel the very fabric of SpecOps.

"We need to move out before we lose that convoy and the general's gone for good."

She swung her rifle to reconnoiter the fleeing vehicles. Lemarti's convoy was accelerating northeast, a boy's face visible in the Hilux's window. Her father's voice echoed in her memory, calm as a Range Fifteen firearms instructor: *Prioritize the mission, Allie. Always the mission.*

The contradiction burned like thermite: *General Martel the asset* demanded immediate action. *David Martel the father* screamed for intervention. But *Hunter element* was dead and dying on foreign soil.

Harley's voice sliced through her neural haze: "Ronin—acknowledge your orders."

Her scope's magnification dialed in tighter—Lemarti's red *shuka* fluttered in the truck's window. The warlord's laughter seemed to ripple across the valley, carried on diesel fumes and broken promises. Behind him, a boy clung to an AK-47 rifle too large for his frame, eyes as wide as a spooked colt's.

Alex's reticle drifted between two targets—Lemarti's grinning profile in the convoy versus shapes moving against a Tier 1 operator, pain contorting his face. She became acutely aware of her rifle's balance, its heft, as if it were begging her to engage.

Her ethical calculus was simple yet complex: Save four proven operators for an immediate tactical gain, or gamble on retrieving one compromised general for his strategic potential and sacrifice Hunter?

Her thumb flicked the safety off.

Blood of my blood.

"Caleb"—her voice emerged steadier than she felt—"request split team. You, Moose, and Rocky suppress hostiles and rescue Hunter at the crash site. I'll take Kurtz and Santiago to intercept the convoy."

Caleb's pause stretched into eternity. "Denied, Alex. We stay together, consolidate forces. We'll rescue Hunter first, then we'll get Condor. We'll get your dad, Alex."

"But Harley's orders—"

"We can't abandon Hunter."

The four hostiles fanned out, closing in on the remaining members of Hunter. Time crystallized. Later, she'd recall the moment as synaptic lightning:

Oath versus creed.

Daughter versus operator.

"I'll make it easier for us," she whispered.

"What?"

Her rifle spoke first—77-grain OTM rounds that shredded the flesh and bone of the enemy soldiers advancing on the Hunter element.

Four shots. Four breaths. Four bodies crumpled mid-stride.

"Crash site's clear!" she barked. "Let's move!"

* * *

LAKE VICTORIA SHORELINE, TANZANIA

Rook tasted copper and regret. Viper's labored breaths fogged the air—pneumothorax, Doc had diagnosed. Five KIA—three teammates and two Night Stalkers lying dead on foreign shores. The math never lied.

"Black Hawk is scuttled," Ghost muttered, watching the helicopter's carcass burn. "Now what?"

Rook reloaded an AK-47 with scavenged magazines. "We stalk north. Link up with the Agency team."

"Assuming they're coming."

"They're coming." Rook's faith felt borrowed. Langley's playbook favored assets over allies. "And even if not, we finish the mission."

Gunfire erupted inland—controlled bursts of 5.56 NATO. American.

"Ronin's here." Rook grinned.

* * *

BUTEMBA OUTSKIRTS, TANZANIA

The ridge trembled under Alex's boots as she sprinted northeast, Kurtz and Santiago flanking her as they raced to keep up. Behind them, Caleb, Moose, and Rocky followed. They made a beeline for the nearest collection of houses, situated between them and the rebel compound, Objective Forge. Her father's convoy dwindled in the distance, dust pluming behind the Toyotas.

"Don't worry." Santiago smiled, breathing deeply as he ran. "We'll find them again."

She wished she felt as sure.

They slowed to a brisk walk along a side street on the outskirts of the coastal village of Butemba. The sky glowing orange behind OP Seagull cast them in an unmistakable glow that they couldn't shake. Their civilian clothing might have helped them blend in better if not for the distinctive impression left by their weapons and gear.

All around them, dogs barked. A rooster crowed. A car traveled past them along the road, its lone occupant giving them a wide berth.

"We don't have long," said Kurtz, watching the car like a hawk. His rifle was slung casually behind him, his hand on his sidearm, as if to say, *Nothing to see here.* Sweat ran along the underside of his square-set jaw. "What's the plan, Alex?"

They were standing in the center of the road next to a Ford Everest, a big four-door SUV.

"We need wheels," she replied through gulps of air.

"No problem," said Rocky, arriving with the others. He reached into his pack and retrieved a tablet computer. He plugged a small wire array into its port and waved it around like a divining rod.

"You better be quick," she added.

"If I had a nickel for every time a beautiful woman said that . . ."

"Hurry up already."

"That, too."

Moments later, the locks popped open.

"One sec," he said, hopping into the right-hand-drive vehicle's driver's seat.

A second later, the engine roared to life.

"There. It'll start now without a fob."

"Wait," Caleb said. Alex shot him a look, one that said *WTF, boss!* "One won't do."

Within three minutes, they had three trucks: two Fords and a Land Cruiser.

"Rocky, you and Moose with me. We're going for Hunter." He pointed to Alex. "You three find the general. From here out, you're call sign Shadow. Got it?"

She nodded. "What about not splitting up?" she asked.

"Improvise, adapt, and overcome, Shooter." He smiled. "We're not leaving Hunter behind. You go after Condor. Don't fuck it up."

CHAPTER 35

PFA COMPOUND, BUTEMBA, TANZANIA

Alex and Santiago climbed into their truck with Kurtz behind the wheel. Their stolen Toyota Land Cruiser fishtailed around a hairpin turn in the dirt. Kurtz white-knuckled the wheel, dodging potholes that cratered the road like mortar strikes. Santiago rode shotgun, his tablet balanced on his knees.

"Turn right up here." They rounded the corner.

"Shit," Alex said. Ahead, the road would pass right outside the gate where the convoy carrying the general had exited Forge.

"What now?" asked Kurtz.

"Just drive past. We have to get to the next cross street."

They approached the gate, constructed out of two-by-fours framing panels of chain-link fencing and chicken wire. As they passed, a smattering of men milled about near the opening of the Nissen hut. Women and children walked between the tents and buildings. Near the opening of the main building, Alex saw a woman wearing a lime-green skirt with a distinctive red-and-yellow kanga cloth tied around her shoulders. She was sure it was the same woman she had seen beside Lemarti as they were loading the general into the trucks.

"Wait!" she said.

"What? You want me to stop?" asked Kurtz.

"No, sorry. Keep going but pull over up ahead."

"What did you see, Alex?" asked Santiago.

"That woman by the door . . ."

"What about her?"

"I saw her earlier."

"So?"

"She was with the group's leader when they loaded the general into the trucks."

"Alex," said Santiago. "We're going to lose your father's convoy. And once they get into the fishing villages along the coast, there's no telling where they could get to. They could even take him somewhere by boat, and then we'd really be screwed."

"I know," she said. "But we're running blind just chasing their shadow. Pull over."

"What? Didn't you just agree?"

"Yeah, but I have a better plan."

The first light of dawn crept over the horizon, bathing the rebel camp in a pale golden glow. The haze of smoke from the dying embers of the central fire pit hung low over the tents, mingling with the faint mist that clung to the ground. The camp was quieter now, its energy subdued after a long night of drinking and boasting. A few rebels still lingered near the fire, their voices low and sluggish as they passed around a bottle of something strong enough to strip paint.

Alex crouched in the underbrush just beyond the camp's perimeter, her Glock secure in its holster hidden under her shirt, a scarf pulled low over her face. The stolen Toyota was parked a hundred meters back, hidden among the trees where Kurtz and Santiago waited, ready to move if things went south.

She scanned the camp. The lime-green skirt caught her eye again—a vibrant splash of color against the drab backdrop of canvas and dirt. The woman wearing it moved between the tents with quiet efficiency, a tin basin balanced on her hip.

"That's her," Alex whispered into her comms.

Kurtz's voice crackled softly in her ear. "You're sure?"

"She was with Lemarti when they loaded my father into that truck. I'm going in."

"Copy that," Kurtz said. "We'll be ready."

Alex slipped the earpiece out and tucked it into her pocket. This was a solo mission now. If she didn't come back, Kurtz and Santiago would know what to do.

The camp stirred lazily as dawn broke fully over the horizon. A few guards patrolled near the edges, their AKs slung casually over their shoulders as they yawned and stretched. Others were just waking up, emerging from their living quarters with bleary eyes, grumbling curses.

Alex moved carefully through the camp, keeping to the shadows cast by the rising sun. Her stolen tunic and loose trousers helped her blend in, but she kept her head down and her movements deliberate, avoiding eye contact with anyone who might question her presence.

The woman in the lime-green skirt stopped near a tent at the edge of the camp, setting down her basin and wiping her hands on her kanga cloth. Alex waited until no one was looking before slipping closer, keeping low and using a stack of crates for cover.

"Hey," Alex said softly when she was close enough.

The woman froze, her head snapping up like a startled bird. Her eyes darted around before landing on Alex.

"Who are you?" the woman hissed, stepping back instinctively.

"I'm not here to hurt you," she said quickly, raising a hand in what she hoped was a calming gesture. "My name is Alex. I need your help."

The woman's eyes narrowed suspiciously. "You shouldn't be here. If they see you—"

"They won't," Alex interrupted. "I'm looking for my father—the man they took yesterday."

The woman's expression flickered with recognition before hardening again. "I don't know what you're talking about."

"Yes, you do." Alex stepped closer, lowering her voice further. "You were walking beside Lemarti when they put him in the truck. You're his woman—you know where my father is."

The woman glanced nervously toward the center of camp, where Lemarti's men were beginning to stir. Her hands fidgeted with the edge of her kanga cloth as if trying to decide whether to trust Alex or call for help.

"I am not that pig's woman. If I tell you anything . . . ," the woman trailed off, shaking her head. "They'll kill me."

Alex wanted to make it personal. "What's your name?"

"Adiya," she replied.

"They won't know the information came from you, Adiya," Alex promised. "I'll make sure of it."

The woman studied her for a long moment before finally sighing and motioning for Alex to follow her behind one of the tents. They crouched low behind a stack of supplies covered with tarps.

"We are dead if they find me talking to you."

"Please, you have to help me find my dad. He's all I have. He's a good man."

Adiya seemed to soften. "He seemed an honorable man."

"Then help me."

"They took him to a village six kilometers from here," the woman whispered hurriedly. "Over the river and into the fishing village along the shore where they keep the boats. He has another place—a factory—next to the water by the docks."

"How many men are guarding him?" Alex asked.

"Eighteen," the woman replied without hesitation. "And tomorrow . . . they will take him across the lake."

Alex's stomach tightened at those words. "Why?"

The woman hesitated before answering, her voice barely audible now. "They want to know what he knows."

"Who does?" Alex pressed.

"*Wachinku,*" Adiya said bitterly, using the local slang for Chinese. "They paid for him—paid Lemarti."

Alex clenched her jaw, forcing herself to stay calm despite the surge of anger rising within her. She had expected something like this, but hearing it confirmed made it all too real.

"Thank you, Adiya."

The woman paused a moment to decide if she should tell the

stranger. "Do not thank me. If Lemarti or Desmond find out I helped you . . ."

"They won't," Alex said firmly. "Stay out of sight today—and if you can leave this place tonight, do it."

Adiya gave a small nod but didn't look convinced.

Alex turned back. "Can you get to the market in the village?"

"What?"

"The market . . . can you get there?"

Panic flashed across the woman's face. Maybe this was a mistake. Alex worried she might suddenly bolt from her.

"Adiya, you must know more. You must know about the place they've taken my father. If we help you, if we take you away from here, someplace safe, a home far away, money, whatever—"

"I used to be a teacher," she said.

"We can do that," Alex said. "We can set you up somewhere with a teaching job again. Here in Tanzania or anywhere you want . . . Can you help me get my father back?"

A slow nod, then a smile.

Alex had to figure it out on the fly. "Okay, go into town. Wear the same skirt and scarf. Someone will find you. Can you be there at noon?"

She nodded. "But how will I know to trust them?"

"They will say to you, 'Alex says hello.'"

Alex slipped back into the shadows and ditched the clothes she stole that she had pulled over her jeans and shirt. She made her way out of the camp, but she couldn't shake Adiya's words: *They want to know what he knows.* The secrets General Martel held were valuable enough for international buyers—and dangerous enough to cost him his life if she didn't act fast.

Kurtz was leaning against the hood of the truck when Alex emerged from the trees, his rifle slung in front of him and his eyes sharp as ever.

"Well?" he asked as she approached.

"Six klicks to go," Alex said grimly as she climbed into the passenger seat. "Over a river and into a fishing village."

"And then?" Santiago asked from behind the wheel.

"Eighteen militia plus Lemarti and his sidekick are guarding my father."

"Maybe we'll be able to take them by surprise before they make it there."

"And what? Hit them with a PIT maneuver along the road? We're badly outnumbered and too outgunned for that. No, we have to hit them at night. Before sunup. They move him in the morning."

The early morning hours were the best time to launch a raid.

Kurtz smirked faintly as he climbed into the back seat. "Sounds like a helluva way to start our day."

"Oh, and I have something for Harley to take care of."

"Oh?"

Alex didn't respond right away as Santiago started the engine and guided them back onto a dirt road leading away from camp. Her mind was already racing ahead to what lay waiting for them. Ideally, she would prefer to hit Lemarti and his crew at night, under the cover of darkness—darkness that would be disorienting to an unaccustomed and ill-equipped fighter. But despite all the hours left in the day to think and plan—maybe too many—how little time they had left would come down to what Lemarti was up to.

"Where to, Alex?"

"We can't hit them now, but I sure as hell don't want to lose them, either. Let's get up there and get eyes on Lemarti's crew."

As they drove, she thought about the gamble she'd taken talking to Lemarti's woman. She could betray her. Double-cross them. It wouldn't be the first time or the last. Hopefully, Adiya had plenty of information to share.

CHAPTER 36

LAKE VICTORIA SHORELINE, BUTEMBA, TANZANIA

Rook tasted blood and diesel fumes. Someone—Ronin, most likely—had eliminated four more Russian fighters who had advanced on them out of the twilight a short while ago, before he and his men had a chance to open fire. Now, his cracked NVGs showed six heat signatures advancing through the scrub—Leopard Group mercs in Russian body armor, AK-12s sweeping the shoreline. Behind them, a Soviet-era BTR-80 armored personnel carrier idled, its 14.5-millimeter KPVT heavy machine gun tracking the boulder where Ghost and Doc sheltered Viper.

"Fucking Leopard Group—the gift that keeps on giving!"

"Three o'clock—suppressing!" Ghost barked, dumping half a mag into the advancing mercs. Rook counted the shots—controlled bursts, conserving ammo. They'd scavenged 120 rounds from dead fighters. Not enough.

The BTR's machine gun roared, stitching the granite with fist-sized craters. Viper stirred, his breath a wet rattle. Doc pressed a fresh combat gauze to the sucking chest wound.

"Stay with me, brother. Cavalry's coming."

Rook's eardrums throbbed. No comms. No extraction. Just the lake at their backs and a Russian kill team closing in.

Then—engines.

He flipped his NVGs up. With dawn came the light.

A Ford Everest fishtailed onto the beach, tires spraying sand.

Moose leaned out the passenger window, an Mk 48 machine gun braced against the roof. "Light 'em up!"

Rocky didn't wait for the truck to stop. He bailed mid-skid, rolling behind a termite mound with an M320 grenade launcher, and targeted the hostile's vehicle. The first 40-millimeter high-explosive round he fired arced over the Russian BTR, detonating in a fireball that lit the mercenaries' flank.

"Hunter—friendly front!" Caleb's voice carried over gunfire as he advanced, his HK416 rifle spitting controlled pairs. A Leopard Group merc crumpled, his armor shattered by 77-grain bullets from Caleb's rifle.

Rook's laugh was a hoarse bark. "Took you long enough!"

Moose's Mk 48 chewed through the BTR's tires. "Welcome to Africa, motherfuckers!"

The mercs pivoted, caught between Ronin's hammer and Hunter's anvil. Ghost flanked left with Viper's Glock, putting two rounds into a shooter's knee before finishing him with a stomp to the throat. Rocky reloaded his M320, eyes cold behind smeared camo paint.

"Fire in the hole!"

The grenade caught the BTR's open hatch. The explosion peeled steel like tinfoil, smoke boiling from its hull. A merc stumbled out, uniform ablaze. Moose cut him down mid-scream.

Rook collapsed against a rock, his adrenaline leaching away. His forearm bandage seeped crimson. "Told you . . . No easy day."

Caleb tossed him a fresh mag for his M4. "Save the quips for the debrief."

"Hey, Viper!" Doc called to Viper, but he was no longer responding. "His pneumo's gone tension."

"Shit!" said Rook.

Doc worked on Viper, slamming a decompression needle into his chest.

"What's happening?" asked Caleb.

A few tense moments later: "Pneumothorax is stabilized. He'll live if we get him to a combat support hospital, but he needs the CSH soon." He pronounced it *cash*.

Ghost ejected a spent magazine. "CSH's a pipe dream. We need exfil—now."

The radio on Caleb's belt crackled. "Ronin Actual, this is Shadow. You copy?"

Alex's voice. Caleb keyed the mic. "Go for Ronin."

"General's convoy has arrived at a location four klicks northeast of your position. About twenty enemy fighters. They're dismounting in a little fishing village. We're moving to intercept—need backup yesterday."

Caleb exchanged looks with Rook.

The Delta operator grinned through bloodied teeth. "I like her style."

Caleb keyed his mike. "Negative, Shadow. Wait for the band to get together again."

His earpiece buzzed again: "Convoy's stopped at grid Sierra-Charlie-Niner. We're at the lake. I think they might be transferring the general to a boat. If they put him on a boat, we'll lose him for good. Get your asses up here—we're going loud in five!"

"Negative, Shadow! Wait for—" Static. "Shooter, I know you can hear me. Do not engage. Wait for reinforcements!"

Moose racked his Mk 48's charging handle. "She's not waiting."

"Then neither do we."

Rook said, "You heard the lady. Let's go hunting."

They stripped the dead mercs for ammo and comms. Moose rigged the BTR's remains with C-4—"A little show for the local tourism board!"—while Rocky and Ghost carried Viper to one of the Fords.

Rook clasped Caleb's forearm. "Owe you a drink."

"Make it two. And tell Viper he's buying."

The teams rolled out—Hunter's survivors in the lead, Ronin flanking. Dawn bled gold across Lake Victoria, but the horizon ahead boiled with storm clouds.

Alone in their truck, Rook said to Ghost, "Hear that? They're loading Condor onto a boat."

"She said she *thinks* they're loading him onto a boat."

"We can't take that risk. We have to assume they are. Fire up your tablet."

Ghost pulled the computer out of his pack. "Are we really going to do this—take out Condor—kill the general?"

"You know our orders. Ironclad comes from the very top."

An overhead image popped up onscreen. The crosshairs rested on their vehicle as they drove up the lake road, the Reaper's sensors having locked in on the signal from the tablet. Ghost manipulated the display as he hunted for Condor. He zoomed out using his thumb and forefinger until he found the village, then pinched back in.

"Got it," he reported. "Looks like Condor and that other cat are parked beside a dock next to a boat, Rook." He held up the display so Rook could see.

"If they get on that boat, arm the missile."

Rook could feel Ghost's stare burning his neck. He turned to him. "You don't have to like it. Just do it. That's an order."

Ghost went back to his screen.

The trucks fishtailed onto a coastal road, engines screaming. Somewhere ahead, Alex was planning to charge into hell. And they'd promised to meet her there.

But there was always plan B.

CHAPTER 37

MWANZA AIRPORT, TANZANIA

Artemi Tarasenko crushed his cigarette against the Antonov's cargo ramp, the embers hissing as they struck pooled jet fuel. Dawn painted the tarmac in bruised hues, the acrid stench of burning rubber mingling with woodsmoke drifting from distant brushfires. He would have preferred the fragrance of the roasting coffee inside his operation in Okavango but today was a day for a different business. The gentility of a fine morning beverage would have to wait.

Behind him, fourteen Leopard Group mercenaries prepped Czech CZ BREN rifles and GP-25 grenade launchers, their movements synchronized by decades of muscle memory imprinted by war.

As the Tanzanian Air Force flag officer receded into the hangar, Anton Kovalchuk approached, tablet in hand, his bald head glistening under the hangar's flickering fluorescents. "Advance teams report: first four operators eliminated the Black Hawk. Ten more engaged Delta survivors at the crash site. All presumed KIA."

Tarasenko's jaw tightened. Fourteen men lost—almost half his force—to a wounded Delta squad, and nothing to show for it. Amateurs. He stared at the tablet's casualty list. "Ultimately, this is Lemarti's doing," he said at last. "That Maasai rat sold us out to the Chinese. If not for his treachery, this would have been over yesterday." The betrayal stung more than the tactical loss. One's wounded pride could be an effective motivator. "A simple decapitation strike against the Americans' Project Aegis—that's all this was supposed to be. Kill the general. It would have set the program back and sent a message that it's time America got out of Africa completely. Nobody wants them here. They don't have the stomach to do what needs to be done anymore, and the whole world knows it. When will they get the message?"

Kovalchuk nodded. "Our intercepts confirm he offered Martel to the Chinese in exchange for Belt and Road Initiative mining rights. It seems our Maasai warrior friend wants to diversify and legitimize his operation. The Chinese are holed up in Dar es Salaam, waiting."

"Waiting for what?" Tarasenko growled, his words as sharp as a wolf circling a bloodied carcass. He snatched the satellite phone, stabbing at a contact labeled Dragon.

* * *

CHINESE MINISTRY OF STATE SECURITY SAFE HOUSE, DAR ES SALAAM

Colonel Zhang Wei sipped *pu-erh* tea from a celadon cup, its fragrance clashing with the safe house's mildew. Through bulletproof windows, the Indian Ocean churned slate-gray under a cloud-choked dawn. His aide, Lieutenant Liu Qiang, monitored encrypted traffic from Butemba—Lemarti's frantic updates, Delta's scrambled SOS calls, and Tarasenko's cargo jet idling on Mwanza's runway.

The satellite phone buzzed. Zhang smiled. Right on time.

"Wei."

Tarasenko's voice crackled, the venom in it thinly veiled. "Your pet warlord has made us both look like fools, Colonel."

Zhang swirled his tea. "You more than me. But nevertheless, Lemarti serves his purpose. As did you."

"He was supposed to kill Martel, not auction him to the highest bidder. Now the Americans swarm like hornets."

"And yet," Zhang said, savoring the Russian's frustration, "you called. Why? How does my arrangement with the Maasai prince concern you?"

A pause. Tarasenko's breath hissed like a leaking airlock. "Let me retrieve Martel. I will deliver him to you. In exchange, you sanction Lemarti's elimination. He can't be of any value to you anymore."

"On the contrary, Artemi, he creates the chaos that allows us to look kind and generous by comparison. He serves China's interests still."

"I suspect that the fallout from this venture will scar your reputation, once the Tanzanian government knows who's actually behind it."

"Are you threatening me?"

"Not at all, comrade. Merely warning you that Lemarti has bitten off more than he can chew, and it is you who will choke on the little rat pieces."

Zhang considered this. There was truth in the Russian's words. "What do you want."

"I will deliver the general and kill Lemarti. You can call it a public relations operation."

"And what will we give you in consideration of these generous services rendered?"

"I want the additional mining contracts you have reserved for China in the west region and in Okavango, for which you will receive a twenty-five percent cut."

Liu Qiang raised an eyebrow. Zhang silenced him with a glance. "Why should we renegotiate?"

"Because I'll burn the general's mind to ash before letting Beijing crack it unless you agree." Tarasenko's threat hung between static cracks. "Or you get him alive and intact. Your choice."

Zhang traced a finger over the teacup's rim. Pragmatism prevailed—the People's Liberation Army needed the Aegis AI's core intact. And even if they shut down the hardware systems, MSS extraction techniques would be able to reverse-engineer the code from what Martel kept locked away in his head.

"Fifty."

"Thirty-five and not a yuan more. I'll put Lemarti's head on a pike and retrieve the general. No interference. And your drones clear our path to his compound in the fishing village."

Outside, monsoon winds rattled the safe house's shutters. Zhang watched a dhow struggle against the waves. "The Ministry does not normally bargain with hired guns."

"No?" Tarasenko chuckled. "Then explain why your Wolf Warriors haven't stormed that camp. You need deniability. I am deniability."

Zhang set down his cup. "Lemarti dies and we get to debrief Martel. But no drones."

Debrief. Ha! "Done."

The line died. Liu Qiang frowned. "He'll betray us."

"Of course." Zhang reopened Lemarti's latest message—a demand for armored transport to the Chinese embassy. "But by then, one of them will have delivered the general to us. Martel's secrets will be ours. Let the Russians and terrorists bleed each other dry."

* * *

MWANZA AIRPORT, TANZANIA

Tarasenko tossed the satellite phone to Kovalchuk. "Have the men get ready. We move in ten."

The deputy hesitated. "The Chinese will double-cross us."

"And we'll triple-cross them. That's business. Now that this debacle has gone from simple execution to rebel militia kidnapping, it might be impossible to effectively mine the data and codes from the American system. But perhaps GRU's Sandworm unit will be able to dig into the Aegis servers and all will not have been lost."

"We should have perhaps considered doing that first—" He almost caught himself before criticizing the Leopard Group commander. But didn't quite stop in time.

Tarasenko strapped on an armored vest, its GOST Level 6 plates clanking.

"Be careful, Anton. Our unit strength has been significantly depleted. We could use a brilliant tactician like you leading the charge." By the expression on Kovalchuk's face, he had caught the rebuke. "MSS wants Aegis? Let them dig its algorithms from Martel's skull. We have achieved our objectives regardless. My plan was to disrupt the American operation in Okavango, and we have done that and then some."

Kovalchuk grinned, hefting a VSS Vintorez sniper rifle. "And Lemarti?"

Tarasenko lit another cigarette, the flame reflecting in his ice-blue eyes. "Save the last bullet for him," he said, indicating toward the sniper rifle. "I want to watch the light die."

The Leopard Group's remaining forces mounted armored vehicles. Somewhere to the northeast, Martel's convoy snaked toward Lake Victoria's shore—and a rendezvous with history.

Tarasenko smiled. Africa had always been a graveyard of empires. Today, it would bury another.

CHAPTER 38

A SMALL FISHING VILLAGE ON LAKE VICTORIA

Alex crouched behind a granite outcrop, a swale overlooking the tiny fishing village below. With the scope on her M38, she tracked Lemarti's convoy as it idled near the dock, fighters swarming around boats like ants on carrion. The fishing village sprawled like a gaping wound along the shores of Lake Victoria, four kilometers northeast of Butemba.

Her father's silhouette flickered in the back of the pickup—alive but hunched over.

"Caleb," she hissed into her comms. "They're going to load him onto a boat. We need to hit them now!"

Static crackled. "Negative, Shadow. Wait! Hunter and Ronin are en route to your position. ETA two mikes."

"If they load him up and leave the dock, he could be in Chinese hands by the time you get here!"

Kurtz materialized beside her, his HK416 scanning the water. "Look."

The men didn't get out of the vehicles. They didn't load the general onto a boat. Whatever they were doing here, it seemed they wouldn't be venturing out onto the water today. Instead, the militiamen returned to their Toyotas.

"They're not crossing," Santiago observed. "They were probably just checking in with these guys—guards, sentries. Whatever they are, they look like they're part of his crew."

Alex agreed. Relief washed over her like waves breaking on the rocky shore next to the dock.

"ISR is online," he said, showing her a map of the area on the tablet.

The vehicles turned around and drove toward their position.

"Down," she said.

They ducked and watched as the convoy drove past and turned left onto a side road overgrown with bushes.

"Where does that go?" she asked.

Kurtz checked the image on his tablet. "That will lead them a couple of klicks up to here"—he pointed—"I'm sure that's the second compound they're heading to."

"Can you zoom in closer?"

He did, and a derelict factory compound came into view. The feed showed several vehicles on-site and men walking around.

"Definitely the second compound. That road doesn't look like it goes anywhere but to that place," she said.

"Hard to tell for sure with the canopy of trees blocking our view, but I think you're right, Shooter."

A twig snapped behind them. Alex whirled with her pistol drawn.

Caleb and Moose emerged from the brush.

"Did you miss us?" asked Moose, his basso voice cheery and uplifting.

Two Delta operators followed out of the trees, another slung between them. Moose introduced everyone.

"Sorry for your loss, Rook," Alex said.

He nodded solemnly. This was the man she had been watching through her scope earlier. Blood crusted the Delta operator's fatigues and soaked through the dressing on his forearm. A bandage covered a laceration below his eyebrow, but his eyes were sharp.

Caleb and Rocky fanned out, completing the perimeter. Moose hefted his Mk 48, its belt feed clinking. He sized up Santiago. Then to Alex said: "I heard you needed a chaperone."

Alex allowed herself a smile and a sliver of hope. The cavalry had arrived.

* * *

The general's convoy had stopped in a fishing village nestled along the shore. Thatched huts leaned against the wind, their bamboo frames lashed together with fraying rope. They stopped long enough for Lemarti to talk to men carrying rifles while others walked down to the docks to inspect boats.

Sentries, thought the general. *We must be near the other compound.*

The convoy had started up again, backtracking to a road concealed by an overgrowth of trees and bush. They turned and proceeded up an unmaintained road, barely a track, and bumped along, with no other conversation than the occasional grunting as the occupants took the blows the truck's suspension couldn't abate.

They passed three checkpoints along the road, each one better equipped than the last to deal with interlopers, with guns of escalating lethality at each stop.

"We are almost there, General."

"Then what?"

"Then you will see. Perhaps you will sleep well tonight, but I am not so sure. What do you think, Kijana? Will our guest sleep tonight?"

Kijana met Lemarti's eyes, but didn't answer. When Lemarti turned back to the front, Kijana looked at the general with almost a look of reassurance. Or was it mere sympathy?

At last, they came to a fence line. A dilapidated guard tower stood sentinel to the east, a man and his rifle leaning over the edge. Someone opened the gate, and the truck drove through. Before them was a large factory, its brown brick broken and crumbling. Instead of going to it as the general had presumed, they curved around the open courtyard and drove to a two-story house sitting squat near the middle of the compound.

Lemarti exited the vehicle first and opened the general's door. "Out," he ordered, yanking Martel by his elbow.

The general stumbled, his leg irons clanking. Four PFA fighters formed a perimeter, their muzzles tracking the tree line.

"Time to go inside, General." Lemarti eyed the sky as if expecting to see something glowing in the morning light.

"Where are you taking me?" Martel growled, buying time. *Maybe if we stay outdoors long enough, I'll be spotted by friendly eyes in the sky.*

"Tonight, you are still my guest, *Mzee*. Tomorrow, though, is another day, and you will have new friends to meet. They are eager to meet you and to . . . talk."

Kijana prodded Martel. "Move, *Mzee*," he said, drawing a smirk from Lemarti.

A plan crystallized.

"You know what they'll do to you," Martel murmured, catching Kijana's eye. "After they're done with me."

The boy stiffened.

"*Rafiki*," Martel pressed, quietly enough that Lemarti didn't hear. "I am your friend, Kijana. Hear me when I tell you that this man"—he indicated in Lemarti's direction with a nod of his head—"cares nothing about you. You are just another soldier to him. In fact, you're worth more to him dead than alive."

Kijana's gaze darted to Lemarti. The warlord was distracted, barking into a satellite phone.

"I want to help you. I want to save your life. My team will be coming for me. Help me, and I can help you."

As he glanced at the sky one last time, he knew somewhere out there, Alex was getting ready. He was sure of it.

He'd bet his life on it.

* * *

The digital musical notes of encrypted static crackled through her comms, followed by Harley's urgent voice.

"Ronin, this is Blackbird."

"Go for Ronin," Caleb responded, pressing his finger to his earpiece. "We've linked up with Delta. We're working out a plan here to proceed to target."

"Negative, Ronin. Fall back immediately to Jengo. I'll send you coordinates. I repeat, you're falling back to the safe house."

Alex frowned, exchanging glances with Caleb. "Blackbird, we had eyes on Condor and now we're two klicks from Lemarti's compound. We can be on target within—"

"That's a negative, Ronin," Harley cut her off, her tone brooking no argument. "Intel says they moved the general to the compound and will hold position until morning. They won't move him again until oh-six-hundred hours."

Viper groaned as the Delta operators adjusted their grip on him. His face had gone ashen, the blood loss clearly taking its toll.

"Copy, Blackbird. We still need an immediate CASEVAC for one of Hunter's crew," Caleb reported, moving to Doc to check on Viper. "One operator needs Dustoff." He used the call sign of US Army Air Ambulance units, a tradition that began during the Vietnam War to request a CASEVAC—a casualty evacuation—for Viper.

"We're working on it," Harley replied. "Get your team to Jengo la Ulinzi, the safe house outside Mwanza."

Caleb looked at Viper, then at Doc, his expression grim. "Copy that. What about Lemarti's compound? Any change in security posture?"

"Negative. ISR shows they've doubled the guard but we aren't expecting trouble until morning from Leopard Group, who are still in Mwanza. Latest signals intelligence reveals that Lemarti and his crew believe they can still get a clean exfil at dawn." Harley paused. "This gives us time to draw up a proper plan, get medical attention for Viper, and hit them when they least expect it."

Alex clenched her jaw, frustration evident in her stance as she keyed her mike. "My father—"

"Is secure for now," Harley assured her. "Intel confirms that once he's on-site, he'll be held in the basement of the main house in the center of the compound. They won't move him again until the Chinese arrive at their rendezvous point."

The rain began to fall and quickly intensified, fat droplets slapping against the leaves overhead. Thunder rumbled in the distance.

"Weather's turning," Moose observed, glancing skyward. "Might work in our favor for a night assault."

Caleb nodded, making the decision. "Blackbird, we're falling back to Jengo."

"Copy that, Ronin. I'll have a full tactical brief ready when you arrive. Blackbird out."

As the comms went silent, Alex stared in the direction of Lemarti's compound. Her father was so close, yet still just beyond her reach. Caleb placed a hand on her shoulder.

"We'll get him, Alex. But we do it right."

She nodded reluctantly. "Let's move."

The team melted back into the trees, carrying their wounded comrade, the promise of the coming assault hanging between them like the storm that washed over them.

CHAPTER 39

CIA SAFE HOUSE (JENGO LA ULINZI), MWANZA, TANZANIA

The rain had finally stopped, but the humidity hung in the air like a wet blanket. Alex wiped sweat from her forehead as the team approached the nondescript building nestled among a cluster of warehouses on the outskirts of Mwanza. The safe house—Jengo la Ulinzi, House of Security in Swahili—looked abandoned, its weathered concrete exterior blending perfectly with the surrounding structures.

Ghost moved ahead, checking the perimeter with practiced efficiency. "Clear," he whispered into his comms.

Caleb supported Viper, whose face had gone ashen from blood loss. Despite the Asherman Chest Seal, his breathing remained labored. And he had taken another round through the shoulder; the dressing Doc had applied soaked through with blood. He needed a hospital to fix his shoulder and see that his lung was properly reinflating.

"We need to get him inside," Doc said, his voice tight with concern.

Moose approached the heavy metal door and entered a six-digit code on the keypad. The lock disengaged with a soft click. "Home sweet home," he muttered, pushing the door open.

The interior of the safe house was sparse but functional—concrete floors, reinforced walls, and minimal furnishings. A bank of communications equipment occupied one corner, while cots lined the far wall. The air smelled of dust and disuse.

"Get Viper on the table," Doc ordered, pointing to a metal examination table near the back. He was already unpacking his medical kit, laying out instruments with methodical precision.

Rocky and Santiago secured the perimeter while Ghost checked the building room by room. Alex helped Doc position Viper on the table, wincing at his groan of pain.

"How bad?" she asked, her voice low.

Doc cut away the blood-soaked bandage, revealing the ragged wound beneath. "Through and through, but he's lost a lot of blood. I can stabilize him, but he needs surgery and a proper transfusion."

Caleb joined them, his expression grim. "What are our options?"

"I'm on comms with Blackbird. They're directing us to get Viper to St. Clement's Mission Clinic." Moose sat across the room where he was monitoring the communications equipment. "CIA asset runs it. About twenty minutes from here. They can handle this level of trauma and arrange medevac if necessary."

Doc nodded. "That's our best bet. I'll get him prepped for transport."

Alex paced the room, adrenaline still coursing through her system. Every fiber of her being wanted to move on Lemarti's compound immediately. Her father was there—so close after all this time. The thought of waiting even hours seemed unbearable.

The communications system crackled back to life, and Harley's voice filled the room. "Ronin, this is Blackbird."

Moose adjusted the frequency. "Blackbird, this is Ronin. Go ahead."

"Status report," Harley demanded.

"We've reached the safe house," Caleb replied. "Viper's down with a GSW to the shoulder and a bullet to the chest—open pneumothorax. We're arranging transport to St. Clement's."

"Understood. Your orders were to follow the general, not rescue Hunter."

"About that," Caleb said. "Tactical decision, Blackbird."

"Regardless, I've got Langley on the line. Patching video through now."

The screen flickered, and Kadeisha Thomas's face appeared. Her expression was tense, but her voice remained steady. "Ronin, what's your status on General Martel?"

Alex stepped forward. "We've confirmed he's at Lemarti's compound. We're ready to move."

"Not in daylight," Thomas replied. "ISR shows Lemarti has doubled his security. A daylight assault would be suicide. They're not moving him until morning."

"How can we be sure?"

"Because the Chinese have promised Lemarti extraction at dawn," Thomas explained. "They've arranged a rendezvous point accessible only by boat. Lemarti believes they're extracting him and the general, but our intelligence suggests it's a setup."

"Tarasenko," Caleb said, the name like a curse on his lips.

Thomas nodded. "We believe the Chinese are working with Leopard Group now. They're using Lemarti to hold the general until they can position their own assets to take custody."

"So we hit them before dawn," Ghost said, rejoining the group. "Oh-four-hundred hours gives us the cover of darkness and catches them before they start moving."

"Exactly," Thomas confirmed. "In the meantime, get Viper to St. Clement's and use the time to prepare."

Doc had done everything he could do to stabilize Viper, who now lay semiconscious on the table, an IV drip running into his arm. "He's ready for transport," Doc announced. "But I'll need help getting him there."

"Rocky, Santiago—you're on escort duty," Caleb ordered. "Get Viper to St. Clement's and stay with him until he's secure."

The two operators nodded, already moving to prepare a litter.

"The rest of us will plan the assault," Caleb continued. "Harley, we need satellite imagery of the compound, thermal scans if possible, and any intelligence on security patterns."

"Already on it," Harley replied. "I'll have a complete package within the hour."

"And what about extraction?" Alex asked, her mind racing ahead. "Once we have my father, how do we get out?"

"We've arranged for a Tanzanian forces helicopter to be on standby," Thomas said. "They'll move in once you give the signal. The Tanzanian government is officially denying involvement, but they've adjusted their attitudes and are eager to see Lemarti removed."

Moose whistled low. "Nice to have friends in high places."

As Rocky and Santiago prepared to move Viper, Alex approached the wounded operator. His eyes fluttered open briefly, focusing on her face.

"Don't worry about me, Shooter," he whispered. "Just get your old man out."

Alex squeezed his hand. "We will. And you better be ready for the after-action party."

A ghost of a smile crossed Viper's pale lips before his eyes closed again.

Once they had departed, the remaining team gathered around the central table, where Moose had spread out maps of the compound and surrounding area. Harley's promised satellite imagery began downloading to their secure tablets.

"Lemarti's compound is here," Caleb said, pointing to a cluster of buildings nestled close to the shoreline of Lake Victoria. "Main factory, main residence, outbuildings, and a dock. ISR analysis suggests the general is being held in the basement of the main house."

"Security?" Ghost asked.

"Approximately twenty men, rotating shifts," Harley replied through the comm system. "Mostly his militia, poorly trained but well-armed. The real threats are Lemarti's inner circle—his deputy Desmond and about five others."

Alex studied the layout, her tactical mind already mapping approach vectors and potential choke points. "What about Tarasenko's men?"

"No sign of them yet," Thomas said. "Which is to say, not in your current area of operations. They're holding at the airport for now, but our intelligence suggests they'll move into position somewhere near the rendezvous point tonight. They'll likely make their move when Lemarti attempts to transfer the general at first light."

"So we have a three-way clusterfuck brewing," Moose observed dryly. "Us, Lemarti, and Tarasenko all converging on the same target."

"Which is why timing is critical," Caleb emphasized. "We go in at oh-four-hundred, extract the general, and exfil before Tarasenko can mobilize."

* * *

Harley's eyes narrowed to slits as she leaned across the table, her voice dropping to a dangerous whisper. "You did what?" Even though Harley was sitting in her office four hundred and twenty kilometers away in Arusha, Alex backed away from her image on the high-definition computer monitor.

Instead, she met her gaze without flinching. "I promised to get her out. She's giving us actionable intel on my father's location."

"We don't have the resources or authorization to run around and save everybody, Martel." Harley's palm slapped against the weathered tabletop. "This isn't a humanitarian mission."

The safe house kitchen smelled of burnt coffee and stale cigarettes. Outside, Lake Victoria shimmered under the midday sun, deceptively peaceful against the urgency thrumming through Alex's veins. Caleb stood by the window, his silhouette backlit by harsh sunlight, saying nothing but watching everything.

"She was a teacher before Lemarti slaughtered her village and killed her husband," Alex said, her voice steady despite the anger coiling in her chest. "She's been living as his captive for three years. And she's willing to risk her life to help us."

"And now we're supposed to set her up with a new identity? A teaching job?" Harley's laugh was brittle. "In Tanzania? Or maybe the Okavango Republic? Jesus, Alex, did you promise her a pension plan, too?"

Santiago and Kurtz exchanged glances from their position by the door. Rocky kept his eyes on his laptop, fingers never pausing as they danced across the keyboard.

"She knows the layout of the second compound," Alex pressed. "She knows the guard rotations, the access points. She knows where they're holding my father."

Harley's expression shifted, the tactical calculus visible behind her eyes. "And she's willing to meet?"

"Noon today. At the market in Mwanza."

"It could be a setup."

"It's not."

"You can't know that."

"I read people, Harley. It's what I do." Alex leaned forward. "She wants out. And we need what she knows."

Silence stretched between them, taut as piano wire. Finally, Harley's shoulders relaxed a fraction.

"Fine. But this isn't a blank check. We extract her, we debrief her, we hand her off to refugee services. That's it."

"That's all I'm asking."

"No, it's not." Harley's smile didn't reach her eyes. "But it's all you're getting."

Alex nodded, accepting the compromise. "I'll make the meet."

"Not alone," Caleb said, speaking for the first time. "Take Rocky as backup."

"I'll drive," Rocky volunteered, closing his laptop. "Been itching to see the local sights anyway."

Harley's gaze swept over them. "Four AM tomorrow, we hit the compound. That's our window before they move the general. Don't be late."

"Wouldn't dream of it," Alex said, already moving toward the door.

"Martel." Harley's voice stopped her. "If this goes sideways, you cut and run. The mission comes first."

Alex didn't answer. She didn't need to. They both knew what came first for her.

CHAPTER 40

MWANZA MARKET, TANZANIA

The market pulsed with life—a riot of color and sound that assaulted Alex's senses. Vendors hawked their wares in rapid-fire Swahili through air thick with the mingled scents of roasting meat, diesel fumes, and overripe fruit. She moved through the crowd with practiced ease, her nondescript clothing—faded jeans, loose cotton shirt, and a scarf draped casually around her neck—helping her blend with the throng of shoppers.

The SIG Sauer P365 pressed against the small of her back was her only concession to the danger. Her Glock 19, fitted with a suppressor, remained hidden in her messenger bag. Both weapons were chambered and ready.

"Eyes on the south entrance," Rocky's voice murmured through her earpiece. He was parked two blocks away in their stolen Toyota, monitoring the market's perimeter. "No movement yet."

Alex checked her watch: 11:58. She positioned herself near a stall selling colorful kangas, pretending to examine the fabric while scanning the crowd. The meeting point—a fruit vendor with a distinctive red umbrella—was ten meters to her right, offering clear sight lines in all directions.

"Movement at the south entrance," Rocky reported. "Woman in a lime-green skirt. Matches the description."

Alex's pulse quickened as she spotted Adiya weaving through the crowd. The teacher's slender frame was draped in the same lime-green skirt and red-and-yellow kanga cloth she'd worn at the compound. But she wasn't alone.

"She's got company," Alex muttered, shifting to get a better view. "Male, early thirties, AK slung across his back. One of Lemarti's."

"Want me to move closer?"

"Negative. Stay with the vehicle."

Adiya's eyes darted nervously around the market, her hands fidgeting with the edge of her kanga. The militiaman shadowed her closely, one hand resting nonchalantly on his rifle's sling, his gaze suspicious as it swept across the crowd.

Alex moved casually toward the fruit stand, keeping her pace unhurried. When Adiya spotted her, the woman's eyes widened briefly before she schooled her features back to neutrality.

"Buy something," Alex murmured as she approached, pitching her voice just loud enough for Adiya to hear. "Act normal."

Adiya nodded almost imperceptibly, reaching for a mango. The militiaman stood a meter behind her, scanning the crowd with bored indifference.

"Alex says hello," Alex said softly, selecting a papaya from the display. Her words weren't necessary, but she hoped they'd give Adiya some added comfort.

Relief flooded Adiya's face. "You came," she whispered.

"Did you tell him why you're here?"

"No. He follows me everywhere now. Lemarti's orders."

Alex handed the vendor a few shillings, her mind racing through scenarios. "When I move, stay close to me."

The militiaman's posture had changed, his attention sharpening as he watched their exchange. His hand tightened on his rifle.

"We need to go. Now," Alex said, abandoning pretense. She grabbed Adiya's wrist, pulling her away from the stand.

"Hey!" the militiaman barked, stepping forward.

"Run!" Alex commanded, shoving Adiya ahead of her.

They plunged into the crowd as the militiaman shouldered his way after them, shouting for them to stop. Shoppers scattered, creating a wake of confusion that Alex used to her advantage, pulling Adiya down a narrow aisle between stalls.

"Rocky, south exit. Now!" she barked into her comms.

"On my way," came the immediate response.

A shot cracked overhead, sending market-goers screaming for cover. Alex pushed Adiya behind a stack of crates, drawing the Glock from her bag.

"Stay down," she ordered, checking that the suppressor was secure.

The militiaman appeared at the end of the aisle, his rifle raised. Alex sighted down the barrel of her Glock and squeezed the trigger twice in rapid succession. The suppressed shots made little more than a dull thwack as the 9-millimeter rounds found their mark. The militiaman staggered, a look of surprise frozen on his face before he crumpled to the ground.

"Come on," Alex said, grabbing Adiya's arm and pulling her to her feet. "We need to move before anyone else shows up. Lemarti must have eyes everywhere."

They sprinted through the panicked crowd, Alex keeping her body between Adiya and potential threats. The south exit loomed ahead, sunlight glinting off the Toyota's windshield as Rocky pulled up, engine running.

"Get in!" Alex shouted, yanking open the rear door and shoving Adiya inside before diving in after her. "Go, go, go!"

Rocky gunned the engine, the Toyota's tires spitting gravel as they accelerated away from the market. In the rearview mirror, Alex could see figures emerging from the south entrance, pointing in their direction.

"We've got company," Rocky announced, swerving around a donkey cart. "Two technicals, coming in hot."

"Take the back roads," Alex instructed, checking her weapons. "We need to lose them before we head to the safe house."

Adiya huddled in the seat beside her, eyes wide with terror and something else—hope, perhaps, or the dawning realization that her nightmare might finally be ending.

"You killed him," she whispered, her voice barely audible over the engine's roar.

"Yes," Alex replied simply.

Adiya nodded. "Good."

The Toyota fishtailed around a corner, plunging down a narrow alley where laundry lines stretched between buildings like colorful spiderwebs. Rocky drove with the focused precision of a man accustomed to high-speed pursuits, his hands steady on the wheel.

"I think we lost them," he announced after several minutes of evasive maneuvers.

Alex kept her eyes on the road behind them, the Glock still in her hand. "Circle back toward the lake, then approach the safe house from the north. Make sure we're clean."

Rocky nodded, executing a series of turns that would confuse any pursuit.

"Thank you," Adiya said quietly, her eyes meeting Alex's. "For keeping your promise."

Alex tucked her weapon back into her bag, suddenly aware of the weight of that promise—not just to extract Adiya but to give her a future. A life beyond survival.

"We're not safe yet," she cautioned.

"But we will be," Adiya said with unexpected certainty. "And then I will tell you everything I know about where they are keeping your father."

Alex nodded, her thoughts already racing ahead to the predawn raid. To her father, held captive in a fishing village six kilometers from Butemba. To the blood oath carved into her palm all those years ago.

"Yes," she agreed, watching the city blur past the window. "And then we'll get him back."

The Toyota sped toward the safe house, carrying them one step closer to fulfilling that vow.

* * *

CIA SAFE HOUSE, MWANZA, TANZANIA

The planning cycle stretched on for hours, the team meticulously working through every detail of the operation. Entry points identified, responsibilities assigned, contingencies established. As darkness fell outside, the safe house buzzed with focused energy.

Alex found herself staring at the satellite image of the compound, her finger tracing the outline of the main house where her father was being held. He had only been captive for two days, but it wasn't the length of his captivity that made her anxious; it was the prospect of what might happen if they didn't get him back. He was less than ten klicks away now. The thought made her heart race.

"We're going to get him out," Caleb said quietly, appearing at her side.

Alex nodded, not trusting herself to speak.

"I know what he means to you," he continued. "But when we go in there—"

"I know," Alex interrupted. "Mission first. Always."

Caleb studied her face for a long moment, then nodded. "Get some rest. We move in six hours."

Alex knew she should sleep, but her mind refused to quiet. Instead, she checked and rechecked her gear, cleaned her weapons, and reviewed the operation plan until she could recite it from memory.

Around midnight, the communications system chimed with an incoming transmission. Moose, who had been monitoring the equipment, answered immediately.

"Ronin, this is Blackbird."

"Go ahead, Blackbird," Moose replied.

"I need a private channel with Rook," Harley said, her voice unusually formal.

Moose glanced at Rook, who had been silently preparing his

equipment in the corner. The team's designated Reaper drone operator nodded and moved to the communications station.

"I've got it," Rook said, taking the headset from Moose. "Clear the channel, please."

Moose stepped away, giving Rook privacy. Alex watched from across the room, a flicker of unease passing through her. Something about Rook's demeanor seemed off—had been off since they'd received the mission brief.

Rook kept his voice low as he spoke into the headset, his back to the room. After a few minutes, he removed the headset and returned to his equipment, his expression unreadable.

Alex approached Caleb, who was reviewing the thermal scans Harley had sent. "Something's not right," she murmured.

Caleb glanced up. "What do you mean?"

"I don't know. Just a feeling." She hesitated. "That private communication with Harley..."

"Probably drone stuff," Caleb said weakly, though his eyes narrowed slightly as he looked at Rook. "But I'll keep an eye on him."

The hours crept by. Rocky and Santiago returned from St. Clement's with news that Viper was in surgery but stable. The team ate a quick meal of MREs, checked their equipment one final time, and prepared to move out.

As they gathered by the door, Caleb addressed the team. "We all know what's at stake here. General Martel isn't just a high-value asset with critical intelligence—he's Alex's father and one of us. Our primary objective is extraction, but if the situation deteriorates, we adapt and overcome. Questions?"

There were none. Each operator knew their role and understood the risks.

"Then let's bring him home," Caleb said, nodding to Alex.

They moved out into the darkness, leaving the safe house behind. The night air was thick with humidity, the stars obscured by gathering clouds. A storm was brewing over Lake Victoria, distant lightning illuminating the horizon.

As they loaded into the two waiting vehicles, Alex felt a strange calm settle over her. The final chapter of her mission to preserve her oath was about to begin.

CHAPTER 41

CIA OPERATIONS CENTER BLACKBIRD, ARUSHA, TANZANIA

While the team had been preparing to depart, Harley sat alone in the Blackbird operations center, the blue glow of multiple monitors illuminating her face. The encrypted communication with Rook had been brief but clear—Operation Ironclad was still active, still necessary.

She pulled up the classified file on her secure terminal, the details of the operation scrolling before her eyes. The directive had come from the highest levels of the intelligence community, bypassing normal chains of command. If General David Martel could not be safely extracted, if there was any risk of him falling into enemy hands, he was to be eliminated.

The weight of the order pressed on Harley like a physical burden. Martel wasn't just a highly valuable and decorated officer; he was part of the CIA family and the father of a fellow paramilitary operator. This was personal. The thought of ordering his death felt like a betrayal of everything she stood for. Yet the alternative—allowing the Chinese or Russians or anyone else to extract whatever information Martel possessed—was unthinkable.

The secure line chimed, and Kadeisha Thomas's face appeared on the monitor.

"Is Ironclad still in play?" she asked without preamble.

Harley nodded. "Rook is prepared to execute if necessary."

"An unfortunate choice of words," noted the deputy director. "He understands the parameters?"

She shook off the remark. "Yes. If Martel is in imminent danger of being transferred to Chinese or Russian custody, Rook will deploy the Reaper and eliminate the target."

Thomas's expression remained neutral, but Harley could see the tension in her eyes. "And Alex? Does she suspect?"

"No," Harley replied, the word bitter on her tongue. "None of them do, except Rook."

"It has to be this way," Thomas said, her voice softening slightly. "You know what's at stake."

Harley did know. The intelligence Martel possessed could jeopardize the most crucial technical advancement in combat over the past decade. Operations worldwide would be at risk. Countless lives could be at stake, and years of diligent effort could be undermined. The risk was too great.

"There's something else," Thomas continued after a moment. "We've received intelligence that Kurtz may have his own orders regarding Martel."

Harley frowned. "From whom?"

"That's unclear. But it appears he's been tasked as a backup plan in case Ironclad fails."

"Jesus," Harley muttered. "Does anyone in this operation trust anybody else?"

"Trust isn't a luxury we can afford," Thomas replied. "Not with these stakes."

After the call ended, Harley sat in silence, staring at the satellite feed of Lemarti's compound. Somewhere in that cluster of buildings, David Martel was waiting, unaware that his own government had contingency plans to kill him rather than let him fall into enemy hands.

And somewhere in the darkness, Alex Martel was moving toward her father, equally unaware that the mission to rescue him carried a deadly alternative.

Harley poured herself a measure of whiskey from the bottle she kept in her desk drawer. She didn't often drink on duty, but tonight seemed to call for it. She raised the glass in a silent toast to David Martel, hoping against hope that Operation Ironclad would remain unnecessary.

The storm over Lake Victoria intensified, lightning flashing across the satellite feed. It seemed fitting somehow—nature's fury mirroring the tempest that was about to be unleashed.

* * *

LAKE VICTORIA FISHING VILLAGE, TANZANIA

The stolen Toyota Land Cruiser's tires sprayed rooster tails of mud as Alex braced against the dashboard, her knuckles white around the grab handle. Her eyes were fixed on the tablet, where thermal imagery illuminated the screen in ghostly greens and reds—heat signatures of armed men lurking in the darkness ahead. The rain had eased into a dreary drizzle, just enough to seep through clothing and gear without offering the concealment of a heavy downpour. Their drone feed from the Reaper flickered, pixels dissolving into static before re-forming into recognizable shapes—the compound, the guards, and the heat bloom that could only be her father.

"Damn atmospheric interference," she muttered, tapping the screen to enhance the resolution.

Caleb kept his eyes on the muddy track ahead, hands steady on the wheel as the Land Cruiser's i-Force Max hybrid powertrain hummed beneath them. Behind them, two more vehicles and the rest of Ronin. Two days since her father's abduction and less than twenty-four hours since they'd started planning this operation. The clock was ticking.

ISR was on station, but they couldn't be certain how long it would last due to a mix of bad weather and bad luck. Still, she didn't place much trust in the latter—good or bad. In her experience, luck was simply preparation meeting opportunity, and they had prepared for this moment since Adiya had given them the compound's layout yesterday. The storm was more than just weather out here; it was a living thing, howling across the vast expanse of Lake Victoria, threatening to erase them from existence as thoroughly as it erased footprints from the shoreline.

"General's heat signature confirmed," Harley's voice crackled through encrypted comms in her earpiece, broadcasting from the CIA ops center in Arusha, where she was debriefing Adiya. The words fought through layers of electronic countermeasures. Static interfered with her transmission, breaking her sentences into fragments. "Boat docked just north of your position, next to the PFA's compound. Intel suggests Lemarti will move him by water to rendezvous with our Chinese MSS friends just after sunrise. Sending coordinates now."

Alex's tablet pinged as the data packet arrived, revealing a satellite overlay of their target—an abandoned factory complex nestled against the lake, partially reclaimed by jungle, its concrete walls stained with decades of tropical growth. The thermal image highlighted a central house within the compound where her father was being held—specifically in the basement, according to Adiya's intelligence.

"Adiya's intel checks out," Alex confirmed, studying the layout. "Heat signatures match her description of guard positions."

Moose shifted in the back seat, the vehicle's suspension groaning under his bulk. The metallic snap of his Mk 48 machine gun's charging handle punctuated the silence as he chambered a round, the sound oddly comforting in its finality.

"Time to remind 'em why we're called Ronin," he said, his Minnesota accent thickening as it always did before an operation. His massive hands cradled the weapon with incongruous gentleness, like a father holding a newborn.

In the Ford Everest following behind them, Rocky maintained a precise distance, his headlights dark like theirs. Kurtz rode shotgun, scanning the road ahead with night-vision binoculars, while Santiago in the back seat checked his equipment—the garrote wire and ceramic knife that had served him well in a dozen countries.

Alex zoomed the drone feed, focusing on the factory's perimeter wall. The concrete barrier bore faded Mandarin graffiti and its English translation, partially obscured by vegetation but still legible in the floodlit compound: BELT AND ROAD INITIATIVE—PARTNERSHIP FOR PROSPERITY.

Kind of on the nose, she thought. *And, anyway, horseshit.* The Chinese weren't building infrastructure out of altruism. They were buying influence, securing resources, and establishing forward operating bases under the guise of economic development. And now they wanted her father's knowledge of Project Aegis—the algorithm that could render America's new autonomous AI-driven drone program obsolete.

"Noise discipline," she cautioned over the team frequency, glancing back at Moose. "If they ID us as NATO, Lemarti scatters. We lose him, we lose my father."

The Land Cruiser fishtailed around a washed-out gully, its headlights dark to avoid detection. The vehicle slewed sideways, tires fighting for purchase on the muddy track before finding grip. Rain pelted through partially open windows, soaking gear bags, weapons, and ammunition crates they'd provisioned from the safe house. The interior smelled of gun oil, wet canvas, and the metallic tang of adrenaline.

"Checkpoint Alpha—two hundred meters," Kurtz warned through the comms from the Everest, his voice clipped and professional. "Sandbags arranged in a standard funnel pattern. Technical with a Dushka mounted in the bed. Two shooters visible at the barricade, one more in shadows to the east. Possible fourth on the ridge above."

Alex's jaw tightened, muscle flexing beneath skin. First test. The plan called for subterfuge at the initial checkpoint, force at the second, and stealth at the third. If they deviated now, the entire operation would unravel.

"Remember," she said, her voice steady despite the tension coiling in her chest, "we're Chinese contractors surveying for the new hydroelectric project. Rook, you're our translator. Everyone else, look bored and entitled."

* * *

CHECKPOINT ALPHA

The roadblock materialized through the thinning rain like a mirage taking solid form: a rusted Toyota Hilux parked sideways across the muddy track, its .50-caliber DShK machine gun manned by a teenager in flip-flops and a tattered AC Milan jersey sitting under a beach umbrella to shelter from the rain. The heavy weapon looked obscene in his adolescent hands—a child wielding the power to end lives with the squeeze of a trigger.

Another militiaman leaned against the cab, an AK-47 slung loose over his shoulder, the weapon's wooden furniture dark with age and use. He chewed something that stained his lips red—betel or khat, Alex couldn't tell in the darkness. A third figure lurked in the shadows beneath a makeshift awning—older, harder, with a Chinese QBZ-95 assault rifle held at the low ready. His eyes reflected the distant lightning, predatory and calculating.

Caleb slowed the Land Cruiser to a stop as Kurtz rolled down his window in the Everest behind them, the drizzle immediately soaking his sleeve and the documents he held out. "*Tunataka kuvuka! Kwa heri ya mradi wa kisasa!*" *We need passage! For the modernization project!*

The teen swung the Dushka's muzzle toward them, the massive barrel tracking across their windshield with jerky, inexperienced movements. His finger hovered near the trigger, a heartbeat away from unleashing a storm of .50-caliber rounds that would shred their vehicle—and them—into unrecognizable scrap.

The older militiaman stepped forward, pushing past his younger comrade. His rifle's barrel drifted toward Kurtz's face, close enough that he could probably smell the cosmoline preservative on its steel. "*Wewe ni mzungu.*" *You're white.*

Alex's hand crept toward her Glock, fingers curling around the grip beneath her rain jacket. One wrong word, one suspicious glance, and this would turn into a bloodbath. They'd win the firefight, but the noise would alert every checkpoint between here and the factory compound.

Rook materialized from the storm like an apparition, moving

with the liquid grace that had earned him his call sign. His soaked black-and-green shemagh clung to his face like a death mask, revealing only his eyes—dark, inscrutable, and utterly calm. He stepped between Kurtz and the militiaman, his body language deferential but not submissive.

"*Marafiki,*" he said, the Swahili flowing naturally from his lips as he pressed a wad of waterlogged hundred-dollar bills into the militiaman's hand. "We're friends. Beijing sent us to survey the site before the ministers arrive next week."

The man hesitated, thumbing through the cash with practiced movements. The Tanzanian shilling may have been the country's official currency, but dollars still ruled the bush—even counterfeit ones like these, printed on the CIA's presses in Langley specifically for operations where deniability was paramount.

"Quickly," Rook urged, jerking his chin toward the darkening sky where lightning forked between cloud banks. "The coming rain will knock down trees. Block the road. Your commander will blame you if the Chinese ministers cannot pass."

The militiaman's eyes narrowed, weighing the risk of letting them through against the risk of angering his superiors. After a moment that stretched like piano wire, he barked an order to the teenager. The Hilux's engine coughed to life, belching black diesel smoke that got lost in the inky light, and it lurched aside, clearing a narrow gap in the roadblock.

"Drive," Alex hissed to Caleb, her fingers still wrapped around her pistol's grip. "Steady pace. Don't rush."

They slipped through the gap, mud churning beneath the Land Cruiser's tires as they accelerated gradually, fighting the urge to floor the accelerator and escape. In the rearview mirror, Alex watched the militiamen shrink into the darkness, the teenager still tracking them with the DShK's barrel until they rounded a bend in the road.

"One down," Caleb murmured, releasing a breath he'd been holding. "Two to go."

CHAPTER 42

LAKE VICTORIA FISHING VILLAGE, TANZANIA
CHECKPOINT BRAVO

The second roadblock was smarter: concrete barriers arranged in a chicane pattern, forcing vehicles to slow to a crawl. Tire spikes glinted dully in the mud, ready to shred rubber and strand unwary travelers. A militia commander in PLA surplus body armor paced between four shooters, their eyes sharp under the harsh glare of diesel-powered floodlights that cut through the gloom like surgical instruments.

"They'll search the vehicles," Caleb muttered, sliding a magazine into his sidearm beneath the cover of his jacket. "Our cover won't hold."

Alex's mind raced, calculating angles, distances, threat assessments. Their cover story—Chinese contractors surveying for infrastructure projects—wouldn't withstand even cursory examination. The C-4 bricks nestled in waterproof cases and the M4 carbines hidden beneath tarps in the back seat were decidedly not infrastructure survey gear.

"Ghost—distraction," she decided, her voice barely audible over the engine's rumble. "Moose—suppress if they twitch. Everyone else, weapons hot but concealed. We go loud only if necessary."

Ghost nodded once, his lean face betraying nothing as he checked the ceramic knife strapped to his forearm—invisible to metal detectors, capable of slicing through cartilage and tendons with minimal resistance. He slid out the passenger side door before they reached the checkpoint, vanishing into the rain-soaked undergrowth with preternatural silence.

The Land Cruiser rolled to a stop before the concrete barriers. The militia commander approached, hand resting on his holstered sidearm, expression suspicious beneath his rain-slicked boonie hat.

"Identification," he demanded in accented English, palm outstretched.

Rook leaned across from the Everest, offering a leather folio of forged documents. "We have clearance from Dar es Salaam," he began.

The commander flipped through the papers, his frown deepening. "These are not—"

A rock clattered against the Hilux's hood, the sound sharp and deliberate in the humid air. The militiamen turned as one, rifles rising toward the disturbance—

"Halt!"

Ghost stepped into the floodlights' glare, hands raised in apparent surrender. His body swayed slightly, a drunken Swahili slur on his lips as he staggered forward. "*Ninaomba msamaha, rafiki . . .*" *I'm sorry, my friend.* "I got lost . . . looking for my brother's village . . ."

The commander's attention shifted, irritation replacing suspicion as he grabbed Ghost's collar, yanking him forward. "You're interrupting official business, fool. How did you get past—"

Moose opened fire from the Land Cruiser's rear window.

Three controlled bursts from the Mk 48 chewed through the floodlights and the Hilux's engine block. Darkness descended like a physical weight as sparks showered from shattered electrical equipment. Chaos erupted as the militiamen fired blindly into the night, their muzzle flashes strobing through the rain.

Ghost dropped to the ground as the commander's grip slackened, rolling beneath the technical's chassis. A flash of ceramic, a spray of arterial blood, black in the darkness, and the commander collapsed, clutching his severed femoral artery.

"Go! Go! Go!" Alex shouted, ducking as rounds punched through the Land Cruiser's bodywork.

Santiago leaned out the Everest's window, his suppressed M4 coughing three times. A militiaman spun and fell, his rifle discharging into the mud.

They plowed through the tire spikes, the Land Cruiser's safari-ready run-flat tires holding just long enough to clear the checkpoint. Behind them, Moose's Mk 48 thundered again, suppressing the remaining militia as Ghost sprinted from the shadows, vaulting into the Everest's open tailgate as they accelerated away.

"Status?" Alex demanded as Caleb swerved around a pothole deep enough to swallow their front axle.

"Compound's on alert," Caleb reported, monitoring radio chatter through his headset. "They know something's happening, but not what or where. We've got maybe ten minutes before they connect the dots."

"Ghost?"

"I'm good," came the reply from the Everest, followed by the metallic click of a fresh magazine being seated. "Commander won't be calling anyone."

* * *

CHECKPOINT CHARLIE

No more tricks. The third roadblock was a kill zone: two technicals with Dushkas flanking the road, their heavy barrels angled to create interlocking fields of fire. Militiamen in Chinese-supplied body armor had dug into foxholes on either side of the approach, creating a gauntlet of death that would shred anything attempting to pass.

"They're expecting trouble," Caleb said, studying the layout through his thermal scope. "Standard ambush configuration. They've got claymores daisy-chained along the drainage ditches."

Alex studied the terrain—thick brush on the east side offered concealment, though not cover. The western approach was more exposed but provided a steeper angle of attack. A frontal assault would be suicide.

"Santiago, Kurtz—flank through the scrub," she decided, pointing to the eastern tree line. "Take out the gunners. Quietly. We need those fifty cals silenced before we move."

Both men nodded, checking their suppressors and combat knives. Santiago's face was a mask of concentration as he slipped a garrote wire into his sleeve—insurance against any target too well-armored for a blade.

"Fifteen minutes," Alex said. "Then we move, with or without you."

Machetes in hand to clear a path through the dense vegetation, they melted into the rain, two shadows among many in the African night.

The remaining team waited in tense silence, weapons ready, ears straining for any sound of discovery. Rain drummed on the Land Cruiser's roof, each drop a tiny explosion in the stillness. Moose's breathing slowed to a meditative rhythm as he entered the calm state that preceded combat—the warrior's mindset that separated professionals from amateurs.

Five minutes passed, then ten. Alex checked her watch, calculating trajectories, contingencies, extraction routes. If they lost the element of surprise now, the entire operation would collapse like a house of cards.

At fourteen minutes and thirty seconds, a choked gurgle carried through the rain—the sound of a man dying with his windpipe crushed. Then another, softer this time, almost lost beneath the patter of raindrops on leaves.

The Land Cruiser rolled forward, headlights flashing once in the prearranged signal. Santiago emerged from the undergrowth fifty meters ahead, his face and hands smeared with mud for camouflage. The bloodied panga in his right hand dripped crimson onto the saturated ground.

"Clear," he reported as they approached, his voice clinical. "East gunner and spotter neutralized. Kurtz has the west technical. Claymores disarmed."

The team advanced through the checkpoint at walking pace, weapons trained on the surrounding jungle. The bodies of the militia had been dragged into the underbrush, hidden from casual observation. Only dark stains in the mud marked their final moments.

A minute up the road and Alex's computer tablet pinged with an incoming transmission. The screen split, revealing Kadeisha Thomas in her DC office—a sterile, climate-controlled environment that seemed to exist in another universe from the humid, insect-filled night that surrounded them. Thomas's crisp suit and perfect makeup were a jarring contrast to their mud-spattered tactical gear.

"Project Aegis is secure," Thomas said without preamble, her voice pitched low despite the encrypted connection. "DEVGRU recovered the core drives and algorithm from the plant in Okavango last night. But if the Chinese crack Martel's knowledge of its blind spots and backdoor protocols . . ."

"We'll get him," Alex snapped, impatience sharpening her tone. Her father wasn't just an asset to be recovered; he was blood of her blood. The oath carved into her palm throbbed with each heartbeat, a constant reminder of promises made and kept.

Harley's feed split the screen again, her Arusha command center a nest of monitors and communications equipment. Dark circles beneath her eyes betrayed the sleepless night spent coordinating this operation across three countries and two continents. Behind her, Alex caught a glimpse of Adiya, the woman's face drawn but determined as she pointed to something on a satellite image.

"Adiya's confirmed the basement layout," Harley reported, fingers flying across her keyboard. "Thermal imaging shows twelve hostiles inside the main structure, four on roving patrol around the perimeter. One in the east guard tower—chain-smoking, probably bored out of his mind. The general is being held in the basement level of the central house, two guards with him at all times."

"Any word on structural details of the basement?" Alex asked, thinking of the potential challenges. Basements could account for up to 25 percent of a building's heat loss, which meant thermal imaging might not give them the full picture.

"Concrete foundation, single entry point via stairs from the main floor," Harley replied, relaying information from Adiya. "No windows, one drainage pipe too small for extraction. The house sits at the center of what used to be the factory manager's compound."

Lightning flashed overhead, momentarily washing out the tablet's display. Thunder followed almost immediately, the sound rolling across the landscape like artillery fire. The satellite uplink whined in protest as atmospheric interference increased.

"Storm's intensifying," Thomas warned, her image freezing briefly before resolving. "We're grounding our birds in sixty minutes. After that, you're on your own until the weather clears."

The compound came into view, scant meters away. They pulled the vehicles off the side of the road. Caleb ejected his HK416's magazine, checking the brass casings before reseating it with practiced efficiency. He adjusted the attached night-vision scope, dialing in the settings for the current light conditions.

"Then we better get a move on," he said, his voice betraying none of the tension that must have been coiling in his gut. "Clock's ticking."

Alex nodded, securing the tablet in its waterproof case. She checked her own weapons one final time—Glock 19 with a suppressor, M4 with hybrid sight system, her father's Ka-Bar knife at her hip. Each item a tool, each tool a potential lifeline.

"Comms check," she ordered, adjusting her earpiece.

The team responded in sequence, their voices clear despite the electronic countermeasures blanketing the area.

"Remember," Alex said as they prepared to move out, "we go in quiet, we locate the general, we extract. No heroics, no deviations. If Lemarti is present, he's secondary to the primary objective."

But even as she spoke the words, Alex knew they rang hollow. If she came face-to-face with the man who had kidnapped her father, who had slaughtered villages and trafficked children across East Africa... Well, some debts could only be paid in blood.

*　*　*

PEOPLE'S FREEDOM ARMY COMPOUND, LAKE VICTORIA, TANZANIA

The rain masked their approach, droplets muffling footsteps and dampening the electronic signatures of their equipment. Alex counted sentries through her thermal monocle: two at the gate, hunched against the drizzle; one on the wall, rifle slung carelessly over his shoulder; another in the tower, the cherry glow of his cigarette a pinpoint of heat in the darkness.

It would all be over soon, one way or another. A lifetime of joy and regrets was sometimes determined by the smallest of miracles—a guard looking left instead of right, a radio failing at the crucial moment, a bullet finding its mark instead of missing by the turn of a man's head.

As they moved into position, Alex touched the scar on her palm—a covenant written in blood and sealed with a promise. Somewhere in the basement of that central house, her father waited. Two days in PFA custody. Two days of who knew what kind of treatment.

She was coming for him. And heaven help anyone who stood in her way.

CHAPTER 43

PEOPLE'S FREEDOM ARMY COMPOUND,
LAKE VICTORIA, TANZANIA

The basement reeked of mildew and decay. A chill seeped through the crumbling concrete walls. A single bulb hung from the ceiling, casting harsh shadows on General David Martel's face as he sat in a chair at the center of the room. The chains around his ankles clinked softly as he shifted, seeking relief from muscles strained by hours of immobility.

Water dripped somewhere in the darkness beyond the light's reach. *Tap. Tap. Tap.* A metronome counting down the hours until dawn—until Lemarti and his crew traded him to the Chinese.

The door at the top of the stairs creaked open. Martel squinted against the sudden shaft of light. Three silhouettes descended—two men with rifles slung across their backs and a smaller figure between them.

Kijana.

The boy carried a metal tray with a chunk of bread and a dented tin cup. His shoulders hunched forward as if bearing a weight far heavier than the meager meal. The guards flanked him, their expressions flat.

"Food," the taller guard grunted, gesturing toward Martel with his chin.

Kijana approached cautiously, his eyes darting between the general and the zip ties binding Martel's wrists. The boy set the tray down and produced a small knife from his pocket.

"Careful," the second guard warned. "No tricks, *mzee*." He directed this last word at Martel, the term for *old man* dripping with contempt.

Kijana sliced through the plastic restraints. Martel suppressed a wince as blood rushed back into his fingers, the sensation like fire ants beneath his skin. He flexed his hands, working circulation back into stiff joints.

"*Asante, Kijana*," Martel said softly. "Thank you."

The boy said nothing, retreating a step as Martel reached for the bread.

"Eat now," Kijana finally said, his voice barely above a whisper.

Martel tore off a piece of bread, chewing slowly. "Beautiful country. Your country."

The guards shifted their weight, eyes narrowing. One muttered something to the other in a dialect Martel didn't recognize—not Swahili, but possibly Maa.

"Eat," the taller guard barked in heavily accented English. "No talk."

Martel ignored him, his gaze fixed on Kijana. "How old are you, son?"

The boy hesitated. "Fourteen."

"Fourteen." Martel nodded, taking a sip of water. "When I was fourteen, I was playing baseball and worrying about math tests. Not carrying rifles for men like Lemarti."

"Silence!" The shorter guard stepped forward, hand dropping to the pistol at his hip.

"These men," Martel continued, his voice calm but penetrating, "they don't love you, Kijana. They don't care what happens to you. To them, you're just another weapon to be used and discarded."

The boy's expression hardened. "You know nothing."

"I know your parents wouldn't want this for you."

Something flickered in Kijana's eyes—pain, raw and immediate. The guards exchanged glances, sensing the shift in the room's atmosphere.

"Enough talk!" The taller guard stepped between them, rifle now in hand. "Eat or we take food."

Martel held Kijana's gaze. "What happened to your village last year—that raid—that wasn't justice. That was slaughter. Your parents raised you for something better than this."

The guard's open palm cracked across Martel's face. "I said silence!"

Blood pooled in Martel's mouth. He spat it onto the dirt floor, never breaking eye contact with the boy. "Think, Kijana. Would your father want you killing for Lemarti? Would your mother want you guarding prisoners who will be tortured tomorrow?"

The second blow knocked Martel sideways, almost tipping him over in his chair. The chains around his ankles rattled as he righted himself, wiping blood from his split lip.

"Stop it!" Kijana shouted, his voice cracking. "Just stop talking!"

"You can leave, son," Martel pressed on, the words coming faster now. "There are people who can help you. People who can get you back to school, give you a real future—"

The guard's boot connected with Martel's ribs. Pain exploded through his chest, but he forced himself to straighten, to keep his eyes on the boy.

"Your mother was a teacher, wasn't she?" Martel wheezed. "Adiya told me. Like her. She'd want you learning, not killing."

Another blow. This time to his kidney. Martel doubled over, gasping.

"I said stop!" Kijana's voice had risen to a shout, his hands balled into fists at his sides.

The taller guard turned on the boy. "You! Out! Now!"

But Kijana stood his ground, tears welling in his eyes as Martel took another blow. The general's face was a mask of blood now, but his eyes remained clear, focused on the boy.

"You can be free, Kijana," Martel whispered, the words heavy.

Something broke in Kijana then. A dam of emotion held back by months of forced stoicism. Tears streaked down his cheeks, cutting lines through the dust on his skin.

"Get out!" The shorter guard grabbed Kijana's arm, shoving him toward the stairs. "Lemarti will hear of this weakness!"

Kijana stumbled backward, his gaze never leaving Martel's face. The general nodded once—a silent promise, a covenant between them.

"Think about what I said," Martel called after him as the guards advanced again. "There's still time to choose a different path!"

The door slammed shut, plunging the basement back into its artificial twilight. Martel slumped against the wall, tasting copper and salt. The pain would come later—the full accounting of bruised ribs and torn flesh. For now, there was only the certainty that he'd planted a seed.

And sometimes, that was enough.

In the darkness, he traced the scar on his palm with his thumb. Somewhere out there, Alex was coming. He just had to hold on.

* * *

PEOPLE'S FREEDOM ARMY COMPOUND, LAKE VICTORIA, TANZANIA

The compound emerged from the darkness like a fortress, its walls glowing faintly in the green haze of night vision goggles. Alex crouched in the underbrush fifty meters from the perimeter with Caleb at her side. The rest of the team was positioned at strategic points around the compound, waiting for the signal to move.

Rain continued to fall, a light drizzle that muffled sound and diminished visibility—ideal conditions for their approach. Thunder rumbled in the distance, the heart of the storm moving steadily closer.

"Ronin actual, this is Ghost. East perimeter clear. Two hostiles on patrol, moving predictably."

"Copy that," Caleb replied softly. "Moose?"

"West side clear. Dock is guarded by one man, looks half asleep."

"Doc?"

"North approach secure. I have eyes on the main house. Second-story lights still on."

Caleb checked his watch: 0355 hours. "Five minutes to execution. Final comms check."

Each team member reported in, their voices calm and focused. Alex felt her heart pounding against her ribs, not from fear but from anticipation. So close now.

"Rook, drone status?"

"Reaper is on station at five thousand feet," Rook replied. "I have thermal imaging of the entire compound. Confirming approximately twenty armed combatants on-site. Main concentration in the barracks building to the west. Three heat signatures in the basement of the house—likely the general and guards."

Alex had swapped her designated marksman rifle for the close-quarters advantage of a suppressed M4. She adjusted its grip, the familiar weight of the weapon reassuring. Her father's Ka-Bar knife was secured at her hip. It felt right to carry it now, as if completing some kind of circle.

"Remember," Caleb said over comms, "we move fast and quiet. Primary objective is extraction of Condor. Secondary objective is elimination of Lemarti, but only if it doesn't compromise the primary. Questions?"

Silence.

"Execute."

The team moved as one, converging on the compound from multiple directions. Ghost and Rocky took out the perimeter guards with suppressed shots, their bodies caught and lowered silently to the ground. Moose disabled the rudimentary alarm system with practiced ease while Santiago covered his back.

Alex and Caleb approached the main house from the south, using the shadows as cover. Doc moved to a position where he could provide overwatch, his rifle trained on the main entrance.

"Rook, what's happening inside?" Caleb whispered into his comms.

"No movement on the second floor," Rook replied. "Basement heat signatures still stable. Wait—movement at the barracks. Two hostiles heading toward the main house."

"Doc, you have eyes?"

"Affirmative. I can take them."

"Negative," Caleb replied. "Ghost, intercept."

"On it."

Alex and Caleb reached the side entrance of the main house, pressing against the wall on either side of the door. Caleb tested the handle—locked, as expected. He nodded to Alex, who removed a small device from her tactical vest and attached it to the electronic lock. The bypass tool worked quickly, and within seconds, the lock disengaged with a soft click.

"We're in," Caleb reported. "Moving to the basement."

They entered the house, weapons at the ready. The interior was surprisingly luxurious—expensive furniture, artwork on the walls, marble flooring. The contrast with the poverty they'd seen in the surrounding areas was stark and obscene.

A guard appeared at the end of the hallway, his eyes widening in surprise. Before he could raise his weapon, Alex put two rounds through his chest, the suppressed shots no louder than a cough. The man crumpled to the floor.

"Enemy down," she reported. "Moving to the stairs."

According to their intelligence, the basement access was through the kitchen. They moved silently through the house, encountering no further resistance. The kitchen was empty, a pot of something still simmering on the stove.

"Basement door should be to your right," Rook guided them.

Caleb spotted it—a heavy wooden door with a modern electronic lock. Again, Alex's bypass tool made quick work of it.

"Thermal shows two hostiles with Condor," Rook updated them. "One at the base of the stairs, one farther in."

Caleb readied a flashbang. "Going dynamic in three, two, one—"

He opened the door and tossed the grenade down the stairs. They turned away, the muffled bang followed by shouts of confusion. Alex moved first, descending the stairs in a combat crouch, Caleb right behind her.

The guard at the bottom of the stairs was still disoriented, clutching his ears. Alex took him down with a controlled burst to the chest. Caleb moved past her, sweeping the room with his weapon.

"Clear left!"

"Clear right!"

The basement was larger than expected, divided into several rooms. The far door was closed, likely where the second guard and her father were located.

"Breach and clear," Caleb ordered.

They positioned themselves on either side of the door. Alex kicked it open, and Caleb tossed in another flashbang. The explosion was followed by a scream of pain.

They entered to find a guard writhing on the floor, his weapon several feet away. Caleb secured him with zip ties while Alex scanned the room—and froze.

A man sat chained to a metal chair in the center of the room, his head bowed. Even in the dim light, she would have recognized him anywhere. But he was in noticeably worse shape than when he had left the PFA compound earlier.

"Dad," she whispered.

General David Martel raised his head slowly, his eyes narrowing as he tried to focus through the aftereffects of the flashbang. His face was bruised, a cut above his right eye crusted with dried blood, the eye swollen all but shut. He looked frailer than she'd ever seen him, and when he sat up, she saw the pain of movement crease his face, but his posture remained military-straight despite the chains and the agony.

Lemarti, you bastard, you'll die for this, she promised herself.

"Who—" he began, his voice hoarse.

"Ronin actual, JACKPOT. We have secured Condor," Caleb reported into his comms. "Preparing for extraction."

Alex moved to her father, holstering her weapon. "Dad, it's me. It's Alex."

The general's eyes widened, disbelief and hope warring on his face. "Alex? My God . . . Allie?"

She knelt beside him, working to free him from the chains that bound him to the chair and around his ankles. "We're getting you out of here."

"Alex, you shouldn't be here," he said urgently. "It's too dangerous. Lemarti—"

"Is being handled," she assured him, finally breaking the lock on his ankle chains. "Can you walk?"

CHAPTER 44

PEOPLE'S FREEDOM ARMY COMPOUND,
LAKE VICTORIA, TANZANIA

General David Martel nodded, rising unsteadily to his feet.

Caleb appeared in the doorway. "We need to move. Now."

"What's happening?" Alex asked, supporting her father as they moved toward the stairs.

"Tarasenko's men have been spotted approaching from the north. And Lemarti's mobilizing his forces. We're about to be caught in the middle."

They ascended the stairs, General Martel moving more steadily with each step. At the top, Caleb handed him a pistol. "Just in case."

The general checked the weapon with practiced ease. "Like riding a bike."

Outside, the storm had intensified, rain lashing against the windows. Lightning flashed, briefly illuminating the compound in stark white light.

"Ronin actual, this is Ghost. We have multiple bogeys converging on the main house. Looks like Lemarti's figured out we're here."

"And I've got vehicles approaching from the north," Moose added. "Definitely Leopard Group."

Caleb cursed under his breath. "Exfil plan Alpha is compromised. Switching to Bravo. All units fall back to the dock. We're going out by water."

They moved through the house toward the rear exit that would lead them to the dock. As they reached the back door, gunfire erupted outside—the distinctive crack of AK-47s mixed with the deeper thump of heavier weapons.

"Sounds like our Russian friends have engaged Lemarti's men," Caleb observed. "Let's use the distraction."

They slipped out the back door into the driving rain. The dock was fifty meters away, two small motorized fishing boats tied at its end. Between them and escape, chaos reigned—Lemarti's militia exchanging fire with Tarasenko's mercenaries, muzzle flashes illuminating the darkness.

"Stay low, move fast," Caleb ordered.

They had covered half the distance when a figure emerged from the shadows—Lemarti himself, his red *shuka* now soaked dark with rain and what looked like blood. His eyes widened when he saw the general.

"You!" he snarled, raising his rifle.

Before he could fire, a burst of automatic weapons fire cut through the air. Lemarti staggered, blood blooming across his chest. Behind him stood Artemi Tarasenko, his face illuminated by a flash of lightning.

"Consider our contract terminated," the Russian said coldly as Lemarti collapsed to the ground.

Tarasenko's gaze shifted to them, his eyes locking with Alex's. For a moment, no one moved. Then he smiled—a predator's smile.

"The famous Alex Martel," he said, his voice carrying over the storm. "I've heard so much about you."

"Let us pass," Caleb called out, his rifle trained on the Russian.

Tarasenko laughed. "I think not. The general and I have business to discuss."

More of Tarasenko's men emerged from the shadows, their weapons trained on Alex, Caleb, and General Martel. The odds had shifted dramatically against them.

"You're outnumbered," Tarasenko said, his accent thickening with satisfaction. "And your reinforcements won't arrive in time."

Alex's mind raced through tactical options, each more desperate than the last. Her father stood between her and Tarasenko.

"Alex," her father said quietly, "stand down."

"What? Dad, no!"

"Listen to your father," Tarasenko smiled. "He understands the situation better than you."

A flash of movement caught Alex's eye—the boy from the compound, slipping behind a stack of crates, his eyes wide with fear. No one else seemed to notice him.

"What do you want with him?" Caleb demanded, buying time.

Tarasenko shrugged. "Originally? His death. Now? His knowledge. The Chinese pay well for American secrets."

"You're working with the MSS?" General Martel's voice was steady, analytical. "Business makes very strange bedfellows."

"A temporary arrangement," Tarasenko replied. "Business is business."

Thunder rumbled overhead as the storm intensified. Rain began to fall in heavy sheets, drumming against the metal roofs of the nearby buildings. Lightning flashed, momentarily blinding everyone.

In that instant, chaos erupted.

* * *

PEOPLE'S FREEDOM ARMY DOCK, LAKE VICTORIA, TANZANIA

The first shot came from somewhere to their left—a single crack that dropped one of Tarasenko's men. Then another. And another.

"Contact left!" one of the Russians shouted.

Through the driving rain, Alex glimpsed figures moving—Ghost and Rook, the Delta survivors, flanking Tarasenko's position.

"Move!" Caleb shouted, shoving Alex and the general toward cover as bullets tore through the air around them.

They dove behind a concrete barrier as Tarasenko's men returned fire, the night erupting into a cacophony of gunfire and shouted commands. Caleb popped up to lay down suppressive fire while Alex worked frantically to find cover for her father.

"Dad, are you hurt?" she asked, her voice barely audible over the firefight. "I mean, besides the obvious."

"Nothing that won't heal," he replied, his eyes fixed on her face. "You shouldn't be here, Alex."

"Where else would I be? Can you run?"

He nodded, flexing his legs. "Just point me in the right direction."

Caleb dropped back into cover, ejecting a spent magazine. "We're pinned down. Tarasenko's got at least a dozen men, and they're moving to surround us."

"What about Ghost and Rook?" Alex asked.

"They're engaging from the flank, but they're outnumbered, too." Caleb checked his remaining ammunition. "We need to get to the extraction point."

General Martel surveyed their surroundings with a practiced eye. "The dock," he said, pointing toward the lake. "There's a couple of boats. If we can reach it—"

"We'll be exposed crossing open ground," Caleb countered.

"It's our best shot," the general insisted.

Alex nodded. "Dad's right. We make a break for the dock."

She keyed her radio. "Ghost, Rook—we're moving to the dock. Need covering fire."

"Copy that," Ghost's voice crackled through the static. "On your mark."

Alex looked at her father, then at Caleb. "Ready?"

They nodded.

"Now!"

Ghost and Rook opened up with everything they had, forcing Tarasenko's men into cover. Alex, Caleb, and General Martel sprinted across the open ground toward the dock, bullets kicking up dirt around their feet.

They were halfway there when the world exploded.

An RPG struck the building to their right, showering them with debris. Alex felt herself lifted off her feet, then slammed back to the ground, the breath knocked from her lungs. Through ringing ears, she heard Caleb shouting her name.

She struggled to her feet, disoriented. Her father lay a few meters away, blood streaming from the cut above his eye. Caleb was already moving toward him.

"Dad!" she called out, stumbling forward.

Then she saw him—Tarasenko, emerging from the smoke with two of his men, advancing on her father.

"No!" she screamed, raising her rifle.

A burst of gunfire from her left—Rook, providing cover. Tarasenko's men dropped, but the Russian commander himself dove behind a stack of fuel drums.

Alex reached her father, helping him to his feet. "Come on, we have to move!"

They staggered toward the dock, Caleb covering their retreat. She moved them to one of the small boats—a weathered fishing vessel with an outboard motor—bobbing in the choppy waters. Freedom was just meters away.

That's when Alex heard the distinctive whine of a drone overhead.

"Reaper!" Caleb shouted, pointing skyward.

Through the rain, she could just make out the dark shape circling above them, low enough to identify. Her blood ran cold as she realized what it meant.

"Rook," she whispered.

Across the compound, Rook crouched behind a bullet-riddled truck, his tablet illuminating his face with an eerie blue glow. His fingers danced across the screen, inputting coordinates.

"What's he doing?" General Martel asked, following her gaze.

Before she could answer, Caleb was sprinting toward Rook, abandoning his position.

"Caleb!" she called after him.

"Get to the boat!" he shouted back. "I'll handle this!"

Alex hesitated, torn between following Caleb and protecting her father.

"Go," her father urged. "I'll make it to the boat. Stop whatever he's doing."

She nodded, squeezing his arm before racing after Caleb.

Rook didn't look up as Caleb approached, his focus entirely on the tablet. "Stay back," he warned. "I have my orders."

"What orders?" Caleb demanded, his rifle trained on Rook.

"Operation Ironclad," Rook replied, his voice hollow. "If extraction fails, Condor cannot fall into enemy hands."

Understanding dawned on Caleb's face. "You're going to kill him?"

"It's not personal. It's national security."

Alex arrived just as Caleb lunged for the tablet. The two men grappled in the mud, fighting for control of the device. She raised her rifle but couldn't get a clear shot with them locked together.

"Stop!" she shouted, trading her rifle for her pistol.

Neither man acknowledged her. Rook slammed his elbow into Caleb's jaw, momentarily stunning him. In that instant, his finger stabbed at the screen.

"Target locked," the tablet announced in a mechanical voice.

"No!" Caleb roared, recovering and tackling Rook again.

The tablet flew from Rook's hands, landing in the mud at Alex's feet. She snatched it up, her heart pounding as she saw the targeting reticle centered on the dock—on her father.

"Missile away," the tablet announced.

Time seemed to slow. Alex's fingers frantically worked the touch screen, trying to abort the launch or redirect the missile. The targeting system responded sluggishly, the crosshairs dragging across the display.

Caleb and Rook continued to fight, oblivious to her efforts. With a final desperate swipe, she dragged the targeting reticle away from the dock—and directly onto Rook's position.

"Impact in five seconds," the tablet warned.

"Caleb!" she screamed. "Move!"

He looked up, saw the tablet in her hands, and immediately understood. He broke away from Rook, diving for cover just as the Griffin missile streaked down from the heavens.

The explosion lifted Rook off his feet, his body silhouetted against the fireball before disappearing in the inferno. The shock wave knocked Alex backward, the tablet flying from her grasp.

When she regained her senses, Caleb was helping her up, his face streaked with blood and soot.

"Are you okay?" he asked.

She nodded, unable to speak. Together, they stared at the smoking crater where Rook had been.

"He was going to kill my father," she finally managed.

"I know," Caleb said grimly. "But he wasn't acting alone."

A burst of gunfire from the direction of the dock snapped them back to reality.

"Dad!" Alex gasped, already running.

They sprinted back toward the lake, weapons ready. Through the rain and smoke, Alex could see her father engaged in hand-to-hand combat with one of Tarasenko's men on the dock. Even after days of captivity, the general fought with the precision and economy of movement that had made him a legend in special operations. As she moved to his aid, he dispatched his opponent into the lake.

But where was Tarasenko?

Her question was answered when she saw the Russian commander dragging Kijana toward a second boat, the boy struggling against his grip.

"Let him go!" Alex shouted, raising her rifle.

Tarasenko spun, using Kijana as a shield. "Drop your weapon, or the boy dies. And I'm taking the general with me as well," he said, pointing a pistol at Kijana's head. "This way, sir," he said to the general.

Alex hesitated, her finger hovering over the trigger.

In that moment of distraction, a figure emerged from behind a stack of fishing nets—Kurtz, bloodied and bruised, his face a mask of cold determination. He wasn't carrying a weapon—he must have lost it during the battle—but he moved with the silent efficiency of a predator, closing in on General Martel from behind.

"Dad, behind you!" Alex screamed.

The general turned, but too late. Kurtz was already upon him, clutching something in his hand—a grenade, its pin already pulled.

"For the greater good," Kurtz said, his voice carrying across the water.

He lunged at the general, the grenade between them. General Martel reacted instinctively, grappling with Kurtz at the edge of the dock. They struggled briefly before toppling into the lake together, the grenade still clutched between them.

"No!" Alex's scream tore through the night.

The underwater explosion sent a geyser of water skyward. For a moment, the entire world seemed to hold its breath.

Alex raced to the edge of the dock, searching the churning waters for any sign of her father. Nothing.

Then, a splash—General Martel surfacing twenty meters out, struggling to stay afloat. Blood clouded the water around him.

Without hesitation, Alex dove in, swimming with powerful strokes toward her father. The cold water shocked her system, but adrenaline drove her forward. She reached him just as he began to sink again, hooking her arm under his and pulling him toward the shallows.

"Stay with me, Dad," she pleaded, feeling his weight grow heavier with each stroke.

They reached the shallows, where she could stand. Dragging him onto the muddy bank, she immediately began assessing his injuries. The grenade had torn through his side, leaving a ragged wound that pumped blood with each weakening heartbeat.

"Allie," he whispered, his eyes focusing on her face.

"Don't talk," she said, applying pressure to the wound. "Save your strength." But where she applied pressure, she found a crater, not a wound.

He shook his head slightly. "Too late for that." His hand found hers, squeezing with surprising strength. "You found me."

"I promised I would," she said, tears mixing with the lake water on her face. "Blood of my blood, until my last breath."

A ghost of a smile touched his lips. "My brave girl." His gaze drifted past her, toward the storm-racked sky. "I'm sorry . . . for leaving you."

"*No!* Dad, stay with me!" She pressed harder on the wound, but the blood continued to flow. "Medic! Doc, I need you here!"

But she knew, with the terrible certainty of someone who had seen too much death, that it was already too late. The light was fading from his eyes.

"Save the boy," he whispered.

"I will, Dad."

"I love you, Allie," her childhood nickname slipping from his lips one last time.

Then he was gone, his hand slack in hers.

For a moment, she couldn't move, couldn't breathe. The world narrowed to this single point of agony—her father's still form cradled in her arms, the promise she had kept too late.

"*No!*" she wailed. *Please, no. No, no . . .*

A movement caught her eye—Kurtz, impossibly dragging himself from the lake a dozen meters away. He was grievously wounded but alive.

Cold fury replaced grief. Alex gently laid her father's body on the shore and stood, drawing her sidearm. She walked toward Kurtz, each step deliberate.

He looked up as she approached, blood bubbling from his lips. "Had to . . . be done," he gasped. "Operation Ironclad. Orders . . ."

"Whose orders?" she demanded, her voice deadly calm.

Kurtz coughed, more blood spattering his chin. "Ask . . . Mustang."

Deputy Director Kadeisha Thomas—*Mustang*.

The revelation hit Alex like a physical blow.

Kurtz's hand moved toward his waist—reaching for a weapon or simply trying to staunch his wounds, Alex didn't care. She fired twice, center mass. Kurtz jerked, then lay still.

She turned back toward the dock, her mind oddly clear despite the chaos around her. In the distance, she saw Tarasenko's boat speeding away, Kijana still his captive. Caleb stood on the dock, exchanging fire with the remaining Russians.

And behind him, Santiago watched the scene unfold, his expression unreadable. For a moment, Alex thought she saw him raise his weapon toward Caleb's back—but then he shifted, firing instead at one of Tarasenko's men who had emerged from cover.

The choice made, Santiago moved to join Caleb, the two of them providing covering fire as Alex returned to her father's body.

"I'm sorry," Caleb said when she reached them, his eyes on the general's still form.

She nodded, unable to speak. Together, they carried General Martel's body to the remaining boat, Santiago covering their retreat.

As they pushed off from the dock, Alex looked back at the shore where her father had died. The rain was washing away the blood, but nothing would ever wash away the memory of this night, this place.

"Tarasenko?" she asked, her voice hollow.

"Gone," Caleb replied. "With the boy."

She nodded, her gaze fixed on the horizon where Tarasenko's boat had disappeared. "We'll find him."

It wasn't a question or a hope. It was a promise written in blood.

CHAPTER 45

CIA SAFE HOUSE, MWANZA, TANZANIA

The safe house felt like a tomb. Alex sat at the table, her father's dog tags clutched in her hand, their metal warm from her constant touch. Outside, the rain had finally stopped, leaving behind a heavy silence broken only by the occasional drip from the eaves.

The team had regrouped here after escaping the fishing village—Alex, Caleb, Moose, Rocky, Santiago, Ghost, and Doc.

No one spoke. What was there to say? The mission had failed in the worst possible way. General Martel was dead, killed not by the enemy but by one of their own. Rook and Kurtz's betrayal hung in the air like poison.

"Why?" Alex finally asked, breaking the silence. "Why would Thomas order my father's death?"

Caleb leaned against the wall, his arms crossed. "Ironclad was a failsafe. If there was any risk of your father falling into Chinese hands, he was to be eliminated."

"They were willing to kill an American general rather than risk what he knew," Ghost added, his voice bitter. "Rook was just following orders."

"And Kurtz was the backup plan," Moose concluded. "In case Rook failed."

Alex's fingers tightened around the dog tags. "Did you know?" she demanded, her eyes locked on Ghost. "Did you know they never intended to bring him home?"

"No," he said softly. "I'm sorry, Alex. I didn't know."

"They hoped to bring him home," Caleb said quietly. "But they weren't willing to risk what would happen if they failed."

The secure communications system crackled to life. Harley's face appeared on the screen, her expression grave.

"Ronin, this is Blackbird. Status report."

Alex stood, facing the screen. "Condor is KIA. Kurtz and Rook, too. Tarasenko escaped with a hostage—a boy named Kijana."

Harley's face remained impassive, but something flickered in her eyes, a question begging to be asked. A long pause. Then, weakly: "I'm sorry about your father, Alex."

"Are you?" Alex's voice was ice. "Was this the plan all along? To make sure he never made it home?"

"That wasn't the primary objective," Harley replied carefully. "But Ironclad was authorized at the highest levels. The intelligence your father possessed—"

"Save it," Alex cut her off. "I know who gave the order."

Harley's expression hardened. "This isn't the time for—"

"Thomas," Alex said flatly. "Kurtz told me before I killed him."

Another long pause. "What happens now is up to you, Alex. But remember who you are and what you stand for."

"I know exactly who I am," Alex replied. "I'm my father's daughter."

The communication ended, leaving the room in silence once more.

Caleb approached her, his voice low. "What's your play?"

"Tarasenko first," she said without hesitation. "He has Kijana. And he's going to pay for his part in all this."

"And then?"

She met his gaze, her eyes cold. "Then I settle accounts with Thomas."

"You know I can't let you do that," he said quietly.

"I know you'll try to stop me." She placed her father's dog tags around her neck. "But not today."

The team gathered around the table as Moose spread out a map of the region.

"Tarasenko will be heading for extraction," Ghost said, pointing to Mwanza Airport. "That's where his Antonov is parked."

"The Tanzanian military has agreed to help," Harley's voice re-emerged through the comms. "They're mobilizing units to intercept at the airport."

"Why would they help us now?" Alex asked suspiciously.

"Because Tarasenko's presence threatens their sovereignty," Harley explained. "And because I told them he kidnapped a Tanzanian child."

Alex nodded slowly. "When do we move?"

"As soon as we confirm his location. Our satellite coverage is back online, and we're scanning for his vehicle."

The team began preparing, checking weapons and gear. As they worked, Santiago approached Alex.

"I saw what happened with Kurtz," he said quietly. "I'm sorry about your father."

She studied his face, remembering her earlier suspicions. "You hesitated back there. For a moment, I thought you might be with Kurtz."

Santiago held her gaze. "He was my friend, but I made my choice. I'm with Ronin now."

Before she could respond, Moose called out from the communications station.

"We've got him! Tarasenko's convoy just arrived at Mwanza Airport. They're prepping the Antonov for departure."

Alex checked her watch. "How long until they're airborne?"

"Thirty minutes, maybe less."

She looked around at her team—battered, exhausted, but determined. "Then we have thirty minutes to stop them."

As they moved toward the vehicles, Caleb pulled her aside.

"This isn't just about Kijana, is it?"

She checked her father's Ka-Bar knife, secured at her hip. "No. It's about justice."

"Just remember," he said, his hand on her arm, "vengeance and justice aren't the same thing."

"Today they are," she replied, and headed for the door.

CHAPTER 46

MWANZA AIRPORT, MWANZA, TANZANIA

Mwanza Airport sprawled before them, its single runway glistening wet in the wake of the storm. The massive Antonov AN-124 stood on the tarmac, its cargo ramp lowered as Tarasenko's remaining men loaded equipment. Armed guards patrolled the perimeter, their weapons at the ready.

Alex watched from the tree line, her binoculars focused on the aircraft. Next to her, Caleb communicated with the TPDF commander, a stern-faced colonel named Nyerere.

"My men will secure the perimeter," Nyerere explained, pointing to positions on a tactical map. "But we cannot risk damaging the aircraft with heavy weapons. Too close to civilian areas."

"We don't need heavy weapons," Alex said, lowering her binoculars. "We just need to get on board before they take off."

Nyerere frowned. "That is extremely dangerous."

"So is letting Tarasenko escape with a child hostage," she countered.

The colonel studied her for a moment, then nodded. "Very well. We will create a diversion at the main gate. That should draw most of their security forces away from the aircraft."

"And we'll handle the rest," Caleb concluded.

The plan came together quickly. The TPDF would stage a security inspection at the main entrance, drawing attention with numerous vehicles and armed personnel. Meanwhile, Ronin would infiltrate via the service road behind the hangars, using the cover of maintenance vehicles to approach the Antonov.

Alex checked her weapons one last time. Her father's Ka-Bar rested against her hip, its familiar weight both comfort and promise. The storm clouds had cleared, leaving behind a sky washed clean, the air charged with electricity.

"You ready for this?" Caleb asked, his voice low.

She nodded, not trusting herself to speak. After everything—the search, the betrayals, her father's death—only one thing remained: justice.

"Remember," he said, "Tarasenko's dangerous. More dangerous than anyone we've faced."

"So am I," she replied.

The TPDF vehicles moved into position. Colonel Nyerere's voice crackled over the radio: "Operation commencing in three minutes."

Alex watched as the colonel's men approached the main gate, their vehicles forming a deliberate bottleneck. Guards emerged from security posts, rifles at the ready but not yet hostile. Perfect.

"That's our cue," Caleb said. "Move out."

Ronin slipped through the perimeter fence where Moose had cut an opening. They moved in pairs, using the scattered maintenance equipment as cover. The massive Antonov loomed ahead, its cargo ramp still lowered, crew preparing for departure.

Through her binoculars, Alex spotted Kijana being escorted up the ramp, his small frame dwarfed by the mercenaries flanking him. The boy's face was blank with shock—the same expression she'd seen on too many child soldiers across too many war zones.

"I see the boy," she whispered. "Tarasenko must be inside already."

Caleb nodded. "Ghost, Doc—secure the perimeter. Moose, Rocky—with me. We'll create a second diversion at the fuel depot. Alex, Santiago—you're on the aircraft."

The team split, moving with practiced efficiency. Alex and Santiago circled toward the aircraft's blind spot, using a fuel truck for cover. At the main gate, the TPDF inspection had escalated into a heated argument, drawing more of Tarasenko's men away from the plane.

"Now," Alex whispered.

They sprinted across the tarmac, keeping low. An explosion rocked the far side of the airfield—Caleb's diversion. Shouts erupted as Leopard Group mercenaries rushed to respond.

Alex reached the cargo ramp first, pressing herself against the massive landing gear. Santiago took position on the opposite side, his face grim with determination.

"Ready?" Santiago asked.

She nodded, drawing her sidearm. "Let's finish this."

They moved up the ramp in tandem, weapons at the ready. The cargo hold was cavernous, stacked with crates, equipment, and the vehicles that had survived the battle. Two guards stood at the far end, their attention drawn to the commotion outside.

Santiago took the left, Alex the right. Two silenced shots, and the guards crumpled.

"Clear," Santiago whispered.

Alex moved deeper into the aircraft, every sense alert. The boy had to be here somewhere, and where Kijana was, Tarasenko would be close.

A noise from the forward compartment drew her attention. She signaled to Santiago, who nodded and moved to flank the entrance.

Alex counted down with her fingers. Three. Two. One.

They burst through the doorway into what had been converted into a makeshift command center. Computer equipment lined one wall, while weapon cases were stacked against another.

In the center stood Artemi Tarasenko, one hand resting on Kijana's shoulder. The boy's eyes widened at the sight of Alex.

"Ms. Martel," Tarasenko said, his voice smooth as polished stone. "I've been expecting you."

Alex kept her weapon trained on him. "Let the boy go."

Tarasenko smiled, the expression never reaching his eyes. "Of course. He has served his purpose." He released Kijana, who remained frozen in place. "Run along, little one."

The boy hesitated, then bolted past Alex toward the cargo hold.

"Santiago," Alex said without taking her eyes off Tarasenko. "Get him out of here."

"Alex—"

"Go."

Santiago retreated, following Kijana. Now it was just Alex and Tarasenko.

"Your father was a remarkable man," Tarasenko said, circling his desk with casual confidence. "A true warrior. It's a shame how things ended."

"Shut up," Alex snarled. "You don't get to talk about him."

Tarasenko raised an eyebrow. "Such passion. Such anger. You remind me of someone I knew long ago—a woman in Grozny who hunted down the men who killed her brothers. She had that same fire in her eyes."

"What happened to her?"

"She found them. Killed them. And then discovered that vengeance is just another kind of emptiness." He studied her face. "Is that what you're seeking, Alex? Emptiness?"

"Justice," she corrected.

"Ah, justice." Tarasenko chuckled. "A prettier word for the same thing."

A commotion erupted outside—gunfire, shouts. The diversion had escalated into a full-blown firefight.

"It seems our time grows short," Tarasenko observed. "So let me offer you a choice, Alex Martel. Walk away now. Live to fight another day. Or die here, achieving nothing."

"There's a third option," she replied. "You pay for what you've done."

Tarasenko's smile faded.

"You're not the first strong woman I've faced, you know. But most are what we Russians call *fear-biters*—dogs that bark and snarl and attack when cornered, not out of strength but out of terror. They are dangerous, yes, but ultimately predictable. When confronted by a true adversary, they piss themselves and run away, tail tucked up their ass." He moved with surprising speed, drawing a knife from his belt. "You, though—you are different. A true warrior. I respect that."

Alex holstered her sidearm and drew her father's Ka-Bar. "Then let's finish this properly."

Tarasenko circled, his knife held low in a fighter's grip. "Your father carried that blade in Desert Storm, did he not? I recognize the pattern on the leather sheath—standard issue for the First Armored Division."

"He carried it his whole life. Then fate gave it to me."

"And now you'll use it to avenge him. Poetic."

He lunged, the blade slicing air where Alex's throat had been a moment before. She countered, her knife catching his sleeve but missing flesh.

They circled again, each measuring the other. Tarasenko was larger, stronger, but Alex was quicker, her movements economical and precise.

"You fight well," he acknowledged. "Better than most men I've killed."

"I'm not most men."

This time when he attacked, she was prepared. She sidestepped, using his momentum against him, and drove her elbow into his kidney. He grunted but quickly regained his balance, spinning to confront her.

The fight intensified, a deadly dance in the confined space. Tarasenko's blade caught her arm, drawing a line of fire across her bicep. She responded by slashing his thigh, blood darkening his tactical pants.

Outside, the gunfire intensified. Time was running out.

Tarasenko pressed his advantage, forcing Alex back against the wall. His knife flashed toward her face—she blocked it with her forearm, pain lancing through her as the blade bit deep.

"You cannot win," he said, his breath hot against her face. "Accept it."

Alex met his gaze, unflinching. "My father taught me something about acceptance."

She drove her knee up, catching him in the groin. As he doubled over, she brought her elbow down on the back of his neck, sending him to his knees.

Tarasenko recovered faster than she expected, sweeping her legs from under her. They both crashed to the floor, grappling for advantage.

He pinned her, his weight crushing the air from her lungs, inching the knife toward her throat. "Your father died begging for mercy," he lied, trying to break her spirit.

The words ignited something primal in Alex—not rage, but clarity. In that moment, she saw through Tarasenko's facade to the hollow core beneath. For all his strength and cunning, he was just another man afraid of his own insignificance.

With a surge of strength born from that understanding, she twisted beneath him, creating just enough space to bring her father's Ka-Bar up and into his chest. The blade slid between his ribs, finding his heart with unerring precision—like a key finding its lock, opening the final door.

Tarasenko's eyes widened in surprise, then understanding. "Not . . . a fear-biter . . . after all," he gasped.

Blood bubbled from his lips as he collapsed beside her. Alex rolled away, retrieving her knife as she stood.

"That was for my father," she said, watching as the light faded from his eyes.

The firefight outside had died down. Through the aircraft's windows, she could see TPDF soldiers securing the tarmac and Leopard Group mercenaries surrendering or fleeing.

Alex wiped her father's knife clean and returned it to its sheath. Blood—Tarasenko's and her own—stained her hands, but she felt no triumph, only a quiet certainty that she had done what needed to be done.

As she walked down the cargo ramp into the African sunlight, she found Caleb waiting for her, concern etched on his face.

"It's done," she said simply.

He nodded, understanding everything she didn't say. "Kijana's safe. The TPDF has him."

"Good." She looked past him to where the rest of Ronin had gathered, battered but alive. "Let's go home."

CHAPTER 47

ARLINGTON NATIONAL CEMETERY, VIRGINIA

Arlington National Cemetery stretched before Alex, a vast sea of white headstones beneath a heavy June sky. She stood at attention as the honor guard folded the flag that had draped her father's casket, their movements crisp and reverent.

The chaplain's words washed over her—duty, honor, sacrifice—while an unseasonably cold wind cut through her dress uniform. Beside her, Caleb maintained a respectful distance, his presence a silent anchor in the storm of grief.

General David Martel was laid to rest with full military honors, his coffin lowered into the ground amidst the crack of rifles and the mournful notes of "Taps." The flag, now a crisp triangle of stars and sacrifice, was presented to Alex with solemn dignity.

"On behalf of the president of the United States, the United States Army, and a grateful nation, please accept this flag as a symbol of our appreciation for your loved one's honorable and faithful service."

She received it with steady hands, though her heart threatened to shatter anew. Around her, a constellation of brass and politicians offered condolences—empty words from people who had authorized her father's death even as they mourned him publicly.

After the ceremony, a reception was held at the Officers' Club. Alex stood in a corner, sipping a glass of bourbon—Four Branches, her father's favorite—as mourners circled like planets around an absent sun.

"He would have been proud of you," a voice said beside her.

She turned to find Kadeisha Thomas, the CIA deputy director's face a mask of professional sympathy.

"Would he?" Alex asked, her voice neutral despite the rage simmering beneath. "Proud that his own government deemed him expendable?"

Thomas's expression didn't change. "He understood the risks. The stakes."

"Did he understand that you had a kill switch ready? That Operation Ironclad was always the fallback plan?"

A flicker of surprise crossed Thomas's face before she recovered. "National security demands difficult choices, Alex. Your father knew that better than most."

"And what about Rook and Kurtz? Were they, too, aware of the stakes and the consequences of *their* choices? Were there any others waiting in the wings?"

Thomas glanced around, ensuring they weren't overheard. "This isn't the place for this conversation."

"No," Alex agreed, setting down her unfinished drink. "It isn't."

She walked away, leaving Thomas standing alone. Outside, the cool air of spring, not yet ready to yield to summer, nipped at her cheeks—a welcome clarity after the stifling formality inside.

Caleb found her there, leaning against a stone pillar, her father's flag clutched to her chest.

"You okay?" he asked, though they both knew the answer.

"I will be," she replied. "Once I finish what I started."

He studied her face. "Thomas?"

"And whoever else signed off on Ironclad."

"Alex . . ." His voice carried a warning. "That path leads nowhere good."

"I'm not looking for good, Caleb. I'm looking for right."

He sighed, running a hand through his hair. "Then at least don't do it alone."

She looked at him—*really looked*—seeing the concern in his eyes, the loyalty, the understanding that went beyond words. For the first time since Tanzania, something inside her softened.

"I won't," she promised.

That night, in her Georgetown apartment, Alex laid her father's flag in a cedar box beside his medals and the photograph of them in Wyoming, fishing poles in hand, mountains rising behind them like sentinels. The unseen photographer behind the camera had been her mother.

Everyone she had ever loved, gone.

The Ka-Bar knife rested on her desk, cleaned of Tarasenko's blood but forever marked by it. She picked it up, feeling its weight, its history, its promise.

Blood of my blood.

The oath remained. Different now, transformed by loss, but unbroken. She would honor it not through vengeance but through justice—the kind her father had believed in, had fought for.

Tomorrow, she would begin. Tonight, she allowed herself to grieve.

When Caleb arrived at her door near midnight, she let him in without a word. They sat together on her couch, shoulders touching, her feet curled under her, the silence between them more eloquent than speech.

"I keep thinking about Kijana," she said finally. "What happens to him now?"

"Tanzanian authorities found the surviving members of his family. He's with them in Mwanza."

She nodded, grateful for this small mercy in a world that offered few.

"And Thomas?"

Caleb hesitated. "She's vulnerable. The operation was sanctioned at the highest levels, but the fallout from your father's death has everyone running for cover. No one wants to be the face of a failed mission that killed an American hero."

"Good," Alex said. "Fear makes people careless."

"What are you planning?"

She turned to him, her decision already made. "The truth. All of it. Every detail of Ironclad, every name attached to it."

"That's career suicide, Alex. Maybe worse."

"I know. But it's the right thing to do."

He took her hand, his calloused fingers warm against hers. "Then we do it together. Ronin stands as one."

For the first time in weeks, Alex smiled—a small, fragile thing, but real. "Thank you."

Later, as dawn broke over the Potomac, they lay together in her bed, Caleb's arms around her, his heartbeat steady against her back. Not passion but comfort; not desire but connection.

"What happens after?" he asked, his voice soft in the darkness.

"I don't know," she admitted. "But whatever it is, I'll face it."

He tightened his embrace. "We'll face it."

Alex closed her eyes, feeling the weight of her father's dog tags against her chest. The path ahead was uncertain, fraught with danger and consequence. But she would walk it with her head high, carrying her father's memory not as a burden but as a beacon.

Blood of my blood, until my last breath.

The oath endured. And so would she.

ACKNOWLEDGMENTS

Thank you to all the readers who have spent their valuable time reading this and other books in the Special Agent Alexandra Martel series. It's because of you that I can keep writing!

I went on a safari in Tanzania with my wife, Lynne, in 2019. I didn't know it then, but that experience would forever reshape me and my perspective on Africa—the land, the wildlife, and its people. Thankfully, Lynne took copious notes, the substance of which found its way into the pages of this novel.

James Urio was our guide. His pride in the country of his birth shone through every moment and word as he demonstrated his encyclopedic knowledge of every bird, beast, and baobab, transforming our Tanzanian adventure into the inspiration for Alex Martel's journey. His patience while we searched for leopards in acacia branches, along with his excitement when we spotted the Verreaux's eagle-owl, showed me what true passion for conservation looks like.

To all the guides and rangers across Tanzania and beyond who rise before dawn and return after dusk, who can spot a cheetah cub from impossible distances and interpret stories in tracks that most would never see: you navigate the endless plains with the same confidence as the Serengeti lions you protect.

You stand between civilization and wilderness, interpreting one world for the other. Through your eyes, we learn to see beyond the spectacle to the delicate balance that sustains these magnificent creatures and landscapes. Your dedication ensures future generations will continue to witness wildebeest thundering across the plains and hear lions calling in the night.

The story in *Blood Oath* was born in the dust of safari tracks and beneath the expansive African sky that you helped me understand. For that gift, and for your steadfast commitment to preserving these treasures, I dedicate this book to you.

Many have contributed to the success of the Special Agent Alexandra Martel series. I am grateful to my literary agent, **John Talbot,** for his unwavering belief in me. You saw the promise before anyone else did. Thank you. To my good friend **Simon Gervais,** who was among the first to welcome me to my first ThrillerFest in New York City in 2018 and the first to read my fledgling Alexandra Martel manuscript, your friendship and calming influence are cherished.

When I think of all the writers I have met who've become friends, I'm truly amazed. So, to all of you, near and far: **John Adams, Jason Allison, Jeff Ayers, Samantha Bailey, Eric Bishop, Linda Hurtado Bond, Bruce Borgos, Brittany Butler, David Darling, Alex Finlay, Tim Hendricks, Claire Isenthal, James (Mad Dog) Lawler, Hannah Mary McKinnon, Taylor Moore, Hannah Morrissey, Chris Mullen, Samuel Octavius, Adam Plantinga, Adam Sikes, Samantha Skal, Ryan Steck, Jack Stewart, Connor Sullivan, Tessa Wegert,** and so many others, know that you inspire me daily. I'm blessed to be acquainted with each of you.

To the luminaries of the writing world whom I count among my friends and acquaintances: **Linwood Barclay, Marc Cameron, Jack Carr, Robert Dugoni, Tess Gerritsen, Mark Greaney, Peter James, Tosca Lee, David Morrell, Brad Thor,** and **Don Winslow,** thank you for giving of yourselves to me and the writing community at large.

The team at Minotaur Books/St. Martin's Publishing Group never ceases to amaze me. Thank you to my editor, **Michael Homler,** for your guidance and patience, and to editorial assistant **Madeline (Maddie) Alsup,** marketing guru **Stephen Erickson,** maestro of publicity **Hector DeJean,** and the rest of the behind-the-scenes cast and crew for all you do. To **Kelley Ragland,** thank you for your encouragement and stewardship of the house of which I'm proud to be a part.

Thank you to the podcasters, reviewers, booksellers, and readers who enthusiastically spread the word. The playing field of authors is crowded, and your support of my work is greatly appreciated. In particular, my profound thanks to **Sarah Pietroski** of A Novel Spot Bookshop in Toronto, Ontario, and **Barbara Peters** from The Poisoned Pen Bookstore in Scottsdale, Arizona. To **Chris Albanese, Sean Cameron, Mike Houtz, Jeff Circle, David Temple and Tammy Temple, Jeff Clark, Nancy Aguilar, The Real Book Spy,** and **Larry Davidson,** you all rock! Thank you!

To my wife **Lynne:** Your steadfast belief in me, your keen and critical eye, and your love of the written word make it easy to be a writer. I'm immensely grateful to have you in my life, sharing this adventure. To our children, **Michael** and **Meghan,** who continue to encourage me on this journey and tell me they are proud of me, you will never truly know how much that means to me. And lastly, to my mom, **Katalin:** Thank you for giving me that spark, my love of reading. How you smiled when I read to you as a child showed me the power of the written word to bring joy and bridge divides. Thank you!

AUTHOR'S NOTE

Tanzania captivated my heart the moment I first gazed upon its sweeping savannahs and witnessed the majesty of wildlife roaming freely across the Serengeti. But beyond the breathtaking landscapes that draw visitors from all over the globe lies the true treasure of this East African nation—its people.

During my time in Tanzania, particularly in the Ngorongoro region, where I was privileged to visit with Maasai families in their traditional boma, I experienced firsthand the extraordinary warmth, dignity, and resilience that define these proud people. The Maasai have maintained their distinctive way of life for centuries, steadfastly preserving their cultural identity despite mounting pressures from the modern world.

What struck me most was their unwavering independence and deep connection to the land. The Maasai's seminomadic lifestyle revolves around their livestock—particularly cattle, which represent not just wealth but their entire worldview. Their vibrant red *shukas* against the golden grasslands, their intricate beadwork, and their profound spiritual relationship with nature all speak to a people who have found harmony in a challenging environment.

Yet this harmony faces serious threats. In recent years, the Tanzanian government has forcibly displaced Maasai communities from their ancestral lands to create game reserves and tourist attractions. These evictions have involved violence, including beatings and arbitrary arrests, violating fundamental rights to land, livelihood, and cultural preservation. Despite promises of consultation and recognition of the Maasai as "good for conservation," communities have been removed from lands they've inhabited for generations.

While one of the antagonists in *Blood Oath* is a fictional Maasai warrior leading a rebel militia, I want to emphasize that this character does not represent the Maasai people as a whole, who have historically stood against violence and even refused to participate in the slave trade. Rather, he emerges from the very real tensions between traditional ways of life and modern political forces.

My experiences with the Maasai were entirely positive—filled with shared meals, cultural exchange, and mutual respect. Their commitment to living by ancestral precepts in the face of overwhelming pressure to change reflects a profound sense of self-worth that commands admiration.

As you journey through these pages, I hope you'll appreciate not just the thrilling narrative but also the complex reality of a people fighting to preserve their identity in a rapidly changing world.

Steve Urszenyi
Toronto, March 2025

ABOUT THE AUTHOR

Raph Nogal

Steve Urszenyi is the critically acclaimed author of *Perfect Shot* and *Out in the Cold*. A former paramedic and police tactical medic specializing in SWAT and special operations, Urszenyi brings extensive real-world experience to his writing. His debut novel, *Perfect Shot*, earned nominations for three prestigious literary awards, including the International Thriller Writers Best First Novel, and *Publishers Weekly* hailed him as "a writer to watch." When he's not crafting intricate international thrillers, Urszenyi enjoys touring on his Harley-Davidson motorcycle, hiking wilderness trails, and capturing the world through his camera lens. He resides in Toronto with his wife, Lynne.